Praise for M. L. Longworth and
the Provençal Mystery Series

"Judge Antoine Verlaque, the ⸻ charges his professional duties ⸻ taste the wines . . . So many ⸻ lovely views. A reader might be forgiven for feeling woozy."

—*The New York Times Book Review*

"The Verlaque and Bonnet mysteries . . . plunge you into a languid world of epicurean pleasures and good living." —*NPR*

"Longworth's voice is like a rich vintage of sparkling Dorothy Sayers and grounded Donna Leon . . . Longworth has lived in Aix since 1997, and her knowledge of the region is apparent on every page. Bon appétit." —*Booklist*

"A beguiling read that will appeal to Louise Penny and Donna Leon fans." —*Library Journal*

"Fun and evocative . . . Best read beach-side with a glass of French wine in hand." —*Bustle*

"Rich with details of daily life in Aix-en-Provence . . . Francophiles will be enthralled." —*Publishers Weekly* (starred review)

"Longworth confirms her long-standing lovebirds as Aix's Nick and Nora; their pursuit of miscreants never interferes with their enjoyment of the good life." —*Kirkus Reviews*

"What keeps you glued to this mystery is its vivid portrait of everyday life in Aix, which deftly juxtaposes the elegance of the city . . . with quotidian woes and pleasures."　　—Oprah.com

"Longworth paints such a loving picture of Provence that it's likely you'll start planning a vacation trip to France the moment you set the book down."　　　　　　　　　—*The Denver Post*

"The best thing about each novel in this series is that they are as much about lifestyle in the South of France as they are about a legal tangle, a disappearance, or a murder . . . Longworth shows the reader why those who love Donna Leon's Brunetti and Martin Walker's Bruno take up her novels with enthusiasm."
　　　　　　　　　　　　　　　　—*Kings River Life Magazine*

"Mystery and romance served up with a hearty dose of French cuisine. I relished every word. Longworth does for Aix-en-Provence what Frances Mayes does for Tuscany: You want to be there—NOW!"
　　　　—Barbara Fairchild, former editor in chief, *Bon Appétit*

M. L. Longworth's Provençal Mysteries

A PENGUIN MYSTERY

The Vanishing Museum on the Rue Mistral

M. L. LONGWORTH has lived in Aix-en-Provence since 1997. She has written about the region for the *Washington Post*, the *Times* (London), the *Independent* (London), and *Bon Appétit*. She is the author of a bilingual collection of essays, *Une Américaine en Provence*. She is married and has one daughter.

The
VANISHING
MUSEUM
on the
RUE MISTRAL

A Provençal Mystery

M. L. LONGWORTH

PENGUIN BOOKS

PENGUIN BOOKS

An imprint of Penguin Random House LLC
penguinrandomhouse.com

Copyright © 2021 by Mary Lou Longworth
Penguin supports copyright. Copyright fuels creativity, encourages diverse voices,
promotes free speech, and creates a vibrant culture. Thank you for buying an authorized
edition of this book and for complying with copyright laws by not reproducing, scanning,
or distributing any part of it in any form without permission. You are supporting writers
and allowing Penguin to continue to publish books for every reader.

LIBRARY OF CONGRESS CATALOGING-IN-PUBLICATION DATA

Names: Longworth, M. L. (Mary Lou), 1963–, author.
Title: The vanishing museum on the Rue Mistral a Provençal mystery / M. L. Longworth.
Description: [New York] : Penguin Books, [2021] | Series: Provençal mysteries
Identifiers: LCCN 2020025291 (print) | LCCN 2020025292 (ebook) |
ISBN 9780143135296 (paperback) | ISBN 9780525506966 (ebook)
Subjects: GSAFD: Mystery fiction.
Classification: LCC PR9199.4.L596 V36 2021 (print) |
LCC PR9199.4.L596 (ebook) | DDC 813/.6—dc23
LC record available at https://lccn.loc.gov/2020025291
LC ebook record available at https://lccn.loc.gov/2020025292

Printed in the United States of America
1   3   5   7   9   10   8   6   4   2

Set in Adobe Caslon Pro   •   Designed by Sabrina Bowers

For my parents

The
VANISHING
MUSEUM
on the
RUE MISTRAL

Chapter One

❧

Friday, April 20

Léa Paulik wished that the little man leading them around the museum had permitted them to leave their backpacks in the front hall. Her back was killing her, the heaviness of her textbook a constant reminder of the Spanish homework she still had to do quickly during her lunch break. It was her own fault, she knew. She had stayed up too late scrolling through Instagram and texting Alexandra until she heard her father pound out of her parents' bedroom and into the living room to unplug the router. How had he known? She looked across the room and winked at Alexandra, who was intermittently yawning and chewing gum.

Léa shifted, trying to balance the weight on her back. She turned to look at the painting that the little man was going on and on about. The painter's last name, Olive, was easy to remember. That would come in handy, as Mme Forbin was going to quiz them on Tuesday about this visit. Léa didn't mind because she always paid attention. She knew how lucky she was to get these kinds of outings at the Collège Mignet, her junior high school in Aix's posh Quartier Mazarin. Many of her classmates were posh themselves, and she looked around at them now. They were either yawning like Alexandra, looking down at the floor, or whispering to a friend. She looked back at the painting, and this time she heard the painter's full name: Jean-Baptiste Olive.

"This charming tableau was painted in the late nineteenth century," the little man said. "I'm sure it's obvious to you all that it's of the entrance to the port of Marseille. Olive did many paintings of this exact same scene, but this one has always been my favorite. Its bright light on the water—"

"Oh! I recognize that spot!" yelled Zoë, probably the richest girl in the whole school. "We go sailing by there all the time!"

At least ten of their classmates groaned, and Léa smirked, but Zoë didn't seem to notice.

"I love the smoke," Mme Forbin said, taking off her glasses and leaning in closer. "Students, look at the bright blue sea and clear sky at the entrance to the port. But if we look up into the old town, the sky is almost black." She pointed to the streets and buildings that surrounded Marseille's port and Léa tried to get closer to see. Sure enough, several chimneys emitted a thick gray smoke. Marseille's sky was always a brilliant blue whenever she visited it with her parents. "Why do French towns no longer have that kind of smoke?" Mme Forbin asked the class.

"Because it's from coal," Léa said.

Mme Forbin smiled and nodded. "Exactly."

The little man seemed to be getting edgy; he didn't know that Mme Forbin, when you got her on an interesting subject, could go off track until the bell rang. Those were always Léa's favorite times at school. "Come along and look at the porcelain," he said.

"Oh, goody!" cried Eddy Peyrot, rubbing his hands together in mock glee.

Léa laughed despite herself—she didn't like Edouard Peyrot, even though her friend Alexandra adored him. She looked over at Mme Forbin, who was covering her grin with the palm of her hand. "*Oui, M Formentin*," she said, pulling her hand away from her mouth. "By all means, the students would love to see the porcelain."

Eddy slid up beside Léa and said, "That painting must be worth a fortune, eh?"

Léa shrugged. "Not as much as a Manet."

Eddy frowned. "You mean Monet."

"No. I mean Manet. Édouard Manet."

Grinning, Léa went to stand next to Mme Forbin, who had again taken off her glasses to look more closely at the porcelain. A few of the students were leaning on the plexiglass case, and M Formentin asked them to step back. He took out a clean white cotton cloth from his jacket pocket and began wiping the case as he spoke. "These porcelain dessert plates are one of the pride and joys of mine . . . of the museum. Mme Quentin-Savary used this service right up until her death in 1900. They were made at the porcelain factory in Sèvres, just south of the capital."

Léa nodded. She had been to that museum with Marine Bonnet and her mother. She looked down at the dozen or so plates, each one with a hand-painted fruit in its center: wild strawberries, fat purple plums, walnuts in their fuzzy green shells, and almost-translucent purple grapes. Some of the other students were pointing and muttering names of fruits, and it quickly became a competition to see who could identify each fruit the fastest. M Formentin stepped back a tiny bit, his arms folded across his chest and a satisfied grin on his flushed face. He reminded her of a television character from a show her parents watched: a short, fastidious Belgian who walked with tiny footsteps, like a penguin.

"*Et maintenant*," M Formentin announced with a dramatic flourish of his right hand, "*les bustes des personnages illustres d'Aix . . . notre chère ville*." He pointed toward the far corner of the room and began walking there as the students slowly followed.

Léa couldn't see that far, as she was stuck at the back of the group. Was it a bust of Cézanne? She hoped so. Or Zola? Léa was proud that she had gotten into the music program at Mignet, a school that boasted such illustrious alumni as the famous painter and his best friend the writer, although in their day Mignet had been a high school. Her parents, too, were over the moon when she was admitted after an agonizing choral audition.

Léa looked to her left and there was Alexandra, looking down at the dessert plates. Léa lifted up her cell phone and quickly took a photo. Léa looked at Alexandra and whispered, "Isn't this a cool museum?"

"Totally," Alexandra replied.

Léa giggled and gave her a thumbs-up. Alexandra smiled, happy to have a friend at last, even if Léa was the other geek in the class. Léa Paulik looked young for her age, but her intelligence and musical talents set her apart. "Léa's on a different planet," one of their fellow students once remarked. But if Léa Paulik was on a different planet, that only made her even more interesting. She was smart and didn't hide it, and Alexandra admired that. Plus, Léa's father was a police commissioner, which was just about the coolest job on the planet.

"*Et voilà!*" M Formentin said, barely containing his excitement about the first bust.

Léa's face fell in disappointment. It was neither Cézanne nor Zola, both of which she could have picked out.

Alexandra raised her arm in the air.

"And who is it, Alexandra?" Mme Forbin asked.

"Mirabeau!" Alexandra answered, almost breathless with excitement.

Léa smiled and looked at the bust; the man's fat head, his pockmarked skin. He was wearing one of those big wigs with rolls of sausage curls and a fancy frilly shirt under a vest with three big buttons. But despite the bad skin and stupid wig, he looked scary in a way. Formidable.

"*C'est exacte!*" M Formentin replied.

"It's in terra-cotta," Mme Forbin said. "Not marble."

"*Ah, oui,*" M Formentin said, sighing with a slight air of apology. "The marble version is in the Louvre."

"In the nation's capital!" Eddy said.

Again, Léa laughed despite herself. Referring to Paris as "the capital" was old-fashioned. Her parents didn't like that expression, "As if there are no other cities in France!" her father would complain. "As if all life revolves around Paris," her mother would add.

"*Ah, oui,*" M Formentin said again with another sigh, disregarding, or not noticing, Eddy's sarcasm. He went on. "But one thing the Louvre doesn't have is this . . ." He gestured for the students to follow him into another, smaller room. He did his penguin walk while the students followed, trying not to laugh.

It was darker here: The walls were a deep red and the only lighting was a chandelier that hung low over a very long polished wooden table. "A feast for your eyes," M Formentin said. "A complete set of porcelain—again from Sèvres—each plate featuring a different French château."

"Why isn't it under a glass case?" one of the students asked.

M Formentin puffed up his chest. "On certain special days, such as your visit today, I set the table with this exquisite service, just as Mme Quentin-Savary would have done."

"More likely the servants would have done," whispered Léa to Alexandra. Alexandra nodded in agreement while their classmates began a competitive guessing game with the plates.

"Villandry," one said, pointing to a plate whose château was surrounded by perfectly geometrical gardens with clipped hedges.

"Very good, Isabelle," Mme Forbin said. "And that one?" she asked, pointing to a plate whose château spanned a river.

"Chenonceau!" Alexandra answered. "The river is the Cher."

"And who was its most famous owner?" Mme Forbin asked.

"Henri II," Léa replied.

"That's right," Mme Forbin said. "He gave it to—"

"*Sa favorite!*" Eddy cried out.

Mme Forbin said, "His mistress. Correct. Next time raise your hand, Eddy. And what was her name?"

Eddy shifted from foot to foot and scratched his forehead in such an exaggerated way that everyone laughed.

A quiet girl named Mélanie raised her hand, which made Léa happy. Léa also knew the answer, but she didn't want to be the one answering all the time because then people would avoid her, as most of them did Alexandra.

"Diane de Poitiers," Mélanie said.

This time it was their guide, the funny little man, who clapped his hands in delight. "Excellent!" he said.

By the time they left twenty minutes later, Léa was sorry to say goodbye to M Formentin and the Musée Quentin-Savary. When she finished school and started working, she wanted a job she loved—not to become rich so that she could buy beautiful things, as Mme Quentin-Savary had done, but so that she could be proud of her work, and not bored. Like M Formentin, who obviously loved his job. And Mme Forbin, who, it seemed to Léa, loved hers most of the time.

Chapter Two

Friday, April 20

"I'd forgotten how beautiful this drive is," Marine said to her best friend, Sylvie. They were heading south on the highway between Aix and the coast, and Marine was craning her head so that she could better see the hills to her right. They were covered in garigue that was brighter than usual because it had rained so much that spring.

"*Oui, c'est vrai*," Sylvie mumbled in agreement, signaling to pass a slow-moving truck. "How are you feeling today?"

"Oh, I'm fine," Marine said, smiling. "It was really just those first three months, you know. I was constantly tired."

Sylvie shifted gears as they climbed the mountain. "Get ready for the view," she said.

Marine did as she was instructed and looked out of the passenger window. She dared not move, as she knew that she'd only have the view for a few seconds. Soon she saw the sheltered bay of Cassis and caught her breath. "The water is sapphire blue and emerald green," she said.

"We're lucky it's so sunny today, after all that rain."

"Look at the vineyards," Marine continued. "How they sweep down the mountain and almost slide straight into downtown Cassis. The contrast is amazing . . . the green blue sea, the orderly rows of vineyards, and the bright white rock of the mountaintops."

"It really is a paradise."

"Yes, that's why I never go in summer. Parking nightmare!" Sylvie laughed. "Give me La Ciotat any day."

"I agree," Marine said. "The underdog. City of dockers."

"And dockers' wives and children."

Marine smiled. "You sound like my mother."

"How are your parents?" Sylvie asked.

"They're both well, thanks," Marine answered. "Maman busies herself with various theological committees and the academic publishing houses where she's a board member. At least I assume she's still a board member." She looked out of the window and smiled. "Maybe she just shows up at the meetings, and they don't protest as they're afraid to get rid of her—"

"Perfect description of Florence Bonnet," Sylvie said, laughing. "And your dad?"

"He loves being retired from his general practice," Marine said. "He sometimes goes to medical conferences but only if they're in Europe. Neither of my parents have ever been great travelers. And he gardens."

"Sounds like a nice life," Sylvie said as she slowed the car down and they exited the highway.

"Even if the ship-building industry has gone bust, those cranes are a constant reminder of the huge ships that were built here," Marine said as the tall cranes that once lifted and lowered heavy metal ships' parts came into view. They looked like monstrous prehistoric birds. "I hope La Ciotat never gets rid of them."

"They won't," Sylvie said. "The cranes are back in use. I just read in *Le Monde* that La Ciotat is now advertising her shipyards as *the place* to get your super-yacht repaired and furnished."

"That's a brilliant idea."

"Yeah, the infrastructure is already in place, and there are so many skilled boat workers here."

"And look," Marine said as they drove downhill and into town, "the sea here is just as beautiful as in Cassis."

Sylvie turned the car onto one of La Ciotat's main streets and changed the subject. "Your parents must be so excited about the baby."

Marine shrugged and looked out of the side window. "I guess."

"What do you mean?"

"Well, they don't really say much. Antoine's father and his girlfriend, Rebecca, are a lot more excited than my parents."

Sylvie glanced at Marine. "Your parents have never been emotionally demonstrative. But they'll come around, you'll see, once the baby is born and your mother can talk its ear off."

Marine laughed, thankful that she was there, in La Ciotat, on a sunny day, with Sylvie. She was happy not to think about the baby for a few hours and to have to respond to Antoine's one million well-meaning questions a day about how she was feeling and if the baby was moving yet. "I'm looking forward to the conference," she said.

"That's great, because late-nineteenth-century Provençal art isn't everyone's thing," Sylvie said, pulling the car into a parking lot adjacent to the harbor. "But some of it is really interesting—precursors to the Impressionists, or to the transition period between them and the boring Academy stuff that went before."

"Painters like Jean-Baptiste Olive and Félix Ziem?"

"Of course you'd be able to list some names," Sylvie said, laughing, as she turned off the car's engine. "Is there anything you don't know?"

"Yes. I have no idea how a camera works, which is your specialty," Marine replied. "What's the theme of your talk today?"

"How the Lumière brothers influenced late-nineteenth- and early-twentieth-century photographers. The older I get, the more interested I am in pioneering photography."

"You're paying your respects," Marine said, smiling.

They got out of the car and walked across the parking lot, every now and then turning around to look at the sea and the bobbing sailboats. "The Lumière brothers were from La Ciotat, right?" Marine asked.

"They came here on holidays," Sylvie said. "But they were from Lyon."

Marine looked up at the pale yellow building across the street, shielding her eyes from the sun. "The Eden," she said. "I don't think I've ever been in it."

"I've only been in once, as an art student," Sylvie replied. "It was a squat back then."

Marine slipped her arm through Sylvie's. "This is doubly exciting, then. Thank you for the invite."

As Sylvie busied herself preparing for her presentation, Marine wandered through the cinema's lobby. She looked closely at a series of photos of turn-of-the-century La Ciotat, the most interesting of which showed a ship being launched from the port where she and Sylvie had just parked the car. It seemed to her that the whole town must have come to watch. In it, hundreds of people of all ages laughed and waved, celebrating the construction of yet another ship made there with their own hands and shoulders and brains. In the next photo, taken a few minutes after the previous one, the same ship, now launched into the harbor, had released a four-meter-high wave in its wake, thoroughly soaking those in the front row. *The days when a whole city took pride in their handiwork are over,* Marine mused. *Most of us now sit in front of a computer. And what had happened to the ship builders?*

"Time to go in," a well-dressed elderly woman said. Marine smiled and nodded, following the woman, who was the sort who regularly attended such conferences: perhaps a widow, or a retired academic. After having taken early retirement from the Aix law school more than a year ago, Marine was happy to be back in an academic setting. She didn't miss teaching or the endless academic meetings, but she did rather miss the camaraderie of colleagues and having a place to go to each morning instead of just shuffling up the stairs to her office in the mezzanine of their apartment. But quitting teaching had allowed her the time to work on writing a biography of Jean-Paul Sartre and Simone de Beauvoir, and, she was quite sure now, had relaxed her enough to get pregnant. She was the nervous, high-energy one in their couple. Antoine was the calm one.

She looked around at the dark red interior of the world's oldest cinema and wondered how many citizens of La Ciotat had met there, sitting in the mezzanine holding hands, watching a Marcel Pagnol movie, in the decades before the cinema was abandoned.

The lights dimmed as a small man with a short, quick step marched onto the stage and set his notes down on the podium. An elderly man—*probably another well-meaning volunteer,* mused Marine—rushed across the stage to lower the microphone. Marine recognized the speaker, who had been introduced by the conference's organizer as M Formentin. He was a downtown Aix regular. She often saw him in the mornings at Les Deux Garçons, and had frequently seen him when she still had her apartment in the Quartier Mazarin. But why? Had he been a neighbor? He was easy to remember: a distinctive old-fashioned dandy who always wore three-piece suits, a folded silk handkerchief in his breast pocket, and a bow tie, regardless of the weather.

M Formentin began to tell the crowd about a museum and Marine realized that he was the director of the Musée Quentin-Savary, a museum in Aix that she hadn't visited since she was in her twenties. She wondered what he was doing there. His museum's collection held mostly porcelain and some old documents and archives, not turn-of-the-century photographs or paintings. At least that's what she remembered. But he soon answered her question, explaining that he was exploring, as an amateur, the work of the painter Félix Ziem and Ziem's importance in Provence. The Musée Quentin-Savary had been bequeathed a Ziem painting of a Venetian canal, circa 1902, by the dear recently deceased

Mme de Montbarbon. Formentin pressed a button and a photo-graph of the painting appeared on the screen behind him.

Marine sat back, mesmerized. She remembered someone had called Ziem the Turner of Provence and she now saw why. The painting featured a rosy pink building in a narrow corner where two canals met, viewed from a striking angle instead of from the front. The dark blue sky was littered with pink clouds and the blue-green water of the canals shimmered with reflections of gold and white. A gondola poled by two men glided past the pink building; the boat was jet black, making the gondoliers' bright white blouses appear even brighter. But it was the loose, hazy brushstrokes that gave the painting its Turneresque quality.

M Formentin, although nervous, was obviously passionate about Ziem's life and work and Marine listened with interest, even taking notes from time to time. It was something she had always done, as a student and then as a professor; the notes aided her memory. She stored them at home in files; one never knew when those bits of information would be useful.

Félix Ziem had lived in Marseille and Martigues, Formentin explained, just west of Marseille, but had traveled to Venice a few times a year until his death at the age of ninety. The Impression-ists had admired his work, most of which had been created well before their first show in 1874, and Van Gogh had remarked that there was no blue like Ziem's. Certainly, Marine saw, the colors were breathtaking, even in a photograph blown up on screen. She couldn't wait to see the actual painting; Ziem's blues were cobalt, his greens touched with lemon, his whites like flashes of light.

Twenty minutes later M Formentin finished his discourse and the crowd politely applauded, Marine a little louder than the others. She found Ziem's life fascinating, especially the fact that he chose to travel by foot, always moving, always exploring, rather than settling down to the bourgeois life that many of the Impressionists had chosen.

Someone in the audience asked if the work had been painted on wood and M Formentin excitedly replied in the affirmative: Ziem felt that wood, especially mahogany, enabled him to add even more color, achieving a glazed effect. After a few other questions, the conference's moderator was about to end the question-and-answer period when a tall, thin man sitting a few rows behind Marine stood up and demanded a chance to speak. He took the microphone and introduced himself as Aurélien Lopez, the director of Marseille's Musée Cavasino on the rue Paradis. Marine knew it but, like the Quentin-Savary, hadn't been there in ages. It was smaller and even gloomier.

"I have some misgivings about this painting," Lopez began.

Marine swung around to get a better look at him.

Lopez went on. "Ziem rarely painted this color but instead painted reds like cherries or rubies—"

The audience muttered in disapproval as Marine looked on, shocked.

"But I have bigger problems with its provenance," Lopez said. "And the papers documenting its ownership that the dear Mme de Montbarbon seems to have put in your trust—"

Formentin spoke up, his voice loud and strong. "She willed the painting to our museum."

Marine swung back around toward the stage and looked at the little man, whose face was flushed with anger.

"Before she died," Lopez said.

"That's correct. You are welcome to come to the Musée Quentin-Savary and read the documents anytime," Formentin answered. A number of questions followed, beginning with more academic ones dealing with provenance and technique followed by many about the painter himself. Formentin revealed more details that Marine found fascinating. Born poor, Ziem had trained as an architect before turning to painting; he was a meticulous bookkeeper of his own sales, very unusual for the time; and, as a true Romantic, he preferred to travel on foot. All the way to Italy.

"And that will be the final question of the session," the head organizer cut in after someone asked about vacationing in Venice, "for we seem to have run out of time! Thank you, M Achille Formentin, for shedding much light on this beloved Provençal painter."

Marine caught Sylvie's eye. She was sitting in the front row with the other speakers. Sylvie made a gesture waving her right hand back and forth under her chin as if to say, "That was intense!" Marine smiled and nodded in agreement. She gathered her purse and jacket, anxious to talk to Sylvie. As she stood up she felt a curious movement in her stomach. Her hand went quickly, automatically, to her stomach, but then the movement stopped. Was that the baby moving? It hadn't happened before. Ecstatic, she made her way past the seats and out into the aisle and ran toward Sylvie.

Chapter Three

Tuesday, April 24

Achille Formentin woke up as he usually did, without the aid of an alarm, at 7:00 a.m. He couldn't remember the last time he had needed to set an alarm. Perhaps for a flight? Berlin, last spring, for the decorative arts conference? He gently set aside the duvet—he wasn't the type to throw back the duvet, ever—got up and drew open the thick silk curtains on his bedroom window. He looked out over the gardens, where beyond the neighboring apartment building he could see the top of Saint Jean-de-Malte's steeple. Swallows furiously flew around it, as if mocking and teasing the stone gargoyles that protruded from each of the narrow steeple's four corners.

After showering and trimming his mustache, he got dressed in a three-piece light wool suit in forest green. Opening the top drawer to his dresser, he carefully chose a cravat. This moment was one of the most pleasurable of his day. The silk handkerchiefs were laid out before him, each one rolled up and resting in a small wooden compartment. After a second's hesitation he chose one with orange and blue stripes, folded it carefully, and set it in the breast pocket of his jacket. He gave himself a final check in the mirror and then walked down the hall of his third-floor, two-bedroom apartment, taking along his cell phone—the only piece of technology he owned—and locking the door behind him.

Once outside, Achille walked down the rue du Maréchal Joffre toward the Place Forbin located at the top of the Cours Mirabeau. He always carefully timed this walk, making sure to leave his apartment before 8:00 a.m. to avoid the 8:15 a.m. rush when parents hurried their small children to primary school. The fact that he had once been their age never occurred to him.

The streets were quiet, and he smiled as he walked through the square and down a block to the Deux Garçons, where he normally ate breakfast. It was breezy but sunny, so by the time he arrived at the café, there were customers already sitting on the terrace, their faces stretched up toward the sun. He passed them and opened the door, walking through the grand dining room full of shining mirrors and gold-gilded trim and turning left to enter a smaller, more intimate room reserved for morning coffees and evening aperitifs. He hurried slightly—trying not to be obvious—to get his usual seat by the window. But halfway through the room he froze; one of the waiters saw him and apologized with a shrug. Achille's corner table had been joined to a bigger one beside it and a group of tourists sat there, speaking English, laughing, and drinking coffee, the table littered with croissant crumbs. Achille turned and quickly looked around the room; all the other tables were occupied. Then to his right he saw a table for four that had only one occupant, a woman of a certain age whose head was buried in a newspaper.

"May I join you?" he quietly asked.

"Of course!" the woman answered, a little too loudly. "I'm by myself," she continued. "I don't think my husband has ever even been here, all these years. My daughter is supposed to be joining me, but there's lots of room. Please, let me move my things from the chair. You certainly don't want to be looking at my old bicycle helmet while having your coffee!"

Achille tried to smile, embarrassed by the excess information he had not asked for or required. "*Merci*," he mumbled, sitting down, before reaching for the *Figaro* that was sitting on the counter wrapped around a wooden pole.

"Perhaps you want this one?" the woman asked, holding up the left-wing newspaper *Libération*.

"*Non, merci.*"

"No, I thought not," she replied, smiling and almost, he thought, winking.

The waiter reappeared. Relieved, Achille ordered his habitual pot of Earl Grey tea and brioche glacé.

"There aren't any more brioches," the waiter said impatiently.

"*Quoi? Mais c'est pas vrai!*" Flustered, Achille tried to think of what he could eat in place of a brioche.

The waiter answered his question for him. "There are only croissants left."

"Very well, a croissant." He opened the paper and tried to concentrate on the first article that caught his eye, but it was about fighting in the Middle East and he couldn't bear that kind of news in the morning.

Antoine Verlaque looked at himself in the mirror just as long as Achille Formentin had. He wasn't as fastidious a dresser as Achille Formentin, but Verlaque would be able to recognize the label of Achille's wool suit as coming from Magee 1866, a small mill located in Donegal that still produced high-quality tweed suits for men and women. Verlaque's paternal grandmother, Emmeline, had been English, and she had dressed, despite living in France for decades, like someone in a *Country Life* article. Except for her shoes and purses, which always came from Hermès.

Verlaque was looking in the mirror *not* because he was fussing over his clothes—a pressed white shirt, a blue wool jacket, no tie or cravat—but because he was worried about his age. Forty-five. Would he have enough energy to take care of a baby? Or when the child got older, to play soccer, or rugby, with them? Regardless of the baby's sex, they'd play one of those sports. Things were changing in France, catching up with North America, where female pro teams were funded, watched, and celebrated, and had been for years. And schooling? He didn't tell Marine, but he was already looking up the ratings for each primary school in Aix. He asked colleagues at the Palais de Justice where their children went to school. What he didn't know was that two of the young officers had started a betting pool on which school he would choose. So far Nativité was in the lead.

His hair was still very thick and wiry, but he was sure it was grayer than it had been the previous week. And his eyes looked tired despite the fact that he was careful to get enough sleep. They went to bed early now, anyway. Marine was tired, too, but ravishingly beautiful, and got more beautiful as the weeks progressed toward that day sometime in September when they would be, hopefully, a family of three.

"Good morning, dear," Marine said as she knocked on the door and came into their bathroom. "Here's your coffee. I'm off to meet Maman."

"Thank you. Your mother? Where?"

"She's having breakfast at Les Deux Garçons." Marine looked at her watch. "I'd better hurry. She said she'd be there at eight, and it's already five past."

"Walk carefully," Verlaque said, taking her in his arms. "You're wearing flats, I see. Good."

Marine smiled and kissed her husband. "Don't worry, I won't fall."

"That red dress looks lovely on you. Is it new?"

"Yes, I bought it during the January sales," Marine replied, twirling so that the fine knit of the wool swirled around her thin silhouette, hugging her body, including the bump in her stomach.

Verlaque smiled. Marine didn't like spending money on herself and always prefaced an announcement of a clothing purchase with the fact that she had bought it on sale. "We need to go to Normandy sometime soon," he said as he followed Marine toward the front door.

"Normandy?" Marine asked, putting on a trench coat. "To your grandparents' house?"

"Yes, there are things we need to go through. Paintings, dishes, Emmeline's clothes. Wouldn't our little girl love playing with Grandmother's shoes and hats and purses?"

Marine smiled. "That's a beautiful image. I'm late, so I have to go." She kissed Antoine and opened the door of the apartment. "Our son might like it, too."

"Normandy? Yeah! Great! I loved it, too, as a kid."

Marine began to walk down the stairs and yelled back up, grinning from ear to ear, "No, I meant the hats and shoes and purses!"

"Sorry I'm late, Maman," Marine said as she leaned down and gave her mother the *bises*.

"No worries," Florence Bonnet said. "I was reading *Libé*. Here, sit down across from me." She picked up her helmet, looked at the man next to her, and asked, "*Ça va?*" as she motioned setting the helmet on the chair across from him.

"*Oui, oui,*" he quickly said, looking back down at his coffee and unread newspaper.

"*Merci!* Now, Marine, what will you have? Are you drinking coffee these days?"

"No, I can't stand it," Marine answered. "Fresh-squeezed orange juice and a croissant," she said to the waiter who had just walked by their table. She recognized the man sharing their table; he had spoken at the conference in La Ciotat on Friday: Achille Formentin, from the Musée Quentin-Savary.

"Just like me," Mme Bonnet said. "I couldn't stand the taste of coffee when I was pregnant."

"Really?" Marine said, leaning forward, happy to have a pregnancy story to share with her mother.

"I can't stay long as choir practice begins at nine fifteen sharp," Mme Bonnet said, quickly changing the subject. "We're practicing for Mme de Montbarbon's funeral mass."

"I heard she died," Marine said, realizing the baby talk was over and taking a sip of the orange juice that had just arrived. She looked around the café. A bouquet of fresh white lilies sat on the marble counter; the walls were a deep patinaed green with gilded-gold edging, the chandeliers crystal, the benches covered in green velvet. She had forgotten how comfortable this small room was. Her mother continued talking and she half listened, taking in every other word. She wondered if she should say something to M Formentin, like how much she had enjoyed his talk, but years of experience of running into people she recognized in Aix had taught her to say nothing, to respect their privacy.

"You wouldn't believe how tricky the Mozart Requiem is," Mme Bonnet continued. "Especially the Kyrie movement for the sopranos."

"Mozart's Requiem?" Marine asked. "Isn't that long and difficult?"

"Well, we're only singing a few minutes of it. Solange Picard is having an especially difficult time, especially at the end of the Kyrie when all of the voices come together. But she's obviously not thinking straight these days, with the break-in and all."

"Break-in?" Marine set her cup down, looking interested.

"You haven't heard? She had to go to the Palais de Justice and be interviewed by your husband's colleagues."

"Her house was broken into?"

"*Mais non!* Mme de Montbarbon's apartment. She wasn't even cold yet when thieves broke in."

Marine set her pastry down, a little disconcerted by her mother's narrative. "Cours Mirabeau, right?" she asked. "I went to school with a Montbarbon. Nice guy."

"Number 8. They own the whole building but rent out the ground floor to a bank."

"I'm confused. What does your choral friend—Solange—have to do with it?"

"Solange Picard is their maid. Don't ask me why, as Mme de Montbarbon was a real taskmaster and Solange has a degree in literature. She's really beyond that kind of work but insists that she enjoyed it. She was with the family for years. No wonder she's so upset."

"What was stolen?" Marine interjected, trying to get her mother back on topic.

"Solange is being rather tight-lipped about it, but she did mention that some very expensive porcelain was missing. A complete set of Sèvres from the eighteenth century."

Marine's eyes widened. She loved ceramics. "That doesn't sound like a normal break-in. These days thieves bypass the silver and china. They're only interested in electronics, jewelry, and cash."

Mme Bonnet shrugged her shoulders.

Marine sat back. She thought of the Verlaque family's country house, sitting empty in Normandy. If it were not for the caretakers, a middle-aged couple who lived in an on-site guesthouse, the mansion would have been ransacked years ago. But she had a romantic idea of northern France, where she imagined, rightly, that there were fewer break-ins. "Do the police have any leads—" Marine was beginning to ask when M Formentin quickly got up, bumping into the table.

"Pardon!" he exclaimed, bowing slightly to the women.

"No problem," Marine said, smiling. She turned around to watch as he paid for his breakfast at the counter and then rushed out of the café, walking like a penguin. "What an odd man," she said, looking back at her mother. "He's the director of the Musée Quentin-Savary."

Mme Bonnet said, "He was listening to our conversation. I tried to be extra-dramatic, to give him his money's worth."

Achille walked quickly down the rue Mistral, clutching the keys to the museum in his right hand. He could feel their metallic teeth cutting into his sweating palm. His heart beat faster and faster as he approached the museum, and by the time he put the key in the lock at number 16 and turned it, his hands were shaking. He opened the door and turned on the foyer lights, closing the door behind him and locking it again. He stood motionless and looked around. The small wooden bench sat against the wall, beside it, a potted fern. He walked slowly through the hall and into an ante-chamber, where there was a small wooden desk—early twentieth century, not a museum piece—at which either he or his secretary, Mme Devaux, greeted visitors and took their three euro admission charge. Continuing into the main room, he switched on the lights and blinked, waiting for his eyes to adjust to the brightness.

But when the room came into focus, he was overcome with horror. He looked around, hoping he was still sleeping. But no, he remembered the swallows taunting the gargoyles and having to share a poorly situated table at Les Deux Gs with a chatty mother and her pensive daughter. He closed his eyes and opened them again. No, it wasn't a dream. It was a nightmare. His museum was empty. Save for the bench and the fern, and the little reception desk and chair, there was nothing left.

He walked through the room, running his finger along the

chimney mantelpiece, where the bust of Mirabeau once stood. The display case was empty. He continued into the dining room and turned on the chandelier, knowing that this room, too, would be empty. Only the long dining room table remained, on it round impressions outlined in faint powdery dust where Mme Quentin-Savary's favorite dishes had been placed. The dark red wallpaper was even more hideous now that everything was gone. And the only sound in his head was Mozart's Requiem.

Chapter Four

Tuesday, April 24

Come in, Bruno," Antoine Verlaque said in answer to the familiar light four knocks—one followed by a pause, then three quick ones—on his office door. He quickly hid the book of popular baby names under a stack of papers and stood up, walking around his desk. He and the commissioner normally met at 11:00 every Monday morning and then had lunch together in town. "Happy Monday," he said, shaking Bruno Paulik's hand.

"Tuesday," Paulik answered.

"Right," Verlaque said, turning on the espresso machine. "Yesterday was Easter Monday. How could I have forgotten? We ate an overcooked leg of lamb at Marine's parents'."

"Yum."

"Thankfully I brought the wine. A magnum of one of your wife's Syrahs."

"That's the same meal we had," Paulik said. "Only the lamb was beautifully pink, roasted on a bed of tiny potatoes and artichokes from my parents' farm, and Hélène steamed great bunches of thin asparagus—"

"Do you want a coffee or not?" Verlaque asked. "Because you're really ticking me off."

"Sorry," Paulik said, sitting down and smiling. "Just a single today."

"That's all you're getting."

Verlaque made the coffees and handed Paulik his, then sat back down behind his desk and slowly stirred a cube of sugar into his espresso, staring into the demitasse as the sugar dissolved. "Quiet weekend in Aix?" he finally asked, looking up at the commissioner.

"Very. Nothing to report crimewise, although our colleagues in Marseille had their hands full with a fight between Russian and French soccer fans after that exhibition game at Le Dôme."

"I read about that this morning," Verlaque said. "When will the world wake up and realize that rugby is the gentleman's game?"

Paulik opened his mouth to reply in agreement when he was interrupted by two knocks on the door.

"Yes, France?" Verlaque said.

France Dubois opened the door. "Officers Schoelcher and Goulin are here to see you," she said. "They say it's important."

"Bring them in," Verlaque said. "Thank you."

"Two knocks?" Bruno asked.

"Yes, that's her sign. You both are privileged."

The two officers stepped inside. After shaking their hands,

Verlaque gestured for them to sit down at a round glass table in the corner of his office. Sophie Goulin sat down and stroked the chair's dark blue upholstery as Verlaque looked on, pleased that someone had noticed his latest auction-house purchase.

"What's up?" Paulik asked.

"We've just returned from the Musée Quentin-Savary," Sophie said. "We were called there just after nine o'clock by the museum's director. I'm still in shock. This is definitely the oddest thing to happen to me in my fifteen years at this job."

Jules Schoelcher raised his hand. "Mine, too. In my seven years on the job."

Paulik looked at the officers. "What happened? No, first of all, where is this museum?"

"Number 16 rue Mistral," Jules replied.

Verlaque said, "I've walked past it a million times—"

"But never gone in, right?" Sophie said.

"Correct. I always meant to . . ."

"Me, too." Sophie Goulin looked at the magistrate and tried to see any signs of change in his outward appearance or facial expressions now that he was going to be a father. She knew about the betting pool on which primary school he would pick; she had bet on Sallier, the public school that had an integrated music program like its neighbor, the junior high Mignet. Violin, she thought, or cello, would suit the child of Verlaque and Bonnet.

"The museum was closed over Easter weekend," Jules said. "The director, Achille Formentin, opened it this morning as he usually does just before nine." He paused and both Verlaque and Paulik leaned forward. Jules went on slowly. "But when M Formentin turned on the lights, there was nothing left."

"What do you mean, nothing?" Verlaque asked.

"Exactly that," Sophie said. "We saw the place ourselves. The museum's been cleaned out except for a bench and a small reception desk."

"And a fern," added Jules.

Verlaque leaned back while Paulik stared at the officers, his arms folded across his chest. "How is that possible?" Paulik asked. "Everything? Paintings? Sculptures? What was in there?"

Sophie got out a notebook and opened it. "M Formentin is preparing a list for us," she said. "Lots of ceramics by the sound of it, some paintings, and the archives about the Quentin-Savary family and Aix."

"Formentin's really in a bad state," Jules said. "He could barely stand up. We told him to rest, but he wants to get the list to us as soon as possible and have someone of great authority—his words—come and speak to him."

"He's not alone, is he?" Paulik asked.

"No, no," Sophie said. "He's at the museum, and just as we were leaving the forensic team showed up to fingerprint and dust the place. Should be easy as, well, it's empty."

Jules added, "He also insists that we question Gilbert Quentin-Savary as soon as possible."

"There's a remaining family member?" Verlaque asked.

"The great-great-grandson of the museum's benefactor," Jules said.

"Three greats, I think," Sophie said. "Mme Quentin-Savary willed the museum to Aix after her death in 1900. Gilbert lives on the top floor above the museum."

"M Formentin kept muttering Gilbert Quentin-Savary's

name," Jules said. "It seems that M Quentin-Savary has a key to the museum, as does M Formentin, of course, and a part-time secretary."

Sophie turned a page of her notebook. "Mme Faustine Devaux."

"Achille? Faustine?" Verlaque asked. "This sounds like a nineteenth-century play."

"That's what the museum feels like," Sophie said. "He showed us photos of it full. But even with it being empty . . . it feels stuck in time."

"Here's an obvious question," Paulik said. "Were there signs of a break-in?"

"The back door, which leads out to a garden and a narrow driveway that is big enough for one car, was open. Unlocked, I mean."

"And M Formentin was sure he locked it, I presume?" Verlaque asked.

"Affirmative," Jules said.

"Did this place not have an alarm?" Paulik asked.

"Yes, but it's broken," Jules said. "The repair was booked for this week."

Paulik put his bald head in his hands and groaned.

"Seems too good to be true, right?" Sophie said. "Inside job. Someone who knew the alarm was off."

"And the above three—the director, the secretary, and the great-great-great-grandson—all knew about the broken alarm?"

"Correct," Jules said. "When we asked about an alarm, that's when M Formentin began muttering Gilbert's name."

Verlaque got up and began walking around the room. "This is

taking some time to sink in. How can a museum be emptied over one weekend? Is that even possible?"

"Apparently so," Paulik said.

Sophie asked, "Could this be related to the theft last week in an apartment on the Cours?"

"The Montbarbon place?" Paulik asked.

"Go on," Verlaque said as he turned around to face her.

"The apartment of Mme de Montbarbon. Clothilde. She died two weeks ago and the robbery occurred a few days after. I overheard some of the officers talking about the break-in; they found it odd that not much was taken."

"You're right. They took a set of porcelain," Paulik said. "She didn't keep jewels or cash in the apartment."

"Pardon me?" Verlaque asked. "Porcelain?"

Sophie nodded. "Like the museum, right?"

"There must be a connection," Verlaque said. "And how does one remove an entire set of porcelain without being seen and without breaking any pieces?"

"Or an entire museum?" Jules added.

"A mover could answer those questions," Paulik said. He got out his cell phone and scrolled through his contacts. "My cousin Renaud in Pertuis moves all kinds of wealthy Parisians down to the Luberon, and sometimes back again when the charm of Provence has worn off and some movie star or fashion designer has decided Provence is no longer fashionable." He got up and began dialing, leaving the room.

"The forensic team is taking photos, I presume?" Verlaque asked.

"Yes," Jules said. "It's very eerie. Even the curtains are gone."

"And the swags," Sophie added.

"Swags?"

"Yes, they were handmade in the late eighteenth century by a famous silk artisan from Paris, or so we were told," Sophie explained.

Verlaque sat down again as Paulik came back into the office. "Renaud can meet us at the museum tomorrow morning at eight. He can't stay long."

"Excellent, thank you," Verlaque said. "And this great-great-great-grandson?"

"We knocked on his door on the third floor, but there was no answer," Jules said. "But we have his phone number."

"Hand it over," Verlaque said. "I'm going to call him right now."

Jules read out the number as Verlaque sat at his desk and dialed, putting his desk phone on speaker. On the third ring a man's voice answered.

"Is this Gilbert Quentin-Savary?" Verlaque asked.

"Yes. Who's this, may I ask?"

"Antoine Verlaque, the examining magistrate of Aix-en-Provence. Are you at home?"

"If you mean in my apartment, no. I'm at my country house near Switzerland."

"How long have you been there?" Verlaque asked.

"What concern is that of yours?"

"You're not aware of what happened this weekend at your family's museum here in Aix?"

"No. What's happened?" M Quentin-Savary asked, snickering.

"A sudden rush of junior high school students came to visit the sorry little place? Or a group of five or six retired civil servants who've made a day trip all the way from Avignon?"

Verlaque looked across the room at Paulik and the two officers and rolled his eyes. "The museum was broken into."

"What? Was there anything stolen?"

"Everything."

A few seconds of silence stung the air. "Pardon me? Is this some kind of prank?"

Verlaque said, "No, I'm afraid it isn't. The museum was closed over the long weekend, so the thieves had three days."

"Someone must have seen or heard them. This is unbelievable!"

"We will be questioning the neighbors as soon as possible."

"Listen, I'll come back as soon as I can," M Quentin-Savary said. "I can be in Aix by early this evening."

"Good. Call me as soon as you're downtown." Verlaque read out his cell phone number. "We'll meet at the museum."

"Do you really mean everything is gone? I'm sorry if I sounded blasé earlier . . ."

"Yes." Verlaque decided not to mention the curtain swags. "I'll repeat my first question. How long have you been at your country house?"

"I got here Friday afternoon."

"Can someone there confirm that?"

"Yes, my housekeeper," M Quentin-Savary replied. "She's right here beside me."

"Put her on, please."

"*Allô?*" a woman's voice asked after a few seconds.

"Hello. This is Judge Antoine Verlaque from Aix-en-Provence.

There's no need to be alarmed, but the museum of M Quentin-Savary's family has been broken into and we are verifying everyone's whereabouts over Easter. Was M Quentin-Savary at his country house all weekend?"

"Yes, sir, he was," she answered. "This is terrible news—"

"And when did he arrive?"

"Friday afternoon. He drove up just as I was leaving. I had been getting the house ready for him. It was about four o'clock."

"Thank you. And you are?"

"Mme Borgia. Gisèle."

Verlaque thanked her again and hung up. "Let's go to the museum, Bruno," he said. Turning to the officers, he asked, "Can one of you have the director and secretary meet us there?"

"Will do," Sophie said.

"I'll go and check my email to see if M Formentin has sent the list of missing objects yet," Jules said.

"Good," Paulik said. "And, Officer Goulin, check the local records for art theft, museum break-ins, that kind of thing. I don't think we can rule out the idea that some art thieves pegged the museum, then got lucky with the alarm being off. Or they were told it was off. Would the back door have been easy to break into?"

"Easy-peasy," Sophie said. "My eight-year-old son could have done it."

"Great," Paulik said, rolling his eyes. "Why didn't this museum have proper security systems?"

"Probably because they didn't think they needed it," Verlaque said, putting his cell phone in his jacket pocket and walking toward the door. "It's a drab little museum that we've all walked by but none of us have ever gone into."

Chapter Five

≈

Tuesday, April 24

A uniformed officer opened the museum's door. Bruno Paulik muttered, "Good morning, Flamant," as he walked into the narrow entryway. Antoine Verlaque followed behind.

"Judge Verlaque," Flamant said with a slight bow.

Verlaque shook Flamant's hand. "How are things?"

"Quiet, as to be expected."

"I'll let you lead me through the museum," Verlaque said. "Is the director present?"

"Yes, sir," Flamant said. "He's upstairs. I'll take you there; the stairs are at the back of the museum."

Verlaque followed and they stopped at a small reception desk, which stood in an alcove between the foyer and the main room. The judge looked down at the desk, his arms folded across his chest. Flamant said, "They've dusted this desk and there are oodles of fingerprints, including the director's. He complained that a group of kids from Mignet were here on Friday and kept touching every single surface."

"Not surprising. Did you get their teacher's name?"

"Yes, sir."

Verlaque looked ahead into the empty room beyond them.

Flamant said, "The museum was still full of its contents, naturally, for their visit."

"Yes. They must have been bored."

Flamant shrugged. "Maybe." He paused. "But Mignet's a really good school."

"I've heard," Verlaque said, still scanning the empty room, trying to imagine its contents.

"It's not too early to be looking into schools, sir, if you don't mind me saying."

"Exactly what I told my wife. She grew up here. Did you?"

"Yes, sir. I went to Sacré-Cœur."

"Really?" Verlaque asked. Sacré-Cœur was high up on his list. "Did you like it?"

"I loved it," Flamant replied, feeling a bit guilty that he was lying. But not many of his colleagues were betting on Sacré-Cœur and he wanted to up the odds.

"Good to know," Verlaque said. "But that must have been a while ago."

"True, but it's one of Aix's oldest schools—"

Paulik arrived and stood next to Flamant. "Can you take the judge upstairs to see M Formentin now? I'm told he's exhausted," he said.

"Right, right," Flamant muttered as he turned around, gesturing with his hand for Verlaque to follow.

Verlaque stopped as he entered the main room, gloomy and dark even during the day. He walked to the center of the room and peered into a glass display case, now empty. Its back was open and Verlaque bent down to look at the small bronze lock. "Was a key used to open this?"

"No," Flamant replied. "A pin or a needle, or so it appears. It would have been as easy to open as the tiny lock on my sister's diary."

Verlaque smiled. "Speaking from experience."

"I only read it once, to be honest. It was boring and I immediately felt ashamed." Verlaque walked behind Flamant, who was so tall and wide the judge could barely see past him. He tried to imagine a twelve-year-old Alain Flamant—probably already tall—curled up in a corner of his bedroom, sneaking a look at his sister's diary, his cheeks flushed from embarrassment and guilt.

The next room was even darker than the first because of the dark red wallpaper that covered the walls. In the center was a long mahogany table. "The table was set with a Sèvres porcelain service," Flamant said. "M Formentin said that normally the service is in that display case against the wall, but he set it out for the schoolkids and didn't bother putting it back as he was getting another visit today. Which he canceled, of course."

"Let's go see him," Verlaque said. "What else is up on the first floor?"

"His office, plus lots of shelves and boxes and filing cabinets. Storage, mostly."

"Above that?"

"The second floor is a two-bedroom apartment rented out to a sales executive, a bachelor, who works for a local chocolate company. He's not here at the moment as they sell worldwide. He's in

Japan, M Formentin thought. We're trying to get ahold of him, but it's difficult with the time difference."

Verlaque said, "Lots of money in sweets." He wondered why Flamant had thought it necessary to specify that the salesman's apartment had two bedrooms. Perhaps to show that he was paying attention to details? Or because he thought it offensive that a single man would have such a large apartment in Aix's most expensive neighborhood?

"I don't like sweets, never have," Flamant said bluntly. He led the way up a narrow service staircase in the back of the museum.

Again, Verlaque pictured a tall, gangly twelve-year-old Flamant, pushing aside his dessert, much to the distress of his frowning mother or perhaps doting grandmother. "Neither do I," he agreed. "I much prefer my calories in wine. And on the top floor is Gilbert Quentin-Savary's apartment?"

"Correct, sir."

A middle-aged man, whom Verlaque assumed was Achille Formentin, stood at the top of the stairs. Unlike Flamant, the museum director was short, and unlike the stocky judge, he was slim and dressed in a three-piece suit. Even from his position down below on the stairs Verlaque could see a bright orange silk handkerchief poking out of Formentin's breast pocket. Formentin was wringing his hands. "Finally you're here," he muttered, stepping aside and half stumbling over a wooden crate labeled FRAG-ILE. "Please come in."

"Antoine Verlaque. Thank you," Verlaque said, shaking his dry hand.

The director pulled up a nineteenth-century wooden chair and tried not to look worried as the judge—who was overweight, in his opinion—sat down upon it. The seat's delicate caning was original and now would certainly be stretched. Thankfully the tall young policeman did not seem to need a chair; he stood with his back against the wall, looking on. Something in his intelligent eyes said that he would be listening carefully.

"The commissioner is downstairs examining the back door, which apparently was easy to break into," Verlaque began.

Formentin continued to wring his hands. "My fault, entirely. I was going to ask the alarm people when they came this week to see about fixing the back door as well."

"Didn't a broken door and a nonfunctioning alarm make you nervous?" Verlaque asked.

"Of course," Formentin replied. His upper brow began to sweat. "But my mother is unwell . . . I've been distracted. When the alarm company couldn't come on the date I had originally booked, I took a chance on waiting until this week to get it fixed. They were the only company who even answered my messages. . . ."

Verlaque nodded, understanding perfectly well how difficult it was to get an appointment out of any tradesman in the south. "Has your mother recovered?"

Formentin looked at him in surprise. "Thank you. But no, she hasn't. She lives in an apartment in the Parc Mozart, but I may have to put her in a hospice."

Flamant made a mental note to check out the apartment complex at the Parc Mozart and make some inquiries about Formentin's mother's health.

"I'm sorry," Verlaque said. "It seems hard to believe that a thief, or thieves, would want everything in the museum. Could it be a ruse? Were they after something in particular? Do you have any ideas?"

"The Ziem painting."

"Félix Ziem?"

Formentin nodded. "An oil on wood of Venice that was recently donated to us by Mme de Montbarbon. I hadn't even had the chance to hang it."

"Do you have a photograph of it? With its provenance?"

"Certainly." With a shaking hand, Formentin handed the judge a file. Impressed by the judge's art knowledge, Formentin took a few seconds to look more closely at him.

"I assume there were other objects of value," Verlaque said. "Paintings? Sculptures? Or important documents?"

"There were some busts, but not of any great value, I'm afraid," Formentin said. "They were in terra-cotta," he added quietly as if apologizing. "And the documents are of value to historians but wouldn't be worth a great deal on the black market except for a few of the maps. We have a map of this neighborhood, for example, hand-drawn, of course, from the early seventeenth century."

"Are you aware that Mme de Montbarbon's apartment was broken into two weeks ago?"

"Yes."

"And that the only thing that was taken was a set of Sèvres porcelain?"

The hand wringing started up again. "That seemed like a prank, Judge, if I may say so. Some youngsters, after a night of drinking . . ."

"Although all of your museum's porcelain was taken as well."

"Yes, but they took everything—perhaps, as you suggest, disguising what they really wanted."

"Do you have any idea who could have done this?" Verlaque asked. "Have there been any visitors lately who have seemed out of place, for instance?"

"No, not while I've been in the rooms," Formentin said. "I split the museum surveillance time with our secretary, Mme Devaux, who'll be arriving any minute." He looked at his watch.

Since Achille Formentin hadn't mentioned the only remaining heir, Verlaque brought it up himself. "And Gilbert Quentin-Savary? I assume he had access to the museum?"

"Yes, yes, of course. But he showed no interest in the collection. Absolutely none."

"One of the police officers claims that this morning you spoke his name more than once."

"I was distressed . . ."

"M Quentin-Savary was away all weekend," Verlaque said. "At his country house. He's coming back this evening."

"*Ah, bon?*" Formentin asked with surprise and, Verlaque thought, slight disappointment. He quickly glanced at Flamant, who blinked twice, very quickly, as if in agreement.

"And your secretary, Mme Devaux? How long has she worked here?"

"For more than fifteen years. You don't think . . . ? No, no, that's impossible—"

"We have to consider everyone, beginning with those who had easy access to the museum." Verlaque didn't add that the general public also had easy access to the museum if they'd bothered to venture down the back alley.

Formentin took out a clean handkerchief from his pants pocket and wiped his brow. Verlaque thought he looked pale. "We'll leave you to get some rest, M Formentin." He stood up and shook the director's hand, which was now slightly moist. "Do you live close by? Would you like someone to accompany you home?"

"I live around the corner, on the rue Pavillon. But thank you."

"We'll see ourselves out," Verlaque said. "The sooner you get the list of the museum's contents to us, the better. But do have a rest first."

The museum director muttered in agreement and Verlaque and Flamant left the office, making their way single file down the stairs.

Formentin got up and walked around to the wooden chair that the judge had been sitting on. He gently pressed down on the caned seat and then let out a sigh.

Flamant and Verlaque stopped in the room with the red wallpaper. They could hear Paulik speaking to a woman at the front of the museum, Paulik's voice deep and gentle and the woman's higher-pitched and broken by sobs.

"What did you think?" Verlaque asked, whispering and gesturing to the ceiling with his head.

"He's beyond nervous," Flamant said. "I thought he was going to pass out. He's guilty, but of what I'm not sure yet."

"I agree. You'll check out the sick mother?"

"Yes, sir."

Verlaque was about to ask about the neighbors when they heard the woman in the front hall continue to weep. "I'll go and speak to the secretary," he said.

"I'll phone the alarm company," Flamant said. "And then pay a visit to the Parc Mozart."

They heard Formentin's footsteps coming down the stairs.

"Excellent, Flamant," Verlaque said in a loud voice, shaking the officer's hand. "See you later."

"I'm going home now," Formentin said as he walked into the room, looking at Verlaque and then at Flamant. "But I'll get you that list as soon as I can."

"Have a good rest," Verlaque said. He and Flamant watched the director walk through the museum and heard him mutter some consoling words to the secretary, then the front door closed.

Verlaque walked toward the entryway where a woman with short gray hair, perhaps in her sixties, sat on the bench, quietly crying and wiping her eyes with a tissue. She looked up at the judge and gasped for breath, her shoulders and upper torso heaving. Verlaque sat down on the bench next to her as Paulik, standing against the opposite wall, looked on.

"Mme Devaux," Verlaque said. "This is quite a shock, isn't it?"

Faustine Devaux tried to control her breathing. She looked at Verlaque and nodded. "Yes," she whispered. "Dreadful . . ."

"Would you like a glass of water, madame?" Paulik asked.

"Please."

"When were you last here, madame?" Verlaque asked.

"Friday. Morning. In the morning there was a school group here, but it was M Formentin's turn to supervise the museum." Her shoulders heaved once more and then she let out a long breath. "Excuse me," she said.

"Are you all right?"

"Yes."

Paulik returned and handed her a glass of water. She smiled and took the glass with slightly trembling hands.

"Were there any visitors Friday afternoon?" Verlaque asked.

"Yes, we had a scheduled visit from an academic who wanted to look at the archives. He came at two o'clock, and left just before I closed at six."

"Do you have his name and phone number?"

"Of course. I'll get those to you as soon as . . ."

"There's no rush for the moment. Did he seem interested in the museum's contents other than the archives? Did anything seem odd about him?"

"No, nothing. I showed him the documents and he worked with them in the back room, at a long table we use for such purposes. He's a historian specializing in eighteenth-century Provence, as are many of the visitors we receive here. He's been here before and is widely published; he usually sends us his articles when he's used the museum for research."

Not a prime suspect, Verlaque thought to himself. "And in recent weeks," he continued, "did anything seem odd or out of place, especially when visitors came into the museum?"

"No, nothing unusual. That's why this is all so shocking. . . ."

"And Gilbert Quentin-Savary? Does he come down into the museum often?"

Faustine Devaux managed a wry smile. "Gilbert? He only comes down to complain about the building—the heat being turned up too high or not high enough. That kind of thing."

"What's your impression of him?"

Mme Devaux wiped her nose and folded the tissue, putting it into her cardigan pocket. "Spoiled."

"I take it you don't like him very much."

"No, not in the slightest," she said. "He's very cruel to M Formentin, too."

"How so?"

"Condescending."

"And with you?"

"He doesn't notice me at all." She smiled again and looked at both Verlaque and Paulik. "I'm invisible to that kind of man. He's only interested in people who impress him with their money or beauty. Where is Gilbert, anyway?"

"He's been away for the weekend but is on his way back to Aix."

"Oh?" she asked, evidently surprised. It had been the same reaction as Achille Formentin's. She didn't ask where Quentin-Savary had been; either she knew about the country house or she didn't care.

"Are you a historian?" Paulik asked.

"No, just a secretary."

"You must have a thorough knowledge of the museum's contents," Verlaque suggested, "as you've worked here for fifteen years."

She looked to her left toward the empty room and sighed. "Like the back of my hand."

Paulik asked, "Any thoughts on what the thieves may have been interested in?"

"As much as I love them, I can't imagine it's the archives," she answered. "There's a new Félix Ziem painting in our possession. It's been estimated to be worth two hundred and fifty thousand euros." She looked at Verlaque and then at Paulik. "Would that be worth a thief's time? Anyway, why did they take everything? A jewelry store in Paris would have more valuable objects than our little museum."

Verlaque nodded, impressed that in a matter of minutes she had come to the same conclusion as he had. But perhaps she had thought about theft before, especially given that in the past year a number of luxury gift shops located in five-star Parisian hotels had been robbed of millions of dollars' worth of jewels.

"And the porcelain?" Paulik asked. He'd been careful to say "porcelain" and not "dishes," the word that originally had been on the tip of his tongue.

Mme Devaux rubbed her forehead, thinking. "There are two beautiful sets, both from Sèvres. But, again, not of any great value. I can get you their insurance estimates. The set with French châteaux is the rarer of the two. If I remember correctly, it's valued at forty-five thousand euros."

"Thank you, madame," Verlaque said, impressed with her knowledge. Achille Formentin hadn't been able, or willing, to give any helpful information.

"We'll need the contact details of the museum's insurance company," Paulik said, thinking that they might provide the police with an itemized list faster than the museum director.

"Of course," Mme Devaux replied. "I'll go upstairs and get you that." She stood up and then asked, "Upstairs. I didn't think to ask . . . Is anything missing?"

"No," Verlaque said, standing up. "M Formentin said that upstairs nothing was taken. But if you could—" He looked over at Mme Devaux in order to make eye contact, but she had already turned her back to him and was walking out of the room.

Chapter Six

❧

Tuesday, April 24

Verlaque looked at his watch as he and Paulik walked up the rue Mistral toward the Cours. It was a few minutes past one and he was ravenous. "There's a new Greek restaurant off the rue Thiers," he said. "Feel like trying it?"

"I'm so hungry I'd eat anything right now," Paulik replied. "But Greek sounds especially good."

"Great. What did you think of Faustine Devaux?"

"Serious, no-nonsense, and smart. But I'm glad we were able to be right behind her when she hightailed it upstairs. She was definitely nervous about something."

"And she seemed disgruntled when we told her that she'd have to turn over her keys to the museum and that she could only be in there accompanied by an officer."

Paulik said, "We'll watch her closely, don't worry. But we need her expertise, too."

"I agree," Verlaque said. "I believe her when she says that she knows the museum's contents inside and out." They turned right on the Cours and walked toward the rue Thiers. To their left, in front of a shop whose windows, it seemed to Verlaque, always displayed out-of-date shoes, stood a teenage girl playing the violin, its case open at her feet. He fumbled in his jacket pocket, feeling the coins he kept permanently there for occasions such as these, until he found a euro. He tossed it into the violin case, nodding and smiling at the girl. She returned the smile and continued to play.

The Greek restaurant was full, but the owner ushered Verlaque and Paulik to the bar and told them a table would be freeing up in a few minutes. "Wine?" he asked. "I have a Greek white; it's a new find."

Verlaque and Paulik exchanged worried looks.

"It's not retsina," the owner went on. "It's an organic wine from Mount Helmos called Tetramythos."

"Organic? That sounds great," Verlaque said.

The owner smiled and went behind the bar, where he poured two glasses of white wine and then set them on the counter along with a bowl of olives. "*Santé*," Paulik said, gently tipping his glass toward Verlaque's.

"*Santé*," Verlaque replied, taking a sip. He shot Paulik a glance, smiling.

"Sun-drenched," Paulik mumbled, putting his nose in the glass and taking another sip.

"Do I detect peaches, but also a sea breeze?" Verlaque asked, swirling the wine around in the glass and smelling it.

Paulik nodded. "Yes, the sea. Definitely the sea."

The restaurant's owner, watching and listening, breathed in a sigh of relief, happy to have made two more converts. He knew what second wine he would offer these two men to follow up on the first crisp white. The waitress—his sister-in-law—motioned to Verlaque and Paulik that their table was free.

As Paulik sat down, his phone beeped with a message. He read it. "Sophie Goulin," he finally said. "She's been interviewing the museum's neighbors. One of them, who lives across the street, saw a white van parked in the museum driveway a couple of times over the weekend. I'm going to step outside and call her back to get more details. Order anything for me."

"Will do," Verlaque said, reading the blackboard listing the daily specials.

The waitress reappeared and asked, "Do you need some help?"

"Yes. I want everything," Verlaque said.

"You could share some starters. I'll bring a plate of shrimp with mustard and a platter of zucchini mint fritters."

Verlaque began to salivate. "Perfect."

"Our main course today is grilled pork chops with roasted asparagus."

"We'll both have that. And for the wine—"

"Panayiotis wants you to try a Greek red." Seeing the puzzled look on Verlaque's face, she said, "The owner. He's happy you like the Mount Helmos white."

"It's very good," Verlaque replied. He looked down at his wineglass and resisted the temptation to have another sip; he'd wait for Bruno to get back and for their starters to arrive.

Paulik returned and sat down, leaning in toward the judge.

"Officer Goulin says the neighbor she talked to sometimes parks in the museum driveway for a few minutes when she's bringing her kids back from swimming and tennis lessons," he said. He looked at Verlaque, sadistically enjoying watching his boss's face darken with dread at the idea of chauffeuring kids around for lessons. For Aixois who lived downtown, most after-school activities were within walking distance, but not tennis or swimming. He went on. "The van was white and unmarked."

"License plate?"

"She didn't notice," Paulik said. "She's a light sleeper and saw the van in the evening and the early morning. But she didn't see anyone around."

"That really was bold of the thief or thieves," Verlaque said.

"Exactly," Paulik said. "Someone will have seen them. Just give us time."

The waitress reappeared and set down two large plates in front of the two men. "The shrimp are fried in olive oil, then set aside while the mustard and lemon sauce is made with onions and a green chili," she told them. "Then the shrimp is added back for another quick fry." She pointed to a larger blue-and-white-speckled earthenware platter and said, "The zucchini fritters are made with feta, bread crumbs, egg, and chopped mint, dill, and green onions. There's a small bowl of Greek yogurt to accompany them."

Paulik tapped the teaspoon that was almost standing upright in the thick yogurt. "No zero percent yogurt here," he said.

She laughed. "Zero percent yogurt should be outlawed. Enjoy, gentlemen."

Verlaque picked up a shrimp by the tail and bit into it, getting a dollop of mustard and lemon sauce. He wiped the corners of his mouth with a cotton napkin and looked around at the full dining room, with the April sun shining in through the windows and the golden wine shining in his glass. "Next time we'll reserve a table," he said. "Just to be sure."

Paulik nodded as he chewed and gave the judge a thumbs-up.

France Dubois was standing at her desk, a stack of papers in her hand, when Verlaque walked into the office. "Have you been standing like that all this time, France?" he asked, teasing her.

"Very funny," she answered, giving him the papers. "Officer Schoelcher brought up files that include photographs of the museum personnel and board members."

"So you've been filled in on what happened this weekend?"

"It's all people were talking about in the canteen at lunch," she replied. "Is it really true? Everything's gone?"

Verlaque nodded. "It's true. Do you know the place?"

"It's around the corner from my apartment."

"Of course it is."

France Dubois, recently hired after Verlaque's former secretary retired, lived on the rue Cardinale, one of Aix's most expensive streets. France had been in her late teens when her parents were killed in an auto accident; the apartment had been purchased by their grieving daughter with their life insurance money.

Verlaque opened the personnel file and saw a photo of a man he didn't recognize. The man was in his mid-forties, with a scruffy red beard and the same color hair—what was left of it—on his head. His eyes were blue and small. "Since you live in the neighborhood, do you recognize this guy?" he asked, showing France the photograph.

"Oh, yes," she said, looking at the photo. "I often see him on the rue Mistral, or buying bread. Does he work at the museum?"

"No, he lives upstairs," Verlaque said. "The museum and building once belonged to his family."

"That explains it."

"Explains what?"

"Why he's so snooty," France said. "He doesn't hide the fact that he thinks he's better than everyone else, especially if he has to wait in line at the *boulangerie*."

"Well, I look forward to meeting him this evening."

"Prime suspect," France said, smiling.

"Noted," Verlaque said, returning the smile and walking into his office. He crossed the room, sat down at his glass-topped desk, and opened another file, flipping through the itemized list until he got to the Ziem painting. The insurance price had been estimated just three weeks previously at two hundred and fifty thousand euros, just as Faustine Devaux had said. He picked up a color photograph of the painting: a view of Venice on a sunny day where two canals met at a bright pink building. He liked it almost as much as his own painting of Venice, done by a student of Canaletto's, that hung in the dining room.

He called France back into his office. "I'd like to meet with the museum's board members this week," he told her. Since Mme Girard's retirement he had been relying on France's organizational skills more and more. It wasn't that the formidable Mme Girard, who dressed in either real Chanel or very good imitations, hadn't been efficient; far from it. But he had inherited her with the job, and she had been working at the Palais de Justice for decades before his arrival. No one had ever explained her role to him, and he hadn't asked, giving her only the minimum of work. She always seemed busy, but now he knew that she was probably arranging her social schedule or writing to her adult children. She had been at the Palais de Justice so long that she was an expert at delegating and knew whom, even in Marseille, Nice, and as far as Paris, to ask for quick answers. France would start at zero. When France, who was single and in her early thirties, had been hired—at his recommendation—she had made it clear to the judge that she wanted, and could handle, as much work as he could throw at her. They now shared their calendars with each other on their cell phones.

"I see you're meeting with Gilbert Quentin-Savary this evening and are going back to the museum early tomorrow morning," France said, looking at her phone. "So let's try for the following day. I saw their names and phone numbers in the file. It looks like the two of them live in Paris, so it will take some luck to get you all together at the same time, but I'll try to set up a meeting as soon as possible." She put her cell phone back in her jacket pocket and looked at the judge. "There's no place to meet at the museum, is there?"

"Not that I saw."

"Here, then? Or do you prefer a hotel?"

"Try the Hôtel Roi René," Verlaque said. "They have proper meeting rooms, it's close to the museum, and we can have lunch or dinner after."

"Will do."

Verlaque's cell phone rang and he answered it. *"Allô, Verlaque ici."* He listened to the person on the line, said he'd be right there, and hung up. "That was your culprit, Gilbert Quentin-Savary. He's already back in Aix."

"He probably never left."

Verlaque looked at France, who was thin and of medium height, with medium-length light brown hair and a fair complexion with no outstanding features. She was polite and soft-spoken; one might, upon first meeting her, write her off as a wallflower or even overlook her. But those with patience and sensitivity were rewarded with France Dubois's intelligence and refinement.

"He was at his country house, confirmed by his maid," Verlaque said. "But if it makes you feel better, I'm going to find out in a few minutes where this house of his is and then call the local gendarmes to ask if anyone saw Quentin-Savary around this weekend."

France smiled and nodded, then turned on her heel to walk out of the room. "Have a nice evening," she said, looking back at her boss. "I may be gone when you return. I have my Chinese class this evening."

"Right, it's Tuesday. How's that going?"

"Besides the several thousand characters, the various tones and sounds, and the huge differences between Chinese and French grammar, I guess it's going all right."

Verlaque laughed and put on his jacket. "Good luck," he said.

"You, too."

Chapter Seven

~≈~

Tuesday, April 24

Verlaque left the Palais de Justice and walked across the Place Verdun, waving to a waiter standing outside the café of the same name. In the Passage Agard, he waited for his turn at the spot where the already-narrow passageway funneled into one claustrophobic lane about two feet across. And then he was out into the brilliant sunshine on the Cours, the plane trees leaving dancing black shadows on the seventeenth-century golden façades. How many times had he done that exact same walk? he wondered. As much as he loved automobiles, this was a town where he could walk to and from appointments, to and from the apartment and the office. Which of course made him think of Venice, the city entirely without cars, and the Ziem painting.

He crossed the Cours and walked down the rue Mistral, past the trendy restaurant whose name seemed to change every year and, below it, a popular nightclub that was as much an institution in Aix as the beloved opera festival. Stopping at number 16, he rang Gilbert Quentin-Savary's buzzer. After a few seconds, the heavy front door popped open about an inch. It irked Verlaque that Quentin-Savary hadn't said anything on the intercom. Was he rude or just socially inept? Or nervous? Verlaque knew from speaking to the heir that he already didn't like him, but as he climbed the tiled steps to the top floor and knocked, he told himself to keep an open mind. The thought made him smile, knowing that he rarely changed his initial impression of someone.

The door opened and Quentin-Savary stepped aside silently to allow Verlaque to walk in. He closed the door behind the judge and held out his hand, nose in the air. "Gilbert Quentin-Savary," he said.

"Antoine Verlaque," Verlaque said, shaking his hand and looking Quentin-Savary straight in the eye. Verlaque's quick assessment matched the photo he had seen: pale skin, a red beard and red hair that was thinning and worn too long, small blue eyes and too-small ears.

Quentin-Savary said, "Follow me." Verlaque did as he was told, following Quentin-Savary down a narrow hallway painted dark green. Now he could check the man out from behind: He walked slowly, with a deliberate swagger, as if bored or entering a room at a party where he knew he would turn heads.

"Have a seat," Quentin-Savary said, gesturing to a Barcelona chair in caramel-colored leather. Verlaque recognized the chair; it was a Mies van der Rohe and happened to be a particular favorite of his, which Marine had vetoed buying for their country house because she thought it uncomfortable. Verlaque noted, once again, the absence of "please" or other such niceties in Quentin-Savary's speech.

"Thank you," Verlaque said, trying to set an example. He sat down and crossed his legs, waiting for Quentin-Savary to sit down opposite him and start the conversation. But when no words came, Verlaque looked around the living room. Except for the modernist chairs, he could have been in Normandy at his grandparents' house. The furnishings had an English touch: lots of patterns on patterns, stripes against checks, and chintz, in faded pinks, blues, and greens. Large bouquets of mixed springtime flowers were scattered about. There were oil paintings on the walls, all of them portraits; Verlaque guessed they dated from the nineteenth century.

"Your family?" Verlaque finally said, gesturing to the paintings.

"Mostly," Quentin-Savary answered, stifling a yawn. "The illustrious gang."

"The family that gave you all of this," Verlaque said, again motioning around the room.

Quentin-Savary huffed. "This poky apartment, yes. And the debt my parents left when they died, which I dutifully paid off."

"Debt?"

"Papa gambled."

"On Friday, before you left for your country house, did you notice anything unusual?" Verlaque asked.

"Nothing," Quentin-Savary said. "But I don't take much notice of things around here."

"Around the museum, you mean?"

"Precisely. That's Achille's little baby, not mine."

"Did you take the highway to the country house?"

Quentin-Savary twitched slightly. "Nope. I never do. I save money by taking the back roads."

Verlaque smiled, hiding his disappointment that Paulik's team wouldn't be able to check the security cameras positioned at each tollgate. "I see that you're on the museum's board despite your disinterest in its contents."

"Have to be. There's always a family member on the board. I show up for the meetings with the half-dead and then leave as soon as I can."

"Not an exciting group, then?"

"They think that the letters of some nineteenth-century Aixois doctor or judge are a fun read."

"No offense taken," Verlaque said. "Speaking as a judge. Do you have a theory, despite the dull contents, on who emptied the museum or why they would do it?"

"None whatsoever. They may have been after the new Ziem painting, which really is a jewel."

Verlaque smiled. "So you do like some of the pieces."

"Only that one. And it's a new acquisition."

"Donation."

Quentin-Savary finally smiled, for the first time. "Right. I don't know how Achille wrangled that one, but yes, a donation."

"You don't like M Formentin?"

Quentin-Savary yawned. "His whole life is his work." He pointed to the floor, suggesting the museum three floors below.

"What's your work?"

Quentin-Savary crossed his legs, swinging the top leg back

and forth. "I've never worked. When I was young, I had a nervous condition, so I couldn't finish my studies. But I'm busy, if you're thinking I'm a slouch."

"Not at all," Verlaque answered. "I would never think that. What keeps you so busy?"

"I read. I know that's not done much anymore. And I cook and take care of my garden."

"At the country house."

"Yes."

Verlaque made a mental note to call the maid and ask her just how busy Quentin-Savary was. "So financially you get by with your inheritance? After the debt was paid off?"

"Yes. Grandmama left me sufficient funds, hidden from Papa, to live simply." He smiled.

"The country house?"

"She left that to me, along with its contents. I was the only grandchild."

"What about Mme Quentin-Savary, who donated the museum in 1900? Was she your great-great-great-grandmother?"

"Yes." Quentin-Savary got up and walked across the crowded room, stopping at one of the portraits. "That's her. She was a formidable woman, from all accounts, as all of the Quentin-Savary women were. Funny, as the women all married into the family."

Verlaque joined him in front of the painting. Mme Quentin-Savary was middle-aged in the portrait, and unsmiling, as they usually were in that era unless they were being painted by an Impressionist or someone like John Singer Sargent. But these were second-rate paintings. Unlike the Ziem. "Do you like these paintings?"

"They're crap. But I like to have them around."

Verlaque looked around the room again and now noticed that every single portrait was of a woman. "Where is your country house, exactly?"

"Near Aix." Quentin-Savary smiled.

Verlaque didn't return the smile as he knew the joke: Quentin-Savary had already told him that his house was near Switzerland. "Where, exactly, in relation to Aix-les-Bains?"

"Northeast, in a village called Allènes."

Verlaque put his hands in his pockets and walked around, looking at the paintings. He did a quick mental calculation of how long it would take to drive up there from Aix-en-Provence, and how long it would take Quentin-Savary to drive to Geneva, where he might have a Swiss bank account. Or Grandmama most certainly had. He guessed Geneva was less than an hour away by car from Aix-les-Bains. "Did you get into the village this weekend?"

"If you're asking if anyone saw me, then yes. I bought bread at the *boulangerie* early Saturday morning."

"Did you go anywhere else?"

Quentin-Savary looked at another painting, taking his time.

"It's not a difficult question," Verlaque said, trying not to sound as impatient as he was.

"My weekends in the country are always so busy."

Verlaque bit his lip.

Quentin-Savary said, "Nope. This weekend that was my only trip into the village. I rang ahead with the grocery list before I left here and had Gisèle buy the food for me."

"Did you entertain? Since you like to cook."

"No, I was alone at the house."

"Thank you," Verlaque said, turning away from yet another unsmiling, ugly face. He shook Quentin-Savary's hand. "This won't be our last meeting."

"As you wish."

"I'll see myself out," Verlaque said. It was obvious that Quentin-Savary wasn't going to accompany him. When he was at the living room door he turned around and said, "Nice flowers, by the way."

Quentin-Savary looked around the living room as if surprised, or as if he had forgotten the bouquet's existence. He opened his mouth to reply, but Verlaque was already at the front door. He opened the door and gently closed it behind him.

Chapter Eight

≈

Tuesday, April 24

When Verlaque got home that evening, Marine was sitting in an armchair, her favorite mohair blanket wrapped around her knees, and a book open on her lap. After hanging up his coat, he saw that she was asleep. He walked into the kitchen and slowly opened the refrigerator door, trying not to make any noise. Taking a large wineglass out of the cupboard, he poured himself a glass of white wine from a bottle that had already been opened. He looked at the label and smiled: it was a Vermentino from Sardinia, one of his favorite white varietals and a region he was beginning to discover. Opening another cupboard, he took out a bag of smoked almonds. He tried opening it with his hands only to have it rip; half of the nuts flew out of the bag, scattering across the counter. "*Merde*," he mumbled.

"Hello, there," Marine said as she stood in the kitchen doorway, rubbing her eyes.

"I'm so sorry to have woken you," Verlaque said, setting down the bag of almonds and hugging her.

"I wasn't sleeping—"

Verlaque laughed. "You were out cold."

Marine smiled. "I've never been so tired in my life."

"Paulik says you're lucky," Verlaque said. "Hélène was tired *and* sick most mornings."

"Could you make me a cranberry juice cocktail?"

"Yes, go back and sit down. I'll be right there." He poured sparkling water into a tall glass of cranberry juice, then added two ice cubes and a segment of lime, stirring it with a spoon. He put her drink on a tray, along with the almonds that he had scooped up and put into a small ceramic bowl, and carried it into the living room.

"Here you go, lovely," he said, setting the tray on the coffee table. "I'll be right back and can't wait to tell you what happened today."

"Oh, good," Marine said, sitting up straight and stretching.

"I'm having a glass of wine," Verlaque said as he came back with his wine and sat across from her. "Sorry about that." He had been trying his best not to drink alcohol during Marine's pregnancy but had been slipping as her pregnancy advanced.

"Don't be silly. I keep telling you I don't mind."

"I'd mind."

Marine laughed. "Yeah, you would. So what happened today?"

Verlaque took a sip of wine and told his story, beginning with the announcement that morning in his office that the Musée Quentin-Savary had been robbed of its entire contents. Every now and then Marine let out a little peep of surprise or shock. Verlaque stood up and began pacing as he talked. He told her of his museum visit: the exhausted museum director, in shock; the faithful secretary who couldn't keep from crying; and then the spoiled heir who lived upstairs. He didn't tell her about the excellent Greek lunch he shared with Bruno; he felt guilty about it but wasn't sure why. Once he was finished, he sat back down and drained his wine.

Marine took a big sip of cranberry juice and sat forward, her elbows resting on her knees. "Maman and I had breakfast next to M Formentin this morning."

"At the Deux Gs?"

"Yes, it was crowded and we had to share a table. But something very odd happened. Something Maman was saying made Formentin nervous or upset. He quickly paid his bill and left."

Verlaque laughed. "Was your mother talking about the choir?"

"Very funny. Yes, but it wasn't that," Marine said. "Oh, dear, Sylvie was right. Pregnancy gives you baby brain." She took another sip and then snapped her fingers. "Now I remember. The apartment of Mme de Montbarbon on the Cours was also broken into."

"That's an interesting reaction for him to have." He reached over and grabbed his suit jacket off the back of his favorite club chair and took out his phone. "She owned the Ziem, right?"

"Yes, up until two weeks ago." Marine smirked. "Mme de Montbarbon's housekeeper sings in the choir . . ."

Verlaque laughed and rolled his eyes.

". . . and she reported that the only thing that was taken was a set of porcelain dishes."

"I just found out about that."

"Eighteenth-century Sèvres. Maman and I talked about how odd it was that no money or jewels were stolen, and that's when he got up and ran out. Or rather waddled out."

"Anything else you can think of? Since you're a wealth of information this evening . . ."

"Yes, in La Ciotat," Marine said, draining her cranberry juice. "I barely told you anything about the conference as we had that dinner party Friday night. But Achille Formentin was there, presenting the Ziem painting as a new acquisition. And afterward, during the question-and-answer period, the director from a small museum in Marseille challenged him, saying that the painting was a fake."

"So everyone at the conference learned that the Ziem was at the Musée Quentin-Savary," Verlaque said, "and not in some apartment on the Cours. Who was this other museum director?"

"His last name is Lopez. I can't remember his first name. The museum is on the rue Paradis. He seemed, well, jealous, and Formentin was furious at his accusation."

"Excuse me, but if you don't mind, I'm going to call Bruno." Verlaque picked up his phone and speed-dialed Paulik.

"Go ahead. I'll heat up our dinner," Marine said, taking their empty glasses into the kitchen.

As they ate in the small but elegant dining room, Verlaque couldn't help glancing at the empty spot at the head of the table, between them, that would soon be occupied by someone else. He tried to imagine how they could squeeze a high chair into the narrow space.

"Gilbert Quentin-Savary doesn't sound like a nice person," Marine said. "But I suppose that doesn't make him guilty."

"I went to high school in Paris with guys like Gilbert," Verlaque told her, setting down his fork. "He's such a prick. So condescending and impolite."

"Good for keeping an open mind, Judge," Marine said, laughing.

"Even France Dubois thinks he's guilty and she hasn't even met him."

She smiled. "Well, in that case."

Verlaque took a sip of red wine and went on. "I gave him a great parting shot."

"Go on."

"Gilbert had just returned from his country house, but the apartment was full of fresh flowers. How is that possible? So I complimented him on the flowers."

"Maybe he bought them on the rue d'Italie as soon as he got back to Aix?"

"Who does that when your family's museum has just been cleared out and you have an appointment with the examining magistrate?"

Marine said, "Maybe he doesn't care about any of that."

"You're right. He made that very clear. It's as if he hates the museum and anyone having to do with it. Formentin and Faustine Devaux confirmed that. And he certainly didn't seem fazed by my visit." He cut a piece of veal and balanced a few peas and carrots on top before putting it in his mouth. He chewed, smiled, and then swallowed. "You really make the best blanquette de veau. Thank you."

"I just follow the recipe, but thanks. Organic happy veal and very rich crème fraîche helps."

"So does fresh dill."

"Thanks for noticing that touch. I had to tour the market twice to find it." Marine leaned forward. "Gilbert doesn't sound as if he's acting like a guilty person. Shouldn't he have been nervous, or at least overly polite?" She was glad that Antoine had an interesting case to work on; it took his mind, and hers, off the baby.

"He's still a jerk," Verlaque said. "He has never worked but claims to be really busy. I'll spare you the air quotation marks around *really busy*."

"Thanks."

"Besides, I can't do them anyway, with my wine in one hand and my fork in the other."

Marine laughed. "Gilbert could be faking it," she said. "Maybe he covets everything in that museum."

"He's an excellent actor, then. But I'll have the board members questioned to see if they agree with the museum's director and its secretary."

"Well, the thief, or the group of them, is interested in something in that museum. And perhaps something at Mme de Montbarbon's. But what? None of it is worth that much money. But perhaps getting its entire contents made the robbery worthwhile? We keep thinking that there's nothing interesting, or of value, in there, but sold all together . . ."

Verlaque looked at his wife and set down his glass. "You may be on to something. Sold as an entire lot. To some billionaire who's always dreamed of having his own collection. A sheikh."

"Or a Texas oilman."

He laughed. "Yes, I can really see a rich cowboy going over those documents and ancient maps before he tucks in for the night. I can't even imagine a painting of Venice being of interest. . . ."

Marine asked, "Was *it* stolen, too? The Ziem?"

"Of course."

"That changes everything." She sat back, twirling her water glass around in her hands. "Is that what the thieves were after in Mme de Montbarbon's apartment? And that must be why Formentin ran out of the café so quickly. He was worried about the painting."

"Possibly," Verlaque said. "But then why would the thieves leave Mme de Montbarbon's with a set of dishes? Why not steal something easier to take with you, or, in your fury over having missed out on the Ziem, why not trash the place? I've seen that before. Besides, the painting's not worth that much. Only two hundred and fifty thousand euros."

"Is that all?" Marine asked. "To think what people pay for a Jeff Koons balloon doggie."

"Now look who's judging!"

"You agree with me," she said.

"Of course I do. I'm teasing. But the art market is even more of a mystery to me than Achille Formentin and, as Gilbert Quentin-Savary calls it, Formentin's dusty little museum."

Chapter Nine

Wednesday, April 25

Renaud Paulik was waiting in front of the museum when Verlaque and Bruno Paulik arrived at 8:00 a.m. sharp. He was as tall, and as bald, as his cousin Bruno, but thin and wiry, without Bruno's bulk. His eyes were the same dark brown, with the same long dark eyelashes. Verlaque wondered who had passed down those dreamy eyes to the cousins.

Renaud nodded shyly when he saw Bruno, and Verlaque imagined that Renaud had always been the defeated cousin, the hanger-on, in the huge Paulik family, the one whom the others played with only grudgingly. Bruno, on the other hand, greeted his cousin with a huge smile—one that Verlaque knew was sincere.

Introductions were made. The cousins exchanged the *bises* and Bruno thanked Renaud for coming on such short notice.

"I have a big house to pack up at nine thirty in Ménerbes, so I can't stay long," Renaud said.

"We won't take up much of your time," Verlaque said.

Renaud held up his half-smoked cigarette, a Gitane. "Mind if I finish this?"

"Go ahead," Verlaque said.

"Another Parisian leaving the Luberon?" Bruno asked his cousin.

"The Ménerbes place? Yeah. They say that the town is too crowded and the countryside too noisy."

Verlaque and Bruno exchanged amused looks. Bruno asked, "Too noisy?"

"The neighbors," Renaud said, taking a long slow drag on his cigarette.

"Ah, yes, tractor noise," Bruno said. "Parisians move down here and forget that there are still farmers around."

"Not farmers," Renaud said. "Their neighbors are other Parisians who have too many parties." This was stated flatly, with no hint of sarcasm or humor. Verlaque and Bruno grinned at each other.

Renaud took a final drag and stubbed the cigarette out on the building's stone front, slowly knocking the ashes off with his index finger. He reached into his pocket and took out a small plastic bag into which he set the stub. Verlaque and Bruno watched as, instead of tossing the stub into the street, Renaud put the bag back into his pocket. Here was a thoughtful citizen, and a tidy man. Perfect for an art mover. He seemed a man of few words, too, but not unfriendly. "Ready," he said, thrusting his shoulders back.

Bruno Paulik took out a key that Faustine Devaux had given

him and let the three of them in. "I have photographs of the museum's contents," he said, "plus photos of the artworks here, in situ."

His cousin nodded and walked in, stopping at the small reception desk. "Late nineteenth, early twentieth century," he said. "No value."

He continued into the first room. "Do you have the room's dimensions?" he asked.

"Yes," Bruno said, walking over to the desk and picking up the museum's floor plan. He'd asked two of the officers to measure the rooms just in case it had never been done before or Formentin or the secretary was unable to find the measurements. It kept the officers from getting bored, too. Bruno also picked up two photographs of the museum still full of its contents and showed them to Renaud, who looked at them for a few seconds. "Thanks," Renaud said, handing the photographs back to Bruno.

Renaud continued to walk around, now and again snapping a photograph with his phone. He stopped at the empty display case that had once held the porcelain set decorated with painted fruits and took out a small notebook and began making notes, using the case as a writing surface. Looking up, he saw the red room and walked into it. Here he also took notes. "Upstairs?" he asked, pointing at the back staircase.

"Nothing was missing from up there," Bruno said.

Renaud made a clicking noise with his tongue against the roof of his mouth. "May I see the photos again?"

"Sure," Bruno said, handing them to his cousin.

"They could have moved the stuff out of here over the long weekend," he said, looking at the photographs.

"In three nights?" Verlaque asked.

"Yes, but only provided they didn't care about breaking any of the pieces," Renaud answered. "And just threw the stuff into boxes."

Verlaque immediately thought of Gilbert Quentin-Savary.

"So an art mover, carefully packing, wouldn't have been able to do it," Bruno said.

"Nope."

"A neighbor saw an unmarked white van parked here over the weekend," Verlaque said. "Wouldn't a professional mover have his logo on the van?"

"Not necessarily," Renaud said. "Some of my vans and trucks are white and unmarked. You don't want to draw attention to the fact that you might be transporting some Jeff Koons work in the back."

Verlaque smiled. "My wife has a particular dislike of his work."

"She has good taste."

"If the collection was stolen for resale," Bruno Paulik said, "wouldn't the pieces have to have been moved out with care?"

Renaud shrugged. "Yes, but maybe they were counting on a breakage percentage. My vans have climate control, remote track and trace, built-in alarm systems, and temperature and humidity controls. And the best air suspension you can get, of course. I can't imagine these thieves having that kind of equipment."

Verlaque looked at Bruno to see his reaction; was this a bit of old cousin rivalry? Was Renaud showing off? But Bruno kept a straight face.

Renaud went on. "This museum wouldn't have been packed up by pros; they'd have had too much to lose. Packing it in the middle of the night, without all the necessary precautions? They'd lose their business, and all that money invested, if they got caught. And they would get caught. Who could dump a whole museum's collection into the art market without getting found out?"

Bruno said, "We should let you go. I don't want you to be late for your next move."

Verlaque thanked Renaud and shook his hand. "Thank you so much," he said.

Renaud nodded and put his hand on the doorknob. "And they always get found out," he said. "Don't they?"

Bruno closed the door after his cousin left and smiled. Verlaque said, "At first I thought he was the quietest person on the planet and then he couldn't stop talking. I liked him."

Bruno laughed. "It's like something goes off in his brain after about ten minutes," he said. "Renaud's always been like that."

"He's obviously a pro," Verlaque said. "And has done well."

"He's hardworking, but it's Yvonne, his wife, who's the brains behind the operation. She oversees the accounts, the trucks, all that."

"I thought of Gilbert when Renaud said that the objects couldn't have been properly packed over the weekend," Verlaque said.

"Me, too," Bruno agreed. "But what's the motive? Did he only want the Ziem?"

"Possibly. What kind of car does he drive?"

"An older Volvo station wagon. White, with dents, the neighbor tells me. Do I have your permission to send some officers up to Aix-les-Bains with photos of the car, and of Gilbert, to ask questions?"

"Yes," Verlaque answered. "And as examining magistrate, I'll soon give you a search warrant for his apartment."

Bruno smiled. *"Merci, mon juge."*

"Miracle of miracles," France Dubois said as Verlaque walked by her desk. She held up a piece of paper with a list of four names. "The museum's board members are all in France at the moment and are willing and available to come to Aix."

Verlaque stopped. "Good news. When can they come?"

"I've started booking train tickets for tomorrow morning. Two are in Paris, one is here . . ."

"Gilbert."

"Yes. And another member lives in Toulouse. He said he'd drive here. The Hôtel Roi René has rooms available, so I've booked one for everyone except Gilbert. When I've sorted everything out, I'll send you an email and copy Commissioner Paulik on it."

"Thank you, France," Verlaque said. "Would you like a coffee?"

"No, thank you," France said.

"All right. I'll be in my office." Verlaque walked into his office and closed the door behind him. He had phone calls to make. But first, an espresso.

As he waited for the small red Italian machine to warm up, he went over to his desk and pulled out the book of baby names, turning to the first page. He looked down and read aloud a name as he made his coffee. "Achille." Verlaque smirked. It was only natural he'd fall upon that name; he'd opened the book on page one. "Greek. Son of Thétis and Pélée; reputed for his warrior talents and his strong physique." He snorted and added a sugar cube to his espresso. This Achille sounded very different from the Quentin-Savary museum director. He carried the book and his coffee over to his desk chair and read aloud, "'Popular in the Mediterranean region.' Naturally." There had been a few saints, too, with the name Achille, the most well-known being a bishop in Larissa in the fourth century. Marine's mother would no doubt know all about him. The name was rated as "unpopular"; this pleased him. And the average age of someone with the name Achille was fifty-nine. Perfect. His son would have the same initials as himself, and he had always quite liked AV, two inverted shapes, perfectly balanced. He closed the book and put it back in its hiding place.

His cell phone beeped and he saw that it was a text message from Bruno Paulik: *We are still interviewing neighbors, but only the light sleeper across the road had seen the white van. None of the neighbors like Gilbert. No surprise there. I'm off to visit Faustine Devaux, this time at her home. I tried to book an appointment with the museum's accountant, but she's away on a two-week vacation.*

Verlaque texted back: *Thanks. I'll interview Mme de Montbarbon's housekeeper, Solange Picard. She's a friend of Marine's mother. ;)* He then scrolled through his numbers and dialed; it was picked up on the second ring. "Hello, Hippolyte," Verlaque said. "I hope I'm not disturbing you."

"Well, hello, Antoine Verlaque. My favorite judge."

"My favorite wine criminal." Verlaque sat back and smiled.

"I'm clean now. You of all people should know," Hippolyte Thébaud said. "If I were still in the wine theft business, I'd have to go to China or Russia, neither of which interests me. I now make enough money from consulting."

"I'm happy for you."

"In fact, I was just opening a '63 Pétrus to drink with dinner this evening. Who would have known that a wine made from one hundred percent Merlot grapes could taste so good?"

"I'm catching the next train to Paris," Verlaque said, intentionally adding a laugh so that Thébaud would know it was a joke. He heard a long, exaggerated sigh on the other end of the line. "Listen," he went on. "There's been a theft of a twentieth-century French painting here in Aix. It's not worth that much money, but I was wondering if you knew . . ."

"Of any art thieves?"

"Retired, naturally," Verlaque said. "Like yourself."

Thébaud laughed. "Marie-Claire is indeed retired. In fact, I think she lives in your neighborhood now."

Verlaque grabbed his pen. "Oh?" he asked.

"Marie-Claire Blay. I know you're writing her name down. Anyway, she was one of the best. Do you remember when the thief went into the museum through the skylight? I can't remember where it was. They used rock-climbing gear."

"Of course. They got a Rembrandt."

"That was her. She's a teetotaler; otherwise we could have become good friends." Again, a long sigh.

Verlaque laughed. "Is she reliable?" he asked. "Despite being a teetotaler?"

"Yes, you can ask her anything. Hold on a second and I'll look up her new address for you."

Verlaque put his phone on speaker, set it on the desk, and lit a cigar. He heard a cork open and some wine being poured into a glass.

"I'm back," Thébaud said. "Here's her number: 04-75-09-09-68. La Ferme de Marie-Claire."

"She's on a farm?" Verlaque asked.

"Yes, but don't ask me what kind. I'm only interested in grapes."

"And you're right, 04 is down here. But where is 04-75?"

"The Ardèche, I think."

"How is the wine, by the way?" Verlaque asked, taking a long drag on his Partagás. "I heard you open it and the cork pop."

"Already exquisite. Are you sure you can't join me for dinner? By this evening it will be perfect."

"Positive. But thanks for the invitation and the help."

Hippolyte said goodbye and they hung up. Verlaque left his phone on speaker and called Marine. "*Salut, ma belle,*" he said when she answered. "How would you like to go to the Ardèche for a couple of days?"

Faustine Devaux lived on one of Bruno Paulik's favorite streets. He coveted several streets in Aix, including the street that his boss lived on, but this one was a close second. Like Verlaque's street, the rue Félicien David was only one block long. It ran between rue Chastel and rue Lacépède, two blocks east from the Palais de Justice. It was quiet, and he could never figure out how, like the Quartier Mazarin, it had escaped the noisy bars and restaurants that the rest of Aix had to put up with. When he was young, there had been more *snacks*, tiny food stands catering to Sacré-Cœur's high school students, here. The school had been behind rue Lacépède; it had since moved to a bigger space outside of the old city center, and so the greasy smell he had associated with this tiny neighborhood was gone. But the school's honey-colored Baroque church still stood at the end of Félicien David. He took out his cell phone and took a photograph of the church. When they were teenagers, one of his brothers had dated a girl who was going to Sacré-Cœur, so he spent hours on the slow bus from their farm in the Luberon going down to Aix to hang out with her. Bruno was about to send the picture to his brother when he hesitated; the girl had dumped his poor brother a few months later for a wealthy lawyer's son, and they had teased him about all the lost time, and money, spent on the bus. But that same year he had won the Spanish prize at their high school in Pertuis. That's what he'd been doing on the bus—learning Spanish, as the girl had moved from Valencia with her family when she was ten. His brother was now the head of the Spanish department at Pertuis's high school, and was happily married to a Luberon girl. Bruno put his phone away; he'd show the picture to Hélène, after dinner, and tell her the story.

He stopped in front of number 6 and rang the buzzer at F ET G DEVAUX. The door clicked open; Mme Devaux was expecting him. The foyer was neat and clean: no colored flyers on the floor; the obligatory potted palm was bright and healthy, given sun by the large skylight four stories up. Running his hand along the wrought-iron handrail, he walked up the marble stairs to the second floor, where Faustine Devaux was standing at her door.

"Bonjour, madame," Paulik greeted her as he shook her hand.

"Come in," she said, standing aside. "Would you like a coffee? I was about to have one myself."

"Yes, thank you." While Mme Devaux went into the kitchen, Paulik walked around her small but neat living room. The sofa was curved and old; he guessed mid-nineteenth century. There were two armchairs in matching red stripes across from it; they, too, were antiques, maybe even older than the sofa. A small contemporary glass coffee table with thin brass legs sat in between. There were no books, but perhaps she kept those in another room. In a corner was a small wooden table with two caned chairs—the sort one often saw in Cézanne paintings. On the polished table was a Chinese porcelain vase of white lilies, the smell of which Hélène and Léa adored but reminded Bruno of funerals.

"Voilà," she said as she walked back into the living room and set a tray down on the coffee table. "We'll sit here, if you don't mind. I'm very tired these days." She sat down on the small sofa and leaned forward to pour the coffee.

"Of course," Paulik said, sitting down in one of the armchairs across from her. "This is a lovely apartment and neighborhood."

"Thank you, yes, I do love it here. And it's much quieter now that the high school has moved out to La Torse."

"You've worked for fifteen years at the museum," Paulik said, picking up his coffee cup, also Chinese porcelain.

"Yes. I worked as a secretary for a travel agency for ten years before that, but one day I was walking past the museum and saw a small ad for a secretary and applied. I love antiques, you see."

Paulik smiled. "I did notice. And M Devaux? Does he work in Aix?"

"I beg your pardon?" she asked. She set down her cup and then relaxed her shoulders. "Oh, the G on the buzzer downstairs . . ."

"Yes."

"My cousin, Ghislaine. She lived with me but died five years ago of cancer."

"I'm so sorry."

"Thank you."

Paulik took a sip of the excellent coffee and said, "It must have been a great shock on Tuesday morning to see the museum empty like that."

"Oh my word, yes, it was. I'm still reeling."

Paulik hoped he would be able to aptly describe Mme Devaux to Hélène this evening. She was like a proper woman out of a 1950s book. He also realized he had no idea how old she was. Between fifty and sixty-five? He'd have to look it up in the records the officers had gathered on Tuesday. "You had no hints that something like this might happen?"

"Oh, no, of course not. Who would go through such a bother or be interested in all of our objects?"

"Yes, who would, indeed. Do you have any ideas?"

She held her thin hand to her chest. "Me? I rather thought that was your affair."

Paulik smiled. "Yes, you're right, but since you know so much about the museum, I thought I'd ask your opinion. I had never been in that museum until yesterday. And you"—he gestured around the room with his hand—"have such an interest in antiques."

"I could help you with who didn't do it," she said, setting down her cup once more. It made a tiny rattle against the porcelain saucer, which seemed to surprise her. "I didn't, nor did M Formentin. We both have too much respect, even love, for that museum and its wonderful history."

Paulik opened his notebook and flipped through it. "What can you tell me about Aurélien Lopez?" he asked, putting on his best neutral voice. "The director of the Musée Cavasino in Marseille?"

She pursed her lips. "Yes, M Lopez is rather a thorn in our side. He calls every week, trying to get us to join forces."

"Really? The two museums?"

"Yes, can you imagine? The Musée Quentin-Savary has been open since 1900. It is the legacy of Estelle Quentin-Savary. She would never have allowed the museum to join another, nor would have anyone in her family."

"What's M Lopez's reasoning?"

"M Lopez believes that if our two museums merged, we'd have more visual power and more resources. He claims we'd have more visitors, too, as the city of Marseille has promised us a prime spot on the harbor in an old building once used as a coast guard office."

Paulik thought that that didn't seem like a bad idea, since he had never met anyone who had ever been to either museum except for Léa with her class on Friday. He also knew the quaint redstone building she was referring to, just at the mouth of the old port. He and a former girlfriend had once sat with their backs against that building, staring at the sea, drinking a bottle of inexpensive champagne out of plastic cups.

"You think that's a good idea," she said, leaning forward as if challenging him.

"Well, wouldn't it be a good thing to have more visitors?"

"Not necessarily," she answered. "Our museum primarily helps researchers and art experts. We are open to the public only as a courtesy. M Lopez doesn't seem to understand the role of small foundations like ours."

"Those experts who come to your museum," Paulik said. "May I have a list of recent visitors?"

"Of course. Last week we had two visitors, one from the university here in Aix and the other came down from Paris. I'll get you their names and numbers." She left the room and Paulik assumed she was going into an office where she had a computer. But she came back a few seconds later with an old-fashioned snakeskin handbag. She sat down, opened it up, and pulled out a black leather agenda. Quickly turning to the correct page, she read out their names and numbers as Paulik wrote them down.

"Old-fashioned technology," he said, smiling.

"Old-fashioned *efficient* technology." She closed her handbag with a snap.

"The neighbor who lives above the museum . . ."

She nodded. "He's a lovely, discreet young man. He works for a local chocolate company."

"In sales." Paulik had ordered the salesman's apartment to be searched, as he was away, but nothing irregular had been found.

"Yes, he travels often, and sometimes brings us chocolates," she said. "Even new flavors that they're trying out. He's very kind."

"You knew he was away?"

"Oh, yes," she replied. "He always lets me know. He's in the Far East right now, for a month. I gave one of your officers his contact information."

"And Gilbert Quentin-Savary? Does he visit often?"

She smirked. "No, as I told you all yesterday. He comes down to complain."

"So he has no interest in the museum."

"None whatsoever."

Paulik asked, "Does he go to his country house every weekend?"

She paused. "I'd say every other weekend, and for most of the summer. He claims that his apartment is too hot."

"Does he have visitors? From what you can tell . . ."

"No, rarely," she replied. "He's a loner, I think. Which is why it's odd . . ."

"Oh?"

"Yesterday I saw M Lopez walking out of the building's front door."

Paulik finished his coffee and let her continue.

"I went to the museum yesterday to finish some filing; a policeman let me in. I had just popped out to the corner mailbox to post some letters when I saw him. M Lopez hadn't been to the museum to see us, you see," she said. "And besides, the museum's closed now."

"Which leaves Gilbert."

She smiled and nodded.

Chapter Ten

❧

Wednesday, April 25

"Mme Devaux makes a mean coffee," Paulik said as he sat down at one of Verlaque's and his favorite small restaurants located in an alley not far from the cathedral and Verlaque's apartment. "I'm completely buzzed."

Verlaque laughed. "I ordered us two glasses of white wine, if that's okay."

"Perfect."

Verlaque turned around to read the blackboard specials. "Do you want to split the rabbit terrine as a first course?" he asked, turning back around to face Paulik.

"Yes," Paulik said, sitting forward and squinting to see the blackboard. "And then I'm having the stuffed leg of lamb."

"Me, too. We'll go light today."

Paulik laughed. "How is it that at lunch I'm already thinking of dinner?"

Verlaque shrugged. "It's a French malady. Most of us have it. Maybe that's why we're never satisfied and always complaining."

"Because we're hungry?" Paulik asked. "Could be."

The waitress came and took their order. They chatted about the weather and then took some time deciding upon which sparkling water to order. She smiled and waited patiently, as if two grown men arguing about the merits of *fines bulles* versus *grosses bulles* was absolutely normal. "You can judge a good restaurant partly on its sparkling water list," Verlaque told her, handing back the drinks menu. They went with the Corsican option, Orezza.

"That's why we only have three," she answered. "Orezza, San Pellegrino, and Chateldon."

"And we'll have red wine with the lamb," Paulik said. "What do you have by the glass?"

"A very good Syrah," she said. "The vines are in the Ardèche, but bordering on the Rhone appellation. Same grapes, lower price tag. I think you'll like it."

"Sounds great," Verlaque said, now more excited about his upcoming trip to the Ardèche.

Paulik squinted again, reading the blackboard. "What else is in the stuffed leg of lamb besides the usual suspects?" he asked.

She laughed, even without knowing that he was the commissioner of police. "Well, besides breadcrumbs, parsley, garlic, onions, and eggs—the usual suspects, as you say—there's bacon, anchovies, carrots, vermouth, and a host of fresh herbs."

Paulik sat back and smiled.

"Happy?" Verlaque asked, looking at Paulik.

"Yes, very," Paulik said.

"I'll be right back with the water, white wine, and your starter," the waitress said before turning around and walking back to the bar.

"How is Mme Devaux holding up?" Verlaque asked.

"Very well, I'd say," Paulik replied. "She comes across as a dainty old lady, which she is, I guess, but I think under that veneer she's tough as nails."

"What's her apartment like?"

Paulik was used to this sort of question from the judge. Not only was he curious about people's abodes, but he was a believer that how they did, or didn't, decorate their living quarters could reveal truths about their personalities. Paulik now believed this, too. "Very dainty, clean, comfortable, and full of antiques, right down to the fragile Chinese porcelain teacups."

Verlaque nodded.

Paulik continued, "She also had one or two bits of interesting information. Namely, she kept insisting, perhaps a little too hard, how impossible it would have been for either her or Achille Formentin to have robbed their own museum."

"I have to agree with that."

"She kept calling it *their* museum," Paulik added. "She also seems to despise Gilbert Quentin-Savary, as does everyone in Aix. She told me that she saw Aurélien Lopez leaving the building last Tuesday and he hadn't been visiting the museum."

"So he's buddies with Gilbert? That is odd."

"It doesn't necessarily mean they're friends."

"True."

"She and Formentin are dead set against the idea of joining

Lopez's museum. Again, it's *their* little museum. If they do join up, they've been promised a primo spot on the *vieux* port for the new museum."

"It seems like a good idea to me," Verlaque said. "They may get fifty visitors in a week instead of two researchers and a junior high school group."

"I thought the same thing."

The waitress returned and poured them each a glass of golden-colored white wine. Both men strained their necks to read the label. "Sorry," she said, turning the bottle so that the label was visible. "Grand Revelette."

"Always a favorite," Verlaque said. "That's one of the first local wines I fell in love with down here."

"I'll be right back with the terrine," she said. "Since you're splitting it, the chef is preparing a larger plate. We aren't that busy today."

"That's very generous," Paulik said. "Please thank him."

"I'll tell her," she said, winking, as she left the table.

Verlaque laughed. "Twenty years ago France didn't have any female chefs except for Hélène Darroze and Anne-Sophie Pic."

"Nor were there many female officers on the force, especially high up."

"Today there are almost as many female examining magistrates as male ones. Which reminds me, my two-day magistrates meeting in Marseille has been canceled tomorrow and Friday, so I may take a long weekend."

"You should," Paulik said. "Why was it canceled?"

"Nadia Hassen in Lille is dealing with a recent murder-suicide, and Thomas Bidon's wife just had a baby yesterday."

"Doesn't he have a bunch of kids already?"

"This makes six, I think."

Paulik mimicked putting a gun to his head.

The waitress returned and set down their terrine. "Enjoy," she said, leaving them to get to it.

"You should pay a visit to this museum director in Marseille," Verlaque said as he cut the terrine in two and put one half on his plate.

"Will do."

"See if you can get any information out of him on this Ziem painting."

"The Ziem painting was the most valuable object stolen. Think Formentin fudged some items?"

"Could be," Verlaque said. "Show the list to Mme Devaux. She probably knows every item in that place by heart. Any luck with the CCTV cameras on the way to Aix-les-Bains?"

"We just received the footage and some of my junior officers are going through it now," Paulik said. "With lots of coffee. I think after lunch I'll swing by Monoprix and buy them some cookies."

"Petits LUs, dark chocolate."

"Naturally."

The waitress came by to collect their shared plate, which she saw had been mopped clean with pieces of bread. The fact that the two men were now discussing cookies was no surprise to her.

Paulik arrived back at the Palais de Justice just after 2:00 p.m. with three boxes of LUs, two dark and one milk chocolate. He had hesitated in the shop, staring at the cookies with the famous schoolboy on the box, and grabbed the milk chocolate after thinking of two junior officers—one really a rookie, still with pimples. Perhaps they were so young that they hadn't graduated to dark chocolate yet? He wanted to make them feel comfortable.

A message was waiting for him as well. M Lopez, the director of the Musée Cavasino, would be available to see him at 3:00 at his museum. Paulik looked at his watch, mumbled something to the group of officers huddled over their video screens, and said he was off to Marseille.

"Do you want me to drive you, sir?" one of them asked. He looked up from his screen, bleary-eyed from the hours of scanning the CCTV footage. "I live in Marseille. There's quite a lot of roadwork right now."

"Nah," Paulik said, grabbing a pair of car keys off the hook. "But thanks."

The officer looked disappointed.

Paulik headed downstairs to the underground parking garage and got into one of the squad cars. He felt sorry for the officer who had offered to drive him, but he needed all eyes on that camera footage right now. Plus, Paulik liked nothing better than driving, and driving alone, with his own thoughts for company. He'd take the scenic route into downtown Marseille, along the docks and past the ferries and the new silvery curved Zaha Hadid building that everyone was talking about. The officer, like all Marseillais, probably had some "fast-track-top-secret" way into Marseille that only he knew about, but Paulik preferred the sea route, which ended at the Vieux Port. He put the key in the ignition and started the car, turning on the radio so he didn't have to search for a station while driving. Someone had programmed the numbers one through six to commercial rock stations. Paulik erased the first one and replaced it with France Musique. The deejay, a woman who had a slight Russian accent but spoke flawless French, introduced a Meredith Monk piece for two pianos titled "Ellis Island." Paulik turned up the volume and headed up the ramp and out into the bright sun.

Once out of Aix and on the highway heading south, he picked up the speed to 100 kilometers an hour, 10 kilometers over the speed limit. The drive between these two archrival cities was only twenty minutes, but he didn't want to be rushed, and he also wanted to have enough time for a quick espresso.

Just as he predicted, twenty minutes later Paulik had turned off the highway and was driving on a raised ramp along the sea, where he had an excellent view down to the monstrous ferries that headed off every day to Corsica and North Africa. Despite the fact that he had grown up in the South of France, he had never set foot on the island of Corsica, nor had Hélène. They hadn't been to the African continent, either. Something told him that Léa would beat them to it.

He looked away from the Mediterranean and back to the road just in time to see the flash of red taillights on the car ahead of him. He slammed on his brakes, stopping less than a foot behind the other car. He leaned over so that he could see out of the middle of the windshield and saw that traffic was stopped all the way into the tunnel. This section of the road was often backed up, but only for a few minutes, so he relaxed, listened to the music, and waited it out.

What was normally a few minutes' wait ended up being fifteen. By the time Paulik got out of the tunnel, he was too frustrated to appreciate the Vieux Port and its sparkling blue water and colorful sailboats. He could see that there was construction ahead—as the young officer had warned him—and he wouldn't be able to drive along the harbor as he usually did. The traffic was getting funneled to the left on a narrow street one block in from the water. No view whatsoever. He crawled along the rue de la Loge, braking for jaywalkers and circling around double-parked cars. When he finally got to the top of the Vieux Port, he stopped for a red light and rolled down his window. He could see more construction on the other side of the port, where he was headed. "*Salut*," he said to a female officer who had been helping to direct traffic. "Construction every-where?"

"You noticed," she said, snapping her chewing gum.

Paulik quickly showed her his badge, hoping he'd get some free parking advice.

"From Aix, Commissioner?" she said. "Don't go back to Aix this way; get on the highway near the train station."

"Thanks," Paulik said. "I'm late for a meeting on the rue Paradis. Is there an easy place to park along the street?"

She laughed. "Forget it. It, too, is all under construction." She looked across the port and gestured across the water just as the traffic light turned green. "Go around the port to the underground parking at Estienne d'Orves."

"Thanks," Paulik said. So much for hot tips. That was where he was going to park all along.

"You might get lucky and find a spot on level three or four," she added as he pulled away.

Paulik was sweating by the time he reached the Musée Cavasino. And he was ten minutes late, with no espresso. He stepped into the museum—at first glance just as dark and gloomy as the Quentin-Savary—and paused to wipe his brow with a handkerchief. He could hear a voice in the next room: someone talking on the telephone. He walked toward the sound, looking to his right and left at the walls, which were hung with nineteenth-century watercolor and oil paintings of Marseille. Most of them were of the Vieux Port. Minus the traffic and construction.

Oddly enough, this museum's layout was very similar to the Quentin-Savary's. Or perhaps that wasn't so odd, Paulik reflected, when they had both been built as noble houses in the late seventeenth or early eighteenth century. He could now see the man who was speaking on the phone, sitting behind an ornately carved wooden desk. The man saw Paulik and quickly ended his conversation. Paulik was almost certain that he hadn't even said goodbye to the person on the other end. "Commissioner Paulik?" he asked, quickly getting up.

"Yes," Paulik answered. "I'm sorry I'm late. Traff—"

"Traffic, yes, yes. Same old story here in Marseille. They spruced it up when it was the European City of Culture in 2013, but as yet haven't finished the construction. I'm Aurélien Lopez." They shook hands. "Please, sit down."

Paulik sat down across from Lopez and looked around curiously.

"We won't be disturbed," Lopez said, seeing the commissioner's eyes wander. "It's rare that casual visitors off the street come into the museum."

"One of the things your museum has in common with the Quentin-Savary."

"One of many," Lopez said, smiling in a way that Paulik found unctuous.

"Is that why you want the two museums to merge? Mme Devaux told me about your plans."

"It makes perfect sense," Lopez said. "As you can see, neither museum attracts much attention. Although we both work very hard at maintaining our collections and keeping the objects and documents in perfect archival shape. But that takes money. You can see that even our national museums campaign for donations and have corporate sponsors. So how do small museums like ours stay alive?"

These were all very good questions that Paulik had no answer for. So he nodded and hoped that Lopez would continue speaking.

"Achille was cooperative at first," Lopez went on. "He liked my ideas and offered to help write up a business plan joining the two museums. But then something happened . . ."

"Do you know what?" Paulik asked.

"No idea. He just stopped cooperating. In fact, he completely switched tacks, telling me that the idea couldn't work and that the Quentin-Savary would never join another museum. It was heartbreaking, and embarrassing as I had already gained support from a few local politicians."

"And the promise of a great spot on the Vieux Port."

"Exactly."

"And you're sure your idea would have worked?"

"It was worth a try," Lopez said dreamily. "We could have shared mailing lists and done events together."

Paulik asked, "And who would have been the director?"

"We didn't get that far into the discussion," Lopez said, "before Achille just shut it down."

"The Ziem painting," Paulik said, turning a page in his notebook to signal that they were moving on. "Were you familiar with it?"

"I'd seen it once before."

"Where?"

"Achille quickly showed it to me before a conference in La Ciotat," Lopez said.

"I understand you thought it a fake."

Lopez hesitated. "I wasn't sure at first. It's very beautiful. The colors just don't fit in Ziem's work history for that period."

"I've never understood how art historians could say things like that," Paulik said. He didn't add that Lopez had only quickly looked at the painting. "Couldn't Ziem have just switched colors one day? Because he was in the mood?"

"It rarely happens like that, you see," Lopez said. "These artists were like accountants in their work habits. Especially Ziem."

Paulik looked around at the seascapes on the walls. "It would have been nice here," he said. "Did Mme de Montbarbon offer it to you?"

Lopez sighed. "No. She had promised it to Achille long before I saw it."

Paulik mused, *It's Achille's museum*. "Do you think the thieves who robbed the Quentin-Savary were after the Ziem painting?" he asked. "Assuming they believed it was the real thing."

Lopez threw up his hands. "That robbery is mind-blowing," he said, this time with real conviction. "It's all we've been talking about in the museum world. I even had a call from a colleague who runs a small ceramics museum in Amsterdam."

"I hadn't realized it was making international news."

"Oh, yes."

"And what are people saying?"

"Some of the pieces are obviously more valuable than others," Lopez said. "What none of us can figure out is, why empty the entire museum?"

"Exactly."

"And so the only thing that makes sense is a personal vendetta."

"Oh, really?" Paulik asked, leaning forward. "Against whom?"

"Achille Formentin, naturally."

"Would you say that you and Achille are on good terms?"

"Surely you're not suggesting . . ."

Paulik stayed silent.

Lopez said, "We don't speak anymore, to be honest. I'm still too angry that Achille suddenly changed his mind about our joint venture with no explanation. But I would never have emptied out his museum! How would I? And why?" He gestured around the room. "I don't have room here for all of *my* museum's objects; hundreds are in a warehouse out by the airport. And the rent on that place keeps going up!"

"Have you seen Gilbert Quentin-Savary recently?" Paulik asked.

Lopez looked at the ceiling as if he were trying to remember. Paulik watched him, thinking that the Cannes Film Festival should have an award for best fake pondering. *Le Prix Lopez*. He couldn't wait to give it to Léa tonight when he asked her if she had cleaned her room and done the living room dusting.

"I may have bumped into him the last time I was at the museum in Aix," Lopez finally said. "But that would have been ages ago. He lives upstairs . . ."

"Yes, I know," Paulik said. He again turned a page in his notebook and read. "In fact, you were seen leaving the building on rue Mistral only yesterday. Tuesday."

"Ah . . . yes, I was in Aix . . ."

"And the museum's closed."

"Gilbert Quentin-Savary asked me to come," Lopez said. "Sorry, it was such a quick visit that I immediately forgot about it. I didn't want to . . . complicate . . . your investigation with Gilbert's silly ditherings. It was a wild-goose chase."

"Oh?"

"He wanted to show me some hideous nineteenth-century portraits. His ancestors. I didn't have the heart to tell him that they were of mediocre quality, but I did tell him I wouldn't have them here in this museum. Again, no room."

"Why not show them downstairs, at Gilbert's own family's museum?"

Lopez shrugged. "Achille must have turned him down as well. Gilbert has an outsized ego."

"Surely he can give them to someone?"

Lopez laughed. "Commissioner, he doesn't want to *give* them away. He wants to *sell* them!"

Chapter Eleven

❧

Wednesday, April 25

Verlaque had never seen so many books packed into such a small apartment. Following Mme Picard down the narrow hallway, he almost had to turn his wide shoulders sideways to fit, as the hall was lined on both sides with bookshelves. Some of the titles caught his eye: some Polish poetry, translated into French. A row of Fred Vargas police thrillers next to Michel Houellebecq's latest controversial novel.

Continuing down the hall, he peeked into a small living room that had two walls, also lined with books. More books were piled under the coffee table.

"Would you like a coffee?" Mme Picard asked as they walked into a small but very cozy kitchen. "Or tea?"

"Tea, please," Verlaque said as he sat down at a small marble table. He'd had two espressos with Paulik after their lunch.

"Fine, I'll have one, too." She busied herself with the kettle and cups while Verlaque sat back, enjoying, as he always did, the neat, well-equipped kitchen of someone who obviously enjoyed cooking. An open shelf above the sink and work surface was lined with large spice jars and various bits of green-and-ocher-colored Provençal earthenware. Over the gas stove hung several bright copper pots and pans and a long magnet holding knives of various sizes.

"It looks like you enjoy cooking as much as reading," he said.

Solange Picard turned around from her tea making and smiled. "We both do," she said. "My husband and me. In our bedroom we have a few hundred cookbooks."

Verlaque pictured the books piled under the bed, like he had seen in the living room. "I have a few dozen cookbooks but certainly not a few hundred. Congratulations, I'm impressed."

She smiled and poured boiling water into a teapot.

"Some, I must admit, I've never cooked from," Verlaque said. "I just look at the photographs and read the recipes and imagine eating the dish. Michel Bras, for example."

Mme Picard laughed. "I have that one, too. And I've never had the courage to cook from it. My husband teases me about it."

Verlaque asked, "Where does M Picard work?" He estimated her to be in her late fifties, so he imagined that they were not quite retirement age.

"Jean-Paul works at the university as a custodian."

Excellent benefits and security, lousy pay, thought Verlaque. *Hence the tiny apartment.*

"We were very lucky to have been able to buy this apartment," she said, as if reading his mind. "My husband inherited a small amount when his father died, and the real estate prices in Aix were still low. There just isn't enough room for books, as you can see."

Verlaque smiled. "An admirable problem. How long did you work for Mme de Montbarbon?"

She sat down and gave him his tea. "Ten years or more."

"Thank you for the tea," Verlaque said.

"You're welcome. Have a madeleine, too. We made them last night."

Verlaque smiled and helped himself to one.

She went on, "I'm sure Dr. Bonnet told you that she thought the job beneath me. Florence, I mean, not your wife, Marine."

Verlaque laughed. "Yes, she did. Florence, not Marine." He bit into the madeleine, and while he didn't have a Proustian moment, he did taste a lovely bit of orange zest.

"It was a pleasure to work for her. Mme de Montbarbon was an excellent employer. Such good company, too."

Verlaque could see from her smile and direct eye contact that this was the truth. "I know that you've been questioned by the police regarding the recent break-in at Mme de Montbarbon's apartment," he said. "But I'd like to go over it with you one more time, if you don't mind."

"Of course not," she answered. "I assumed that was why you were here."

Verlaque had a sip of tea and tried not to look at the plate of remaining madeleines. He said, "I read in the police report that a window was left open, and that's how the thieves entered."

Mme Picard cringed. "Yes, and that would have been my fault. As I told the police, the problem is that I can't remember closing it. With Madame's death and my mourning, I may have been careless and left it open."

"The window opens onto a terrace."

She nodded. "Yes, unfortunately. I was told by the officer that it would have been easy for the youths, or thieves I should say, to hop down from the roof onto the terrace. Although I've never seen them do that, everyone in Aix says that's how it's done."

"Yes, that's true in the old town. But this one was an odd break-in, wouldn't you say?"

Mme Picard mumbled in agreement and took a sip of tea. "Do you mean because they stole porcelain?" she asked after setting down her cup.

"Exactly."

"Well, I suppose that's all they had to steal. Mme de Montbarbon never had great amounts of cash in her apartment. Her bank was right downstairs, and if she needed money, she'd call the manager and he'd run it up to her and she'd sign for it."

Verlaque smiled. "I wish I could do that."

"A favorite client."

"Did she have jewelry?"

"No," replied Mme Picard. "That was one of the things I admired in her. She lived very simply. She rarely bought clothes, but when she did they were very good quality, and the jewelry she did inherit she passed on to her granddaughters."

"Who live in Australia."

"Yes."

"But why take the porcelain?" Verlaque asked. "Why didn't they just leave?"

She tilted her head to one side and smiled. "You're the

magistrate, so I'm assuming you've already asked that question, but now you'd like my opinion."

"Yes, you're right. You worked for her and knew the apartment. I'm puzzled by this robbery, which, as I've said, isn't straightforward. No cash or jewels taken, as there were none. Just some—to quote one of our junior officers—old-lady dishes. You were familiar with the dishes, I would think."

"I loved that set," she said with no trace of dishonesty or shame. "So I guess I have old-lady tastes, although I'm not yet sixty. The dishes were painted with a pattern of Brazilian flora and fauna. They were stunning. Eighteenth century."

Verlaque said, "I saw a photograph of them that you gave to the police and insurance people. Were they valuable?"

"That I have no idea. While I love cooking, I'm no antique dinnerware expert. And I'm told the insurers haven't yet been able to estimate their value."

"Which might mean that they're rare," Verlaque suggested. "Mme de Montbarbon didn't tell you of their origins?"

"No. I can't even remember her ever using them. They sat in a sideboard in the dining room."

Verlaque asked, "And the thieves took the lot?"

"Yes."

"What did you make of it at the time?"

She smiled. "I don't know whether to be flattered or confused by your questions. Well, at the time I was just angry, but after I had made coffee for myself and the police who were there, I became puzzled." She leaned forward, getting about as excited as Verlaque imagined Solange Picard could get. "Why take only the porcelain? They had an empty apartment all to themselves, thanks to me. Madame did have silver and some expensive paintings. That's why I suggested they were teens. Who else couldn't recognize a Corot?"

Verlaque nodded. "I agree. It's very odd. Could they have been alarmed by something and left in a hurry?"

"I thought of that," she said. "But as the apartment opens onto the back garden, it's very quiet." She laughed and added, "Unless there was another team of thieves on the roof!"

Verlaque laughed as well. "Given the break-in rate in Aix, that's entirely possible."

She helped herself to a madeleine and passed the plate across the table to Verlaque, who gladly took another. "I'm interested in the Félix Ziem painting," Verlaque said. "Did very many people know that she had a Ziem in her collection?"

"I wouldn't think so, except for her son, who of course doesn't live in France, and perhaps one or two of the curés who would come for tea or before-dinner drinks." She smiled and added, "With the priests it was usually before-dinner drinks, which Madame had a particular liking for. She said it kept her healthy."

"She lived into her nineties, so she had reason to believe so," Verlaque said. "At any rate, the Corot would be worth more than the Ziem."

"Yes, it would."

"Was she a solitary person?"

"Yes, she shied away from strangers and social situations. She loved to read, and she hated fools. But she continued to invite the priests over. Why, I'm not sure, as she was an atheist like myself. Perhaps she was just carrying on a tradition."

Verlaque now saw how the two women could have been good

company for each other. "Or perhaps it was because, as you suggested, she and the priests all enjoyed a little tipple. Did she know Gilbert Quentin-Savary?"

Solange Picard bit her lip. "He did visit, only once, just last month."

Verlaque tried not to look surprised. "That was odd, I take it?"

"Well, yes. He had never been before."

"Do you know why he went to visit Mme de Montbarbon?"

"No, it wasn't my place to ask. But I did hear raised voices. His, mostly." She pulled on her apron and winced. "I should have intervened, but to be frank, I didn't think it my place to do so."

"What kind of mood was M Quentin-Savary in when he left?"

"I don't know, as I was in the kitchen. But he did slam the door." She picked at a crumb on the kitchen table. "The next morning I overheard Mme de Montbarbon on the telephone with the Quentin-Savary director, offering him the Ziem painting. I don't know if my hunch is right, but it seemed to me that perhaps Gilbert Quentin-Savary asked for the painting for himself—perhaps he offered to buy it—and she refused. She didn't need money, you see."

"You may be right," Verlaque said. "But the museum is, after all, in the Quentin-Savary family."

"Yes, but Madame told me later that day that Gilbert wasn't interested in the museum at all. She grinned a bit when she told me that. It wasn't a spiteful grin, mind you, but a playful one."

Verlaque smiled. "Mme de Montbarbon was quite shrewd."

Mme Picard nodded and smiled back. "That's why you can reassure Florence that I was quite content to work for her."

Verlaque took this admission as a cue that their conversation was over. And it had been entirely worth his time. The fact that Gilbert and the old woman had argued was highly interesting news. He got up to leave, thanking Mme Picard for the tea and delicious madeleines. "Please, take a few for your walk back to the Palais de Justice," she urged him.

He took two madeleines, amazed by her acute awareness of everything around her. Of course he was going back to work, and of course he'd love to eat them when he got back to his desk. She probably even knew what floor his office was on. "Will you be looking for another job?" he asked out of genuine curiosity and concern.

She opened the front door for him and smiled. "I won't have to," she said. "Mme de Montbarbon was very generous in her will. My husband is also going to retire, and we will stay here, in this apartment, but travel, which is something we've never been able to do."

Verlaque beamed as he shook her hand. "Congratulations," he said. "I'm sure it was very well earned."

"Thank you," she said. "You know, I've never been to Venice."

"If you do go, please let me know and I'll recommend some of my favorite restaurants. I mean that in all sincerity."

"Thank you," she said again, closing the door. "I'll do that."

It was only at the end of the workday that Verlaque and Paulik had time to meet up and debrief each other of their respective earlier interviews. "It's strange that we call them interviews," Verlaque mused. "When really they're interrogations."

"But with tea," Paulik said.

Verlaque told Paulik of the argument between Mme de Montbarbon and Gilbert. For a reason he couldn't explain, he kept the information about Mme Picard's madeleines to himself. He then asked about Paulik's trip to Marseille.

"I came away with three questions that Lopez raised or didn't raise," Paulik said. "One: Why did Achille Formentin support the joint museum idea, then abruptly change his mind? Two: Why and how does Gilbert Quentin-Savary expect to sell his family portraits, which you told me weren't very good? And by the way, Lopez didn't want to tell me that he saw Gilbert yesterday. And three: Lopez rents a big warehouse out by the airport; could this space possibly be where the museum contents are now stashed?"

He went on to inform the judge that he had assigned a young officer to comb the internet for porcelain listings and recent thefts. "Two other officers are still going through the CCTV cameras between here and Aix-les-Bains," he continued. "And the traffic violations."

"Good," Verlaque said. "If it *was* Gilbert, he might have been speeding. That's a lot of driving to do over one weekend."

"We are looking into Gilbert's friends and acquaintances," Paulik added. "If he did do it, he must have been helped. The problem is, he doesn't seem to have any friends."

"Not surprising." Verlaque asked to see the officer who was going through the records of porcelain and Paulik pointed to a room down the hall. Verlaque found the officer rubbing his eyes, hunched over a computer screen.

"Judge!" the young officer said when he saw Verlaque standing in the doorway.

"Good evening," Verlaque said. "Find anything interesting?"

"No." The officer straightened his back and stretched his arms toward the computer.

"Make sure you look up the porcelain missing from the break-in at Mme de Montbarbon's two weeks ago. Eighteenth century with tropical images."

"I saw the file. Will do."

Verlaque turned to go while the young officer stifled a yawn. Verlaque reached into his pocket and took out the two madeleines, which Mme Picard had wrapped up in a paper towel for him. He placed them on the desk. "These are delicious, made by Mme de Montbarbon's cleaning lady. Enjoy."

"Thank you!" the officer said, trying not to show his surprise. Antoine Verlaque wasn't at all a Parisian snob like some of his colleagues said.

Verlaque walked away, wondering what was for dinner and if it was all right to refer to the elegant bookworm Solange Picard as a cleaning lady. "Maid" didn't sound right, either, and certainly not "servant," which is what his mother had called their staff in Paris on the rue des Petits-Pères. He remembered one in particular, Luis, from Madrid, who spent most of his time polishing the silver, as if the Verlaques lived in the nineteenth century.

As he left the building and walked up the rue Rifle-Rafle toward home, he again thought about Solange Picard; he decided that she wouldn't mind the term "cleaning lady" at all, as she was completely without an ego complex, nor was she concerned about social hierarchies. She had kept the job because she enjoyed Mme de Montbarbon's company. He found himself thinking of the Picards on the deck of a vaporetto chugging down the Grand Canal, seeing that city for the first time. He broke into a wide smile.

Chapter Twelve

✝

Thursday, April 26

The next morning Verlaque remembered that the museum board members were coming to town. After a morning of administrative meetings he arrived at the Hôtel Roi René just before noon. The board members were there, hovering together in the rather grand but, he thought, too nouveau riche lobby. He had looked up their names before coming and thought he could pick out each one. The sole female was easy enough: Myriam Peronne, director of the Musée de Sèvres near Paris, an expert in ceramics. The other Parisian, he thought, must be the tall, slim man on her left wearing a double-breasted bright blue suit: Raymond Policante, an antiques dealer with a gallery in Paris's sixth arrondissement. The painting expert. The short, fat man with the thick, out-of-fashion white mustache would be the academic from Toulouse, Gérald Lagouanere. He'd be the documents and maps guy.

"I'm Antoine Verlaque. Thank you for coming," Verlaque said

as he greeted them, shaking hands with each board member, starting with Myriam Peronne.

"Valet parking!" the mustached man cut in. "This hotel is quite a step up from the usual place Gilbert books for us. I'm Professor Lagouanere. Pleased to meet you."

"We will be finished by tomorrow afternoon, right?" asked the blue suit. "I have to be back in Paris for a dinner."

"You will, M Policante," said Verlaque.

"We will help in any way we can," said Mlle Peronne, seeming to bring her colleagues back to important matters. "What's happened at the museum is shocking and, in my memory, unprecedented."

Policante mumbled in agreement. The professor asked, "Your boys come up with anything yet?"

"My commissioner, Bruno Paulik, has extra officers working on the case. He will be here at any minute."

"Along with Gilbert," said the professor, "who's always late."

"It's a psychological trick," said Raymond Policante. "He keeps us waiting to show us he's the boss."

Mlle Peronne snickered. "Pathetic, and true. He does it every time."

"Who does?" the professor asked.

Mlle Peronne calmly replied, whispering, "Gilbert." She quickly glanced at Verlaque, who pretended not to have noticed.

"Ah, here's the commissioner," Verlaque said as he saw Paulik's tall, wide figure and bald head come through the lobby's glass doors. He was relieved to see him. He already found the company of the three board members tiring, however interesting their opinions of Gilbert. And now they had to eat lunch together.

Paulik arrived and introductions were made. Verlaque thought he saw Myriam Peronne flush when shaking Paulik's hand. It had never, or rarely, occurred to Verlaque that the commissioner could be a lady-killer. But when he looked at Paulik now, he noticed his large eyes with their long dark lashes, which his lack of hair only drew attention to; his wide, honest smile; and the obvious muscles in his upper arms. He had also, Verlaque realized, recently lost some weight.

"Let's go into the dining room," Verlaque said, gesturing with his hand. "We'll eat and then go to a meeting room with our coffees."

At that moment Gilbert Quentin-Savary arrived and coolly shook hands with the party. He made no apology for his lateness, and Verlaque saw Mlle Peronne and Policante roll their eyes at each other. Instead of flushing when shaking Paulik's hand, Verlaque saw that Gilbert slightly—very slightly—trembled.

As they walked to the dining room, Verlaque fell behind to speak to Paulik. "Gilbert is afraid of you."

"I noticed," Paulik answered. "Too bad we can't take him in for questioning right now."

"Even as magistrate, I can't do that yet. We have zero evidence."

"It won't be long. By the way, we got ahold of the chocolate seller last night."

"The guy who lives above the museum?"

"Yes. We Skyped with him. He told Mme Devaux he'd be gone and gave her his dates and hotels, as he always does. He left the weekend before Easter and will be gone for a month."

"Did he tell Gilbert?" Verlaque asked hopefully.

"No, he says he only told Mme Devaux."

"*Merde*." Verlaque looked over at Paulik's smooth stomach. "Have you lost weight?"

"Yep. Running."

"What? Where?"

"Through Hélène's vines and around the village," Paulik said. "I try to do it every morning."

"Traitor. I'm gaining weight."

"Your wife's pregnant. It's normal."

Verlaque grunted. He hated being normal. And he couldn't wait to see what was for lunch.

After a very adequate lunch that had been ordered ahead by France Dubois—duck breast with orange sauce and a green salad accompanied by sparkling water, no wine, and finished with a slice of lemon tart—the group got up to move to a large conference room. Professor Lagouanere left the dining room and walked the wrong way, only to be redirected by Mlle Peronne, who gently took him by the elbow and turned him around. As they walked, they tilted their heads together, laughing over a private joke. Verlaque noted Mlle Peronne's discreetness and compassion.

A waiter brought in espresso and more water as the guests sat down at an oblong walnut table. Verlaque pretended to fuss with the coffee, which the waiter had placed on a side table, until Gilbert sat down. In a flash Verlaque sat down across from him, and Paulik, obviously seeing his chance and the judge's tactic, took a seat next to Gilbert. If Gilbert had noticed their actions, Verlaque didn't care. Even better if he had; he'd be nervous and might slip up, offering some new information that he had previously been able to hide. Despite his alibi, Gilbert was still their number one suspect, but Verlaque couldn't figure out why. What in the world was his motive? The museum's contents weren't worth that much.

Verlaque once again thanked the board members for their presence and for having made the trip to Aix. "Any information that you can give us will be a help," he said. "Even if you think it's inconsequential."

"Why isn't Achille here?" Myriam Peronne asked. "Or Mme Devaux, for that matter."

"You'll meet with them tomorrow morning," Paulik answered.

Mlle Peronne smiled. "I'm not sure that's an answer to my question, but I'll accept it."

"It's because they're suspects," Gilbert said, leaning back in his chair with his hands behind his head. "Especially Formentin. He loves those dishes as much as his mother."

Paulik said, keeping his cool, "We've already questioned them, and they are still in a state of shock. To put it quite simply, there are some questions that we will ask you this afternoon that may be easier for you to answer among us, without the museum's director present. For example, were you satisfied with his work? Do any of you have any reason, besides M Quentin-Savary, to suspect any odd movements or intentions on his part?"

"Not at all," Raymond Policante replied. "Achille, while slightly eccentric, is wholly dedicated to the museum. But in a good way." With this last phrase the antiques dealer glared at Gilbert.

"Agreed," Mlle Peronne said.

"Same," Gérald Lagouanere said. "While Achille may not be

the world's best administrator, he's a walking encyclopedia when it comes to eighteenth- and nineteenth-century art, especially the decorative arts."

"The real administrator is Mme Devaux," Mlle Peronne added. "And that's why they are a perfect team."

"Where would one go to sell off the museum's contents?" Verlaque asked. "This is another reason why we didn't want M Formentin or Mme Devaux here this afternoon. As the commissioner said, they are in shock, and that kind of question would be very difficult for them to hear."

"One would have to go abroad," Policante said. "If you listed any of those objects in Europe, alarm bells would go off. I know I'm on the lookout for the missing art, as are many of my colleagues."

"That's very kind of them," Verlaque said.

Policante laughed. "They are antiques dealers, dear Judge. They are not doing it out of kindness. They are hoping to grab some of the goodies."

"Do you think that the thieves were after one specific piece?" Mlle Peronne asked.

"That's one of the theories we're considering," Paulik said. "Any ideas on which piece?"

She shrugged. "The new Ziem painting, I would think. Sadly, the ceramic arts are still undervalued. At least French ones are."

Out of the corner of his eye Verlaque caught Gilbert flinching.

"There are some quite valuable seventeenth-century maps in the museum," Professor Lagouanere added, not wanting to be left out.

Gilbert laughed. "Right," he said. "Some freak has taken

everything out of the museum just to get a map of what Aix looked like back in the glory days, when they routinely hanged people on the Place des Trois Ormeaux."

Verlaque thought about the professor's comment. Was it such an odd idea? Whoever had done this might be a touch crazy, and someone who would steal a map might be the kind of person obsessed enough to empty a museum to do it. They should explore that idea.

"We have an officer working full time on looking for the ceramics on the internet," Paulik said. "What should he be looking for besides the patterns on the dishes?"

"Sèvres porcelain is marked on the underside with two blue-painted interlaced *L*s," Mlle Peronne said, her voice noticeably getting at once authoritative and excited. "This in turn often encloses a letter or double letter, which acts as a code for the year in which the piece was produced. Most of the painters, and even the gilders, left their mark as well." She opened a file and pushed forward a color photograph toward Verlaque, who looked at it and then passed it to Paulik.

"The crescent?" Paulik asked as he looked at the photograph of a small blue bowl.

"Yes, that moon mark is for Louis-Denis Armand the elder," she said. "Painters were celebrated for their particular skills; some, for example, excelled in birds, others, flowers. The châteaux pieces missing from the Quentin-Savary were painted by Erwan Broc'han. His mark was a stylized wave, as he was, as his name suggests, Breton."

"Would the porcelain, and the other missing objects, be more valuable if sold as a group?" Verlaque asked.

The antiques dealer whistled. "Yes, but almost impossible to sell. Anywhere."

Verlaque thought to himself: *Supposing they were wealthy and didn't want, or need, to sell? A hoarder?*

"The John Shepherd collection sold a few years ago at Christie's for millions," Mlle Peronne added.

"An American collector?" Verlaque asked.

"Yes, he began to collect eighteenth-century Sèvres in the 1970s up until his death in 2002. He had pieces that Marie Antoinette, who was a big Sèvres fan, had ordered."

"I'd say that as a whole the collection may be worth a million euros, perhaps more," Professor Lagouanere said. "We could add up the estimated value of each piece, which I'm sure you've done, but that doesn't give us a realistic idea of the value of a collection that has been together for more than a hundred years. Its provenance adds to the value, surely."

"I'm going to go out on a limb here. It's worth more than just a million," Mlle Peronne said. "It's priceless."

Verlaque nodded and tried to look serious as he noticed that the others shifted uneasily in their chairs. The Quentin-Savary collection priceless? Perhaps the Wallace Collection in London was, but this? He remembered his last visit to the Wallace, over a year ago, with Marine; when she took too long looking at the Italian majolica ceramics, Verlaque jokingly threatened to divorce her. Marine pointed him in the direction of the rather splendid courtyard restaurant, where he had a glass of white wine—Italian, in honor of the majolica—which immediately improved his mood. In a few months, they'd have a child. How would they visit museums with a rug rat? He'd seen other parents wheeling toddlers around through museums and it had always exasperated him.

Gilbert Quentin-Savary brought Verlaque out of his reverie. "Hilarious! More than a million? You're dreaming."

"M Policante?" Paulik asked, turning to look at him. "What do you think? Could someone sell the entire collection?"

"It's a thought," Policante said slowly, rubbing his chin. "The stolen contents could be stored in a warehouse near Marseille somewhere, ready to be put on a boat when the time is right."

Verlaque tried not to look at Paulik. They had already discussed this possibility.

Gérald Lagouanere held his head in his hands and moaned.

"I think it more likely they are waiting to sell it piece by piece," Mlle Peronne said. "I've drawn up a list, with M Policante, of his best Sèvres buyers and of my donors. The names would be easy enough to find if you asked around Paris, Zurich, and London. They are a surprisingly small group and most of them know one another."

Verlaque couldn't imagine a local thief being that savvy; they wouldn't know the first thing about asking questions around Zurich or London. Paris, maybe. "Thank you," he said. "We'll have an officer contact them to see if they've been approached by anyone. Although, as you say, it's still early."

"But the clock is ticking," the professor said. "If the collection gets on a boat to North Africa, we're doomed."

"I've also drawn up a list of collectors who buy twentieth-century Provençal paintings," Raymond Policante said. "The Ziem painting is worth quite a bit of money."

"Thank you. Had you heard that its authenticity is being challenged?" Verlaque asked.

"Let me guess. Lopez?" Policante asked.

Verlaque nodded.

"He's jealous, and is always full of half-baked opinions," said Policante. "It's real, all right. We wouldn't have accepted it into the collection otherwise."

Lagouanere and Mlle Peronne nodded in agreement. "I've even been there," the professor said.

"The pink building on the canal?" Paulik asked.

"Two weeks ago. It's still there, in all its glory. Not much has changed in Venice."

"Except for the cruise ships," Myriam Peronne said.

As Verlaque walked home, he thought about the meeting. Three of the board members seemed entirely innocent and he crossed each one off his list of suspects. That left Gilbert. Paulik had stayed back to speak to them individually and Verlaque would get Paulik's reading of the situation tomorrow. He stopped to cut and light a cigar and smiled at the thought of Mlle Peronne alone in a room with dog-eyed Bruno Paulik. A young woman walked by him and scowled; was it because he was smiling to himself? He may have even been chuckling out loud. He then realized it was probably the cigar.

By the time he got home, his cigar was only a third finished, so he gently stubbed it out on the wall of his building before going inside the front door. He'd save it and smoke it later, out on the terrace. Now that Marine was pregnant, he no longer smoked inside. As he walked up the stairs, he thought of Marine and tried to psych himself up for the now nightly conversation about the baby. Baby, baby, baby. It wasn't that he didn't want it; he just didn't know how to think about it or what to say about it. Childhood, and definitely infancy, wasn't something that had ever been spoken about in the Verlaque home, so the whole thing was a mystery to him. He couldn't imagine Marine's parents having been much more open about it, either, but Marine seemed to be taking pregnancy in her stride, calmly and with the amount of excitement that seemed normal to Verlaque and not at all annoying. She wasn't preoccupied about painting the guest bedroom with balloons or flowers or funny little animals or whatever people did when expecting a baby. He realized, between the second and third floors, that her daily need to talk about the pregnancy and the baby was not so demanding after all.

"*Coucou*," he called out as he opened the door to their apartment.

"I'm in the living room," Marine shouted back.

He walked into the living room to find her curled up on the sofa with a book, her legs covered with a favorite mohair blanket. Verlaque leaned down and kissed her. "I'm going to step out onto the terrace and put this half-smoked cigar in an ashtray," he said. Marine nodded and smiled.

"Rereading Proust?" he asked when he came back in.

"As a matter of fact, I am."

Verlaque laughed and told her about the madeleines. He sat down next to her and began rubbing her feet. "Did the baby move around today?" he found himself asking.

"I felt a little something," she said. "But now I think I'm

imagining it. That day in La Ciotat, at the lecture, it definitely felt like the baby was moving. But since then, nothing."

Verlaque continued to rub her feet. He wasn't sure what to say. Was this a normal occurrence? He could stay up late and try to find out on the computer, but he knew that looking up medical information on the internet wasn't a good idea. He couldn't really ask anyone at work about it; Paulik would think him off his rocker, and perhaps he and Hélène hadn't talked about this kind of stuff. His secretary, France, was single with no children. Then he thought of Sylvie, Marine's best friend. She had a thirteen-year-old. He'd call her.

"I think your phone's ringing," Marine said, nudging Verlaque with her foot.

"Right! Thanks!" he said as he hopped off the sofa and jogged to the kitchen, where he had left his cell phone to charge.

"Bruno," he answered, seeing Paulik's caller ID.

"*Salut*," Paulik said. "I hope I'm not bothering you."

"No, no."

"Officer Roche has found something on the internet."

"Roche?"

"The young officer I have looking for porcelain. Patrice Roche."

"Oh, right, that poor kid," Verlaque said. "What did he find?"

"One of those châteaux plates. Or so we think. It has the painter's mark—that stylized wave that Mlle Peronne told us about—and the date fits. The photograph is crap."

"The Breton painter."

"Exactly."

"Wow. Good work. Where is it?"

"On leboncoin."

Verlaque said, "You'll have to fill me in."

"You've never heard of it?" Paulik whistled as Verlaque waited patiently. "It's a website across France where people buy and sell stuff they don't want anymore. Everything from cars to furniture to clothes."

"Like a junk sale online?"

Paulik paused. "It's not all junk. We found our antique walnut kitchen table on it."

"Sorry. So who's the seller? Can you contact them?"

"There's a phone number. No email."

"A price?"

"It's listed for one thousand euros or best offer. Doesn't seem like an antiques dealer given that they're selling it on leboncoin and their pseudonym is DJ Kool, with a *K*."

"Can Roche tell who the seller is?"

"No. Only that they are in the Paris region."

"Paris? Did he call them?"

"He's left several messages."

"Fine; keep me posted," Verlaque said. "Send my best to the girls." He hung up and wondered if Marine would be going to bed early, as she'd recently been doing. He couldn't wait to look at leboncoin.

Chapter Thirteen

Thursday, April 26

Early evening was France Dubois's favorite time of the day. She loved "the golden hour," which lasted a few bewitching minutes in Aix, lighting up the buttery-yellow stone buildings into almost a hot pink. She stopped at a building on the corner of rue Sallier and rue Mistral and felt the warm stone with the palm of her hand. Walking on, she waited for the green light at the boulevard Roi René and continued her way toward *la faculté*, where her Chinese language classes were held. Here, seventeenth- and eighteenth-century Aix changed to postwar Aix, as if the nineteenth century had been forgotten. She mused that there had probably been many fine nineteenth-century buildings in southern Aix, but they had been replaced in the 1950s for better and cheaper versions. She knew from her books that after the Second

World War it was sheer bliss for people to have small, cozy homes with central heating and plumbing, and she couldn't really blame them.

As she passed in front of the Hôtel Roi René, she saw Bruno Paulik speaking to a small group of people outside the hotel's front doors. She looked at them curiously, knowing that they were the board of directors at the museum and she had spoken to most of them on the phone or by email. She quickened her pace as she didn't want Bruno Paulik to see her and feel like he had to stop what he was doing in order to say hello. Gilbert Quentin-Savary stood at the edge of the group, smoking a cigarette and staring at the sky. A woman's laugh rang out and she saw Bruno Paulik throw his head back in returned laughter. Whatever could they be laughing about? France wondered, a bit surprised by their gaiety. But then she realized that they had been in a meeting all afternoon and it was probably nervous, or exhausted, relief, not any disrespect or antipathy for the empty museum that had been under their care.

A few minutes later she walked into the languages building, thankful for the recent renovations and clean bright rooms. France had been invited to her boss's house for Christmas and Marine Bonnet had entertained the group with stories of the Aix *faculté* when she was a junior professor. She had had to make sure to use the bathroom at her apartment before coming to campus to teach as half of the toilets were out of order and the other half were padlocked by the secretaries of each department for their own use. Bruno and Hélène Paulik, neither of whom had been to that university, had looked at Marine in disbelief while Antoine Verlaque had laughed uproariously. "When was this, exactly?" he had asked his wife. To the shock of everyone, Marine replied, "Not so long ago. After 9/11, so around 2002."

France took her seat in the middle of the classroom. She would have preferred to sit in the front row, in order to hear better, but she had arrived a bit late for the first class and those places had been taken. From then on, the same people had occupied those seats for each class and France didn't think it polite to try to intercept them to change now. Besides, from the middle of the room she could observe her fellow students, who represented a mismatch of ages and desires and interests. What most of them were doing learning Chinese every Tuesday and Thursday nights she couldn't tell, although the same was true even for herself. Partly it was boredom; as much as she liked her apartment, it did get lonely at night, especially in the winter. Was she interested in the Chinese language or culture? Only slightly; she had a vague connection to China, as her father had worked there on a couple of occasions and had thoroughly enjoyed it. Ever since both her parents had died in a car accident when she was a teenager, she had struggled to find connections to them, especially now, so many years later. She knew from reading newspapers that many young people were learning Chinese to help them in the job market, and she looked around the class, judging at least three-quarters of the students to be college age. There was only one other thirtysomething like herself, an odd-looking man with thick glasses and oily hair who always brought a sandwich in a small Tupperware and ate it daintily as he took notes. A fifty-year-old drove up from Marseille, usually complaining about the traffic. There were a few senior citizens, who raised their hands too often in order to show off. The teacher would smile and nod, patiently waiting to continue. And then there was the teacher himself, and France knew that he was the real reason she was still there.

The museum was dark and deathly quiet. Achille Formentin turned on the lights and walked into the main room, studying its sad emptiness. He blinked to stop the tears from coming to his eyes; he had been having trouble controlling his emotions ever since all these troubles began. He moved slowly around the room, in his head re-creating the full museum with each object in its proper place. A noise from upstairs stopped him and he held his breath. All was silent again and he returned to his pacing, deciding that the noise had probably come from the renter upstairs, back from one of his chocolate-selling trips.

He racked his brain, trying to understand why he felt the need to return here each night when the police had gone. It was partly out of grief for the lost objects he had so lovingly tended all these years. Without them, he had no profession. At his age, he would never find work again. He walked over to the window and looked out onto the even darker courtyard. He had always planned to plant a garden there but had never gotten around to it. Now it was too late; no doubt the museum would close. He rubbed his index finger along the windowsill, making a line in the dust. Turning around to face the empty room, he saw the stairs and remembered that in his office were his ideas for a small exhibition of historic maps. He was beginning to walk up the stairs when he heard

the same noise again—like a shuffle. He took the last steps two
at a time.

Myriam Peronne was vaguely disappointed that Commissioner
Paulik wouldn't be joining her and the other board members for
dinner. Only vaguely because she had seen his wedding ring, and
she in no way harbored any interest in a love affair with a married
man, but nonetheless she had enjoyed his company. He was hand-
some, too, in a nonconventional way; she usually fell for that type
of big, muscular man with soft eyes and an easy laugh. And that
kind of man was virtually nonexistent in the Paris museum world.

Fortunately, Professor Lagouanere was a gourmand and had
chosen what appeared to be a fantastic small restaurant off the
Cours Sextius, on the less-smart side of town. Myriam had tea
with the professor beforehand and helped him with his tie, and
they went down to the lobby together at 7:30 p.m. Raymond wasn't
there yet, so they decided to leave for the restaurant without him,
as the professor was a slow walker. They chatted the whole way
there.

Once inside the restaurant, Myriam looked around and was
comforted by the warm décor—a few tables with antique but comfortable chairs, the tables dimly lit with small lamps—and, most
important to her, the absence of music. She had just returned from
a weekend in London visiting her sister, who lived there with her
English husband, and although Myriam had been delighted in
the quality and variety of London food, the restaurants had been
so noisy that she'd had trouble following the conversation.

They studied the small list of enticing choices on the menu in silence. It seemed that the other two board members were running late, so they each ordered a cocktail and resumed their conversation.

After thirty minutes, Gilbert finally arrived and sat down at the end of the table, looking his usually unkempt and ruffled self. A waiter walked by and Gilbert loudly demanded a whisky with ice; the professor groaned and Myriam bit her lip.

"Where's Raymond?" Gilbert asked.

"Late, as you can see," Myriam replied. "Are you having another aperitif?" she asked the professor.

Professor Lagouanere sighed. "Well, I'd be quite happy with another flute of champagne. This has been a rather trying day."

The waiter smiled and nodded, then walked back to the small bar to order their drinks. "I didn't find it trying at all," Myriam said. "The police weren't as intimidating as I'd expected."

"That's because you were gushing over the bald commissioner," Gilbert said with a snicker.

"I beg your pardon?" she asked. "You're a real twit, Gilbert."

Raymond Policante finally arrived, appearing frazzled. "A million pardons," he said as he sat down. "I'm so sorry."

The waiter reappeared with a tray full of cocktails. "A cocktail, monsieur?" he asked.

"No, I'm fine," Raymond said with a wave of his hand.

Myriam looked on, perplexed, as Raymond usually liked his flute of champagne. He was also disheveled, which was very out of the ordinary for the antiques dealer; his hair was uncombed and she noticed that he had missed the middle button on his waistcoat.

"To get back to the conversation," the professor said. "I only meant today was trying because of the lost objects. On the drive from Toulouse I kept thinking that when we got to Aix we would be told that the police had found them, or at least were on track to do so. But now I've given up that hope."

Myriam was relieved that the professor's memory seemed to be working this evening.

"Have faith, dear Professor," Raymond said. "We are all experts in our own domains—well, almost all experts." He threw a glance at Gilbert, who hadn't noticed as he was intently studying the menu. "And if we put our heads together, we should be able to come up with some useful information to help the police."

As they finished their cocktails, Myriam mused over Gilbert's comment about Achille being the prime suspect. At first she had thought it ludicrous, but now she saw that it made sense. But only a tiny bit. Achille was at times overly attached to the museum's objects. Would he steal them in order to keep them? To keep them away from Gilbert, who, if the museum ever closed, would do . . . what with his family's legacy? She had no doubts he would sell them to the highest bidder, probably a Russian oligarch or a Saudi prince. Was the museum under threat of closure and none of them knew about it? Their past few board meetings had been fraught with monetary arguments: money was scarce, as were paying visitors. Mme Quentin-Savary had left a legacy, but that, too, would run out in under ten years; on the TGV to Aix, she and Raymond had talked about the museum's dire straits.

As if reading her mind, Raymond said, "Gilbert, do you have anything to say? You know as well as we that the museum is running out of money. Doesn't that concern you?"

"Where in the world is the waiter?" Gilbert asked, looking around the room. "We need to order."

Raymond sighed. "Gilbert?"

Gilbert rolled his eyes. "Of course it concerns me. The museum is owned by my family."

The professor snickered. "It hasn't been a bad job for you, has it?" He poked Gilbert in the side as their colleagues exchanged worried looks. Gilbert opened his mouth to comment, but the professor beat him to it. "Have we ordered yet?" he asked, looking worriedly at Myriam.

"No, Professor," she said, laying a hand on his forearm. "I'll try to get the waiter's attention."

"I'll go and get him," Raymond said, getting up.

She watched Raymond cross the room, grateful that he was such a help. She turned her head back to their table. The professor was playing with his napkin, folding it into what looked like Napoleon's hat, and Gilbert scrolled through his telephone messages. She decided that the next morning she would tell the commissioner about the museum's financial problems. For some reason it was an embarrassment that none of them wanted to talk about. It was time to come clean.

Raymond returned with the waiter apologizing behind him. When he took their orders, she ordered a steak, suddenly very hungry and in need of some protein.

Chapter Fourteen

Friday, April 27

Faustine Devaux felt guilty about two things. She'd forgotten that she kept a second set of museum keys in her apartment, at the back of her desk drawer. She'd found them by chance looking for her checkbook. She needed to give them to the police. She was hoping to rectify that just now, after she dealt with the second thing she hadn't told them about. The second thing she had not forgotten about; it had been intentional.

She checked her watch; it was just before 7:00 a.m. She must get to the museum before the police did, if indeed they were still going there. She had no idea if they had finished their work, dusting and fingerprinting or whatever it was they seemed to take ages doing. She would have been more efficient. She walked quickly, now and then glancing down at the sidewalk to make sure she didn't step in any dog feces or trip on any uneven stones.

Aix was lovely at this time in the morning; hardly anyone was about except for the café owners who were already open for business and the butchers and bread makers. Her father had owned a *boulangerie* in northern France, as had his father before him. Bread just wasn't as good anymore; it was empty and full of air, and the crust wasn't crispy enough. Their apartment had been above the *boulangerie* and she remembered the wonderful smells, and the heat, which hadn't bothered her even in the summer. It had been a dry, comfortable kind of heat. She remembered the flour being delivered in big bleached-white burlap sacks that read VER-LAQUE. She knew that Aix's judge came from that family; she'd read it in the local paper. But most of all she remembered the flour delivery boy, just a year older than her, and his smile, and how she would wake up early in the hopes of seeing him, perhaps speaking to him. And then her parents died, one after the other within eighteen months, and she was sent to Provence to live with cousins.

Now she was standing at the door of the museum. She realized she had walked there in complete unawareness of the streets, as if her body could get her there without her brain having to instruct it. Putting her key in the lock, she opened the door and slipped inside. The museum was as she expected: empty. A bit of morning light shone through the windows, helping her see. She stepped into the main room and noticed Achille's long black umbrella leaning against the wall. Odd. But then she remembered it had drizzled the day before, so perhaps he had come and then forgotten the umbrella here. She quickened her pace and headed for the stairs that led to their office, worried that he had taken the document she had come for.

Flipping the light on, she walked up and into the office, heading straight for her hiding place, a plastic box under the coffee maker that she knew Achille never bothered with. He hated coffee. Leaning down, she took the lid off the box and pulled out the document, but for reasons she couldn't understand, she put it right back and stood up, turning around and looking toward the next room, where the archives were stored. The door was ajar and some sixth sense made her walk hesitantly toward it and push the door open. She blinked, not sure she was seeing correctly.

There were two figures on the floor, one whose head was surrounded by a dark reddish liquid she slowly realized was blood. She stood there, frozen, putting a hand to her chest. She opened her mouth to scream, but nothing came out. Now she wished that the police were there; the sight before her was unimaginable. Taking a deep breath, she walked toward the two bodies. They were both men, and bending down at the feet of the first one, she saw that it was Achille.

"No!" she cried, and quickly took his wrist in her hand. She thought she could feel a pulse, but she was no expert. She ran to the desk, picked up the telephone, and dialed 18, almost dropping the receiver. A woman answered on the second ring and she gave the museum's address, whispering that something horrible had occurred.

"What exactly has happened, madame?" the woman asked. "Please explain."

Faustine tried to answer, but once again, no words escaped her now-parched mouth. Her stomach heaved and she dropped the receiver and fell to the floor.

In less than thirty minutes the museum was abuzz with emergency workers. Faustine Devaux had been revived by the first to arrive, two police officers who gently put her in a chair and offered water. The ambulance team followed, and Bruno Paulik, who insisted that Mme Devaux be accompanied home. "Will he be all right?" she asked Paulik faintly as she was led out of the office by a female officer.

"I hope so," Paulik replied. He put a hand lightly on her shoulder. "The doctor says you arrived just in time. Please don't worry."

"And the other gentleman?"

He glanced in the direction of the archival room. "No," he replied simply. "He was killed late last night, by a blow to the head."

Mme Devaux looked worriedly around the office, something that did not escape Paulik. Then she nodded and obediently let the officer take her by the arm.

"One question before you leave," Paulik said. "You were to give your keys to us . . ."

"I did," Mme Devaux replied quickly, looking down at the floor. "But I found an extra set in my apartment, a set I thought lost long ago. I was going to give them to you . . ."

"Very well," he said. "We'll talk later today about it, when you're feeling better. You understand how it looks."

She was still looking at the floor. "Yes, I do. And the others as well, with their keys . . ."

"Excuse me?"

"The board members."

Paulik sighed. "The board members all have keys to the museum?" He was about to ask if all of Aix also had keys, but the look of weariness on both the secretary's face and that of the officer, who thought he was being too hard on the old woman, stopped him. "Please go home now, and try to relax for the rest of the day," he said.

"Yes, and I'm sorry," she said, letting herself be led down the stairs.

Paulik turned around and walked over to where the chief medical examiner was bent down over the dead body. "Do you know him?" Dr. Cohen asked, looking up at the commissioner.

"I think he's Aurélien Lopez," Paulik replied. "But I can't be certain . . ."

"In the state his head's in," she said bluntly, finishing his sentence for him. "As I said earlier, he was killed late last night by a blow to the head."

"Please excuse us," a forensics photographer said.

Paulik and Cohen got to their feet and moved aside. She pulled off her plastic gloves and tossed them into a bag. "I'll keep you posted."

"Thank you, Doctor," he replied. "And M Formentin? Will he be all right?"

She shrugged. "Touch and go. He, too, was hit pretty hard. I'm off."

Paulik thanked her again and sat down in a chair and began taking notes. Officers Goulin and Schoelcher arrived, looking almost as shell-shocked as Mme Devaux. Paulik motioned with his head toward Lopez's body and briefed them.

"Who found them?" Goulin asked.

"The secretary."

"Mme Devaux?" Schoelcher asked. "What was she doing here?"

"I'll ask her that same question when she's feeling better. She fainted. We need to know what Lopez and Formentin were doing here at night. Did they come together? Sophie, make the rounds of the neighbors and see if anyone saw anything, especially the neighbor across the street who sleeps poorly."

"All right. And the judge?" Goulin asked. "Does he know about the attack yet?"

"No," Paulik replied. He looked at his watch. "He's on his way to the Ardèche for the weekend. I'll call him later. Jules, let's round up the board of directors. They'll need to stay in Aix longer than they thought. Any one of them could have come in last night."

"Right," Schoelcher replied. He stood up and then asked as he scratched his head, "They have keys, too?"

"Apparently, yes. I just found out."

"Geez, does all of Aix have keys to this place?"

Chapter Fifteen

꙳

Friday, April 27

It was hard for Verlaque to describe what made the Ardèche different from Provence. It was scrubby and rocky here, *sauvage*, but so was Provence, even around Aix. It was mountainous, almost as soon as they ventured off the highway, and the two-lane road they took just out of the tollbooth south of Montélimar turned into one lane in no time. As he drove, he looked out of the window and saw low stone walls almost touching either side of his car. Was that the difference? Provence didn't have as many stone walls, and here, he now realized, there were fewer houses. Neighbors seemed to be miles away, not just up the road.

"It's so wild here," Marine said, looking out of the passenger window.

"I can't figure out why it's so different from Provence," Verlaque said. "It was only a two-and-a-half-hour drive."

"Vines."

Verlaque looked at her. "You're right. There aren't any."

"It's rockier, too," Marine said. "There are famous cave paintings south of here." She looked at the Michelin map that was open on her lap.

He smiled. "Do you have a complete set of those maps, just like your parents?"

"Almost a full set," she replied flatly, still looking at the map. "Chauvet–Pont d'Arc. But we won't have time to go. It's too far south on tiny curvy roads."

"I thought they were never going to open those caves," Verlaque said. "To save the paintings."

"They didn't. They made a replica. Like at Lascaux. My parents, when they were small, each saw the real thing at Lascaux."

"Mine did, too," Verlaque said. "At least I know my father did." He looked over at Marine again. "How are you feeling?"

"Good. I slept on the highway, didn't I?"

"Yes, for about an hour."

They arrived at a crossroads and he turned right, following the sign for the town of Privas. Marine opened her purse and took out a piece of paper. "Our hotel is called the Auberge de Privas. It's on the main square."

"How many stars does it have?"

"Probably none," Marine said, smiling. "I don't think they rate auberges with stars like they do hotels. But don't worry, it looked nice on the website. The restaurant has great reviews."

"Excellent, because I'm more than ready for lunch."

Thirty minutes later they were checked in and sitting in the dining room. A huge open hearth stood at one end of the room, and the walls were covered in a collection of black-and-white photographs of Privas from the nineteenth and early twentieth century. Marine smiled, moving her hand along the red-and-white-checked tablecloth.

"You're happy," Verlaque said. "This is your kind of place."

"I wish we had them in Aix."

"You'll be even happier when your meal arrives on an antique flowered plate."

As if on cue, the waitress arrived and set Marine's omelet before her. The plate was ivory-colored porcelain with a ruffled trim and pale pink flowers around the edge.

"Are those mushrooms on the side?" Verlaque asked.

The waitress replied, "Yes, sautéed in butter with cream and Madeira wine."

Verlaque grunted, wishing he had ordered the same thing. They had agreed to order light and eat a more substantial meal in the evening, after their visit to Marie-Claire Blay. The waitress set down his ham sandwich and he whistled. "It's huge!" he said, smiling.

"The sourdough bread is from the village," the waitress announced. "As is the pig. *Bon appétit!*"

"Do you suppose that your Marie-Claire Blay owns the pig farm that gave you your sandwich?" Marine asked as she put her fork into the puffy omelet.

"My guess is that she owns goats."

"*Chèvre,*" Marine said. "You're right. I think there's a lot of goat's cheese in the Ardèche." She quickly leaned back and put her hand on her stomach.

"What is it?"

"I felt a little something."

"There you go," Verlaque said, smiling. "Twenty weeks is normal. It can take even longer to feel the baby kicking when it's your first pregnancy."

Marine looked at her husband in surprise.

"I looked it up," he said.

"I'm at twenty-four weeks."

"First pregnancy," Verlaque repeated.

"One thing's for sure," she said.

"What's that?"

"I think we're going to eat very well this evening."

Verlaque laughed and reached across the table and took her hand.

"There's something else about this terrain," Marine said as Verlaque drove the car out of the village along a tiny winding departmental road. "The trees are different here. There aren't any cypress and few pines. You know, those tall Cézanne pines. Here there are lots of chestnut and scrubby oaks."

"You're right," he said. "And I like that."

"Yes, when you're not used to it, it's refreshing. They probably say the same thing when they come to Provence. If they can come to Provence. We must seem very wealthy to them."

"Yes. Life is hard here and the salaries low."

"We should be getting close," Marine said, "according to her instructions. Voilà! I see a sign up ahead."

Verlaque slowed the car down and she sat forward to better read it. "La Ferme de Marie-Claire."

"This is it." He signaled and turned the car into the drive. They drove for a few more minutes, Verlaque swerving the car gently to the right or left to avoid the potholes. "There are some animals," Marine said, pointing off to the right. She laughed and added, "I feel like a schoolkid from the city out on a country field trip."

"They're cows," Verlaque said. He looked again. "Or not."

"Cows with very long hair," Marine added. "How bizarre. Some rare breed?"

Verlaque stopped the car in front of a single-story stone house. A much bigger building, a barn, and a large shed housing a tractor stood beyond the house. A tall woman with graying curly hair walked out of the house, drying her hands on an apron.

"Mlle Blay?" Verlaque asked as he got out of the car.

"That's me," she said, shaking his hand.

"I'm Antoine Verlaque, and this is my wife, Marine Bonnet."

"Pleased to meet you," Mlle Blay said, shaking Marine's hand.

"Thank you for letting me come along," Marine said. "I quite enjoy farms."

"I assumed that you were here to ask me questions about art theft," Mlle Blay said, smiling.

Verlaque laughed. "If we can do both on this visit, that would be great."

"I have to feed the animals," Mlle Blay said. "Why don't you both come with me? We can talk as I work."

"Sounds great," Verlaque said, thankful that he had thought to wear a boot version of his beloved Westons.

They followed Mlle Blay through the thankfully dry field. "They're the strangest-looking cows," Marine said.

Mlle Blay stopped and turned to them. "Oh! I should have explained. They're water buffalo."

Verlaque laughed. "I've never seen one before."

"I haven't either," Marine said. "Are there many in the Ardèche?"

"There are more over in the Cévennes," Mlle Blay said. "But they do quite well here. I have twenty cows and a bull. I supply milk to a few cheese companies that make their own buffalo mozzarella; in fact, I can't keep up with the demand."

They stopped at a trough and Mlle Blay reached down and opened a trapdoor; out fell what seemed like an enormous amount of grain. "They eat a lot," she explained. Hearing the metal trapdoor open and the grain fall, the buffalo began to move over to the trough. "We'd better step aside," she advised.

"Just tell us what to do and we'll follow," Verlaque said.

"They're very friendly, but it's always a good idea to leave them some space while they're eating," Mlle Blay said. "Like anyone, I suppose."

Verlaque and Marine smiled. Verlaque asked, "Had you heard about the museum break-in before we spoke on the phone? You didn't seem surprised."

Mlle Blay said, "I saw it on the news, and a friend from Paris rang me up to tell me."

"Any ideas?" Verlaque asked. "Either from you or your friends in Paris . . ."

"Friends in the art theft world?" she asked, a crooked smile forming at the edges of her mouth. She didn't wait for Verlaque's answer and quickly said, "Someone insane."

Verlaque and Marine exchanged looks. "I beg your pardon?" he asked.

Mlle Blay took a breath. "Listen, it would be next to impossible to sell any of that stuff on the open market in the next few years. Everyone will be looking out for it."

"What about the closed market?" Marine asked.

Mlle Blay shrugged. "No offense to Aix-en-Provence, but the Quentin-Savary collection wouldn't attract the illegal market. There are no Impressionists or Greek or Roman antiquities. But someone obsessed with, let's say, French porcelain, or old documents, could be interested. Nuts are out there. I met plenty, both outside and inside of prison."

Verlaque remembered Gilbert's quip about the thief being antique map obsessed. "Know any offhand?" he asked.

"Nah," Mlle Blay answered. "I did know a guy up in Normandy who was obsessed with medieval armory." She laughed. "You can imagine how hard it was for him to steal the stuff; he was creative, though. He once walked out of a château in the Loire wearing a medieval knight's armor, pretending he was part of the museum staff! It was credible, as a medieval fair was going on at the same time, but all the same . . ." Her anecdote got laughs from her guests and she smiled, patting one of the buffalo on the rump. "Hey there, Artemisia! Slow down!"

Marine asked, "Artemisia, after the Italian painter?"

"Yes," Mlle Blay replied. "That's Georgia O'Keeffe beside her."

"And the one bull?" Verlaque asked. "Named after a male artist? Which one?"

"I'm sure you can guess," Mlle Blay said. "He's out in another field; he's been too frisky lately."

He laughed and scratched his head. "It wouldn't be Pablo, would it?"

"You guessed it," Mlle Blay said. She gave the buffalo more

food and murmured endearments as they ate. She then turned to Verlaque and asked, "Did the thief take absolutely everything from the museum?"

"Yes," he said. "Except for the front desk. Which is why your nut theory is beginning to sound plausible."

Marine was watching the buffalo. "They look very friendly," she said.

"They are," Mlle Blay replied. "And they're more intelligent than cows, but more stubborn, too. But the more time you spend with them, the friendlier they are. School groups from the region come here for visits; the buffalo, and the kids, love it. And now should we go inside for some tea? It's getting cold, and you," she said, gesturing at Marine's stomach, "might like a rest."

"I would," Marine said. "And I need to use your bathroom."

"Let's go then," Mlle Blay said. "Once inside, I can show you my Ziem painting. Bought with my own money years ago, not stolen, I assure you."

Verlaque reflected that if Marie-Claire Blay was able to buy a Ziem painting, even years ago before Ziem was rediscovered, it was with money she had gained from thieving, but he kept quiet. "You knew that there was a Ziem stolen from the museum?" he asked as they walked back to the house.

"Yes, they mentioned it on the news. Mine is very small, just a landscape of a river with an old stone bridge. It reminds me of here, but I think he did it in Italy."

Marine was thankful that the hotel proprietor had lit a fire in the dining room's enormous hearth; it was decidedly cooler in the Ardèche than back in Aix. When he saw that she was pregnant, he gave them a table close to the fire. As they sat down, Verlaque's cell phone buzzed. "It's Bruno," he said. "I'm going to take this out in the lobby. Do you mind?"

"Not at all," Marine said. "I'm going to order a cranberry juice and sparkling water."

"I'll be right back. Order me a glass of white," Verlaque said, taking his phone with him and regretting having to leave Marine, and the fire, and the wine list that the waiter had just set down on their table.

"Bruno," he said.

"I'm sorry to bother you," Paulik said. "But there's been a sad turn of events here in Aix. I tried calling earlier."

"I saw that," Verlaque said. "I'm sorry. I was in a field surrounded by water buffalo. I'll explain later. What's happened?"

"Achille Formentin was hit on the back of the head. He was found unconscious upstairs in the museum and is now in intensive care. Dr. Cohen said it happened last night. The poor guy lay there all evening until Mme Devaux found him."

"Mme Devaux?" Verlaque asked. "Any idea who did it or with what?"

"No," Paulik said. "Well, some kind of blunt instrument, Dr. Cohen says. But there's worse . . ."

"Pardon me?" Verlaque asked, sitting down in an armchair in the lobby. "This doesn't sound good."

"Lopez was found next to him. Dead. Hit on the back of the head."

"Are you serious? Sorry. You normally don't joke about these things."

"Yes, I'm serious," Paulik said. "I wish I was joking."

"Lopez was attacked by the same person and with the same object, I would guess," Verlaque said.

"Yes. He was killed just before Formentin was hit. Formentin may have seen the attacker, so I'm having the ICU manned day and night. I've also stopped the board directors from returning home this afternoon. I caught them just as they were leaving the hotel. They all have keys to the museum."

"What?" Verlaque asked. "Did they all forget to tell us that? It's sounding like a conspiracy." He walked to the dining room's open doorway and caught Marine's eye. He gestured for her to eat. She gave him a thumbs-up just as the waiter set a small plate of food down in front of her. Verlaque smiled, relieved that she'd gone ahead and ordered a starter. "Should I cut my Ardèche weekend short?" he asked.

"Nah," Paulik said. "I can do everything from here. I'll call you if I have any updates."

"Thanks, and good luck," Verlaque said.

"Yes, go eat," Paulik said. "Ciao."

Verlaque returned to the dining room and sat down, putting the napkin on his lap. "Terrible news," he said. "There's been a murder in the museum."

"*Quoi?*" Marine asked, setting her fork down. "That's awful! Who?"

"Lopez, the museum director from Marseille."

"Did they catch the murderer?"

"No."

"Do you think M Formentin did it?" she asked. "Do you remember that I saw them arguing in La Ciotat at that conference?"

"We're sure that Formentin didn't do it, as he, too, was hit on the head and is in the ICU."

"*Mon dieu*. He might have seen it happen." She sat back. "All of a sudden I'm not very hungry. Does Lopez have family?"

"I didn't think to ask," Verlaque said. "I should have."

"You were probably as shocked as I am. Don't worry, Bruno will handle everything well," Marine said.

"This investigation is taking too long."

"Don't beat yourself up," Marine said. "And it hasn't been that long."

"What if Lopez has a family? Kids?"

She reached across and took his hand. "Let's talk about Mlle Blay instead. She was very odd."

"Eccentric, yes."

"No, I meant her behavior was odd," Marine said. "She didn't seem very curious about the theft . . ."

"She's left those thieving days behind," Verlaque suggested.

"Yes, I know, and yet she seemed to know exactly what was in the Musée Quentin-Savary. Even though it's just a tiny provincial museum."

"True. She knew there was a Ziem."

"Exactly. I'm not saying she should be treated as a suspect, but it's odd, that's all."

Chapter Sixteen

❧

Friday, April 27

Gilbert Quentin-Savary shifted uneasily in his plastic chair. "You'd think the police could use some of our tax money to buy proper furnishings," he said to no one in particular.

"If they did that, you'd be the first to complain that they were wasting public funds," Myriam replied sharply.

"Do you know how much longer we have to wait?" Professor Lagouanere asked her.

"Not much longer, I hope," she answered, looking toward the closed door. The professor yawned and Myriam put her hand on his arm. "I'll ask the commissioner if you can go next," she said. She looked around the waiting room and tried to concentrate on the informational posters instead.

"This is ridiculous," Gilbert grumbled. "We were all there together last night, at the restaurant."

"Except you arrived later than us," Myriam said, lifting her eyes off a poster about battered women and resting her eyes on Gilbert.

"But not as late as Raymond," Gilbert said. He glared at Myriam.

The professor looked worriedly at his outspoken colleague. He would never have been bold enough to have said what she'd just said, although he, too, had thought it. Now it didn't matter if he kept silent, as he was an old man, and seniors were permitted to sit back and let everyone else make fools of themselves.

The office door opened and Raymond Policante stepped out, wiping his brow with a silk handkerchief. Paulik looked at the remaining board members and saw the fatigue on the professor's face, especially in his milky eyes. "Professor?" he said. "Could you please come in?"

The conversation with the professor lasted ten minutes. After he left, Paulik took a few minutes to finish writing up his notes. "How did the professor seem to you?" Paulik asked Officer Roche, who was sitting silently beside him.

"Well," began Roche, "he isn't a very reliable witness, is he?"

"Why do you say that?"

"He can't seem to remember much."

Paulik nodded. "But he did remember that both Gilbert and Raymond Policante got to dinner late," he offered.

"But he wasn't sure of the time," Roche added. "And he got the two men mixed up at one point."

Paulik smiled. Patrice Roche was one of his favorite young rookies, and would do well as his career progressed. "You can ask Myriam Peronne in now."

A few seconds later Mlle Peronne sat, her back erect, opposite

Paulik and Roche. "This is hard on the professor," she said. "He's very tired."

"Yes, I noticed," Paulik said. "Will you accompany him back to the hotel?"

"Yes, I told him to wait for me."

"I'll try to be quick then," Paulik said. "Where were you the night of the attack on Achille Formentin and the murder of Aurélien Lopez?"

"As you know, we all had dinner together that night. Before dinner I was in my hotel room," she answered. "Then around six thirty I started getting ready. A little after six thirty my room phone rang; it was Professor Lagouanere, inviting me next door to his room for a cup of tea." She smiled and continued, "He was quite excited by the fact that our rooms are equipped with coffee- and tea-making facilities. He also needed help with his tie; his wife usually knots it for him."

"So the two of you were together until dinner?"

"Yes. We stayed in his room, chatting, then walked to the restaurant together since Raymond wasn't in the lobby."

"You arrived at the restaurant just before eight with the professor?"

"Yes, that's correct," she said.

Paulik asked, "And the others?"

"Gilbert was a half hour late. As usual."

"As usual?"

"Yes," she said. "He's always late to our meetings. It's a power-trip thing."

"I see. And M Policante?"

"Now that's what's unusual. Raymond is always on time. But he, too, was late. Forty-five minutes or so. We had time for two cocktails, which I realized too late was too much for the professor."

"Professor Lagouanere told me about their tardiness as well," Paulik said. "But he said it was M Quentin-Savary who arrived last, forty-five minutes late."

"Oh no," she replied. "Gilbert came first."

"And how were their moods?"

"Gilbert was the same as usual. Testy, and obviously wanting to be somewhere else. But appreciative of a free meal."

"And M Policante?"

"Frazzled," she said after a moment's hesitation. "That, too, is out of character for him."

"Did you see any of your colleagues leave the Roi René hotel early, before your dinner?" Paulik asked.

"I'm not sure," she said. "I did hear Raymond arguing with someone on his cell phone out in the hallway around six o'clock, so I opened my door slightly to see what was up, but he got on the elevator."

"Thank you," Paulik said. He already knew what Policante was doing, if his alibi checked out. "And Aurélien Lopez," he said. "How well did you know him?"

Mlle Peronne said, "He came to one of our board meetings."

"And that was the only time you met him?"

She hesitated. "Yes, I believe so."

"Achille Formentin?" Paulik asked. "How is your relationship with him?"

"Fine. He was . . . is easy to get along with and to work with.

He's utterly dedicated to the museum. It's his life." She realized she hadn't mentioned the museum's financial problems, but quickly decided that now was not the time.

"Thank you. That will be all for now."

Mlle Peronne quietly left the office and in a few seconds Gilbert Quentin-Savary was sitting in her place, his legs spread apart and his body slouched. Paulik almost asked him to sit up straight. He could tell that Roche was thinking the same thing as the young officer had subconsciously corrected his own posture.

"You arrived late last night for dinner," Paulik began.

Gilbert smiled. "I figured they'd squeal. Yes, about a half hour late, which for me is pretty good."

"You're often late?"

"Yes. I know Myriam thinks it's a power trip."

"Is it?" Paulik asked, thinking Quentin-Savary one of the most conceited people he had ever met.

Gilbert shrugged but didn't answer.

"Why were you late?" Paulik asked.

"Paperwork."

"What sort?"

"Bills, mostly," Gilbert said. "I pay the bills on the building. It's a lot of work."

Paulik nodded, knowing that Gilbert might sign the checks and mail them, but the money came out of the family account. Paulik wished their accountant was back from holiday; he'd try calling her cell phone again as soon as he got back to the office. "Did you know Aurélien Lopez?"

"Yes, of course. He came to a board meeting once, all fired up about our museum joining his."

"How did that pan out?"

"Well, it didn't happen, did it?" Gilbert said with a smirk. "I was against it, as were Raymond and Achille."

"And Mlle Peronne and Professor Lagouanere?"

"They were for it," Gilbert said.

"Why?"

"They thought it would bring more visitors to each museum."

"Isn't that a good thing?" Paulik asked.

"It still wouldn't have brought in enough money. Remember, I pay the bills. I know how expensive it is to run a museum. Myriam and the dotty professor are both civil servants, living in their cocoon world."

"Did you ever meet Lopez after that?"

"No."

"Did you hear M Lopez and/or M Formentin last night?"

"No, why would I?" Gilbert asked. "I live two floors above the museum."

Paulik pressed on. "You saw nothing either?"

"No."

"When did you get home from dinner?"

"Around eleven o'clock. Ask the others, I walked back with them. We almost had to carry the professor."

"Yes," Paulik said. "I understand he had too many cocktails while waiting for all of you to arrive. There's something else. What were you and M Lopez meeting about last Tuesday, in your apartment?"

Gilbert paused but then quickly recovered. "I asked to see him."

"What about?"

"The paintings in my apartment."

Paulik pretended he didn't know what Gilbert was talking about. "You'll have to fill me in."

"I thought they might be of interest to Lopez and his museum."

Paulik put on his best naïve look. "Oh, I see. You wanted to donate them."

"No," Gilbert replied slowly. "I was hoping to sell them. But I don't see what this has to do with—"

Paulik cut in. "Do you know what M Lopez and Formentin were doing in the museum at night?"

"No idea," Gilbert replied. He stared at the commissioner, who stared back. "Maybe Lopez was making a last-ditch attempt for Achille to agree to his proposal?" he finally suggested. "Is it true that Mme Devaux found them?"

"Yes."

"That's so interesting . . ."

"How so?"

"What was *she* doing there?" Gilbert asked.

Paulik said nothing, as it wasn't of any concern to Gilbert. But he did wonder how Gilbert knew that Mme Devaux had been the person who reported the murder.

Gilbert went on, "The dutiful secretary, almost as obsessed with antiques and our little museum as her dreary boss."

"More obsessed than you?" Paulik asked, based on what Verlaque had told him about Gilbert's antiques-filled apartment. He realized immediately that he shouldn't have said it, but he was sick of Gilbert Quentin-Savary.

An hour later the next interviewee arrived, amid a flurry of hand flapping and semi-bowing on the part of three young male officers.

Many of the employees at the Palais de Justice hadn't recognized the young man; he just looked like a young, wealthy, well-dressed southerner, one involved in somewhat shady businesses. Perhaps a mafia informant. But some *had* recognized him, even without his blue-and-white soccer jersey marked with the celebrated number 3, and by the time he got to the second floor there was a handful of officers, now both male and female, hanging around in the hallway pretending to discuss urgent police matters. Luis Sandoval was led into the interrogation room and shown to a chair opposite Bruno Paulik. "Thank you for getting here so quickly," Paulik said.

"*C'est normal*," Sandoval replied with his celebrated Spanish accent. "It was the least I could do." He took his designer sunglasses off and opened his jacket—Paulik caught a glimpse of the Gucci tag—and placed them in a side pocket. As he pulled his hand away it trembled, causing the tattooed butterfly that covered the back of his hand to twitch, as if in flight. Paulik knew there were lots of other tattoos as well, now covered up by about five thousand euros' worth of clothing. Sandoval's jet-black hair was slicked back from his high prominent forehead, his eyes every bit as blue as in the thousands of photographs Paulik had seen of him over the years. His chiseled face was already tanned. "To be honest," Sandoval went on, "I thought that the sooner I got here, the better the chances that none of this would get out. To the press, I mean."

Paulik nodded. "We'll do our best. I promise." He opened his notebook to the pages where he had taken notes after speaking to Raymond Policante. "M Policante claims he got to your house last night just before seven o'clock."

"That's right," Sandoval replied. "I didn't want him to come. It's too risky. We argued about it on the telephone."

Paulik nodded, remembering Mlle Peronne's observation in the hotel hallway.

Sandoval continued, speaking quickly, "But I gave in. I missed him and wanted desperately to see him." He coughed and his face flushed. "Like I said, Raymond arrived just before seven and left after eight thirty. He said he was going to be late for dinner, but neither of us could . . . draw ourselves apart."

"Have you known each other a long time?" Paulik asked. He saw Sandoval's face cloud over and added, "This is confidential."

"About four months. He redesigned our living and dining rooms, with antiques from his shop and from abroad."

"Did anyone see M Policante arriving or leaving your home?"

"No, I don't think so. It's a quiet street, and as I told your officer on the telephone, my wife is in Paris this week and the staff is off for a short break."

"That's too bad," Paulik said.

Sandoval frowned. "I thought that was a good thing. This . . . can't get out to the press."

"Had someone seen M Policante, his alibi would be more secure."

"But I'm his alibi," Sandoval argued.

"Yes, but you're not a very reliable one," Paulik said. "You've been lying to your wife about your affair with Policante."

"That sounds like a judgment."

"Not at all," Paulik said. "It's a fact. But M Policante was overheard arguing on the telephone at the hotel shortly before he says that he went to your place, so that helps your story."

"I'll show you my cell phone," Sandoval said, his hand shaking again. "If that would help. Raymond called me around five thirty and then again at six o'clock."

Paulik took the cell phone and passed it to Roche, who jotted the phone numbers and times down. "Thank you, sir," Roche said in a nervous whisper as he handed the phone back to its owner.

"If I need any more information, I'll call you on your cell phone," Paulik said. After seeing Roche's awe, Paulik decided that he should be the one to have all future contact with Sandoval. "You may leave now. I'll accompany you out of the building."

"Thank you," Sandoval replied quietly. He got to his feet and Paulik opened the door for him, following behind. Turning around, he saw Roche staring at Sandoval, his mouth agape. Paulik rolled his eyes.

Chapter Seventeen

⁂

Saturday, April 28

I'm not going to eat much for breakfast," Verlaque said the next morning.

Marine looked up from her herbal tea and smiled. "But you never eat that much for breakfast."

"I know." He opened the Michelin restaurant guide that lay to the right of his coffee, holding a page with his cell phone.

"Oh, I see," Marine said, choosing a croissant out of the basket that had been set on their breakfast table. "You have ideas for lunch? Or dinner? Or both?"

"I thought we could revisit Mlle Blay, then go out for lunch. There's a restaurant not far from her farm."

"So you agree that we should speak to her again?"

"Yes. I'm going to come up with an excuse why. Something I had forgotten."

"Good idea." She peered into the basket. "Well, I'm going to have a second croissant. I'm ravenous."

Verlaque smiled. "We'll be taking the baby to its first starred restaurant."

"Starred? I didn't bring the right clothes."

"Just one star, so don't worry," Verlaque said.

"I should have known that a trip to the country with you would include fine dining."

"The restaurant is the last civilized place on earth."

"Who said that?" Marine asked. "I'm not sure that I agree, but I think I know what they meant by it."

"A Parisian chef I know."

"And the restaurant you're taking us to for lunch?"

Verlaque put his reading glasses back on and looked at the opened page. "It's in the country, near to what this writer says is one of France's most charming villages. The restaurant is called Adoux. It's been in the same family for four generations." He paused. "They grow a lot of their own food."

Marine quickly set down her half-eaten croissant. "You always manage to convince me. Let's call and reserve."

He looked at his watch. "It's still a bit early yet. We can call from the car."

"Okay. Time to revisit Georgia and Artemisia."

"Don't forget Pablo."

Marine smiled at her husband. "How could I?"

This time Marie-Claire Blay was already outside when she saw the dark green Land Rover pull into her drive. She had expected them to return. She set down the trowel and wiped her forehead with the back of her hand. She looked over at her buffalo and saw that Georgia was happily rolling around in the mud, in the puddles that Marie-Claire had made for the animals with her garden hose, as the ground was now quite dry. She smiled, knowing that at least her love for these beasts was honest, unlike her conversation with the judge and his beautiful wife would be.

"*Salut*," she said, walking toward the car and taking off her gardening gloves.

"Hello again," Verlaque said. "I hope we aren't bothering you. There were just a couple of things . . ."

"That you forgot to ask."

"Yes."

Marine walked around the car and shook Mlle Blay's hand. "You're planting?" she asked.

"Tomatoes for the summer," Mlle Blay said. "The other vegetables I buy locally at the market, but there's nothing like fresh-picked tomatoes."

"I agree," Marine said.

Mlle Blay looked from Marine to Verlaque and said, "But you didn't come back to talk about tomatoes."

"No," Verlaque said. "I neglected yesterday to ask you if you've ever met, or had dealings with, Achille Formentin at the Quentin-Savary or Aurélien Lopez at the Musée Cavasino."

"As a farmer?" she asked. "No, why would I?"

"I was referring to your past life," Verlaque said.

"Not then, either."

"It's just that you seem to be very familiar with the Quentin-Savary collection."

"I did my homework," Mlle Blay replied with a wry smile. "Back then, as you say, in my past life."

"But the museum didn't interest you? Back then. As a potential . . . project?"

"No," she said. "Provincial tripe."

"Not worth your time?"

"Exactly. Which brings me to a theory that I was thinking about all last night after you left. It's a long shot, but there could be an item in the museum that's been undervalued and hence overlooked, even by me, I'm embarrassed to admit, something worth millions, and the thief knows it but you don't. He or she took *everything* to confuse you."

"Which they have," Verlaque said.

"I'd get experts going over every missing piece with a fine-tooth comb," Mlle Blay said. "They might discover that one of the pieces is highly valuable and none of us knew about it."

Marine shot her husband a quick look. Mlle Blay was once again using the royal we, as if she had a vested interest in the museum. Perhaps she had seriously considered robbing it at one point, despite the fact that she had just told them that the collection was too provincial for her.

Verlaque, on the other hand, was thinking of what valuable piece could have gone unnoticed. The images of the porcelain plates and the dark, murky oil paintings flashed through his head.

Mlle Blay went on. "I hope you appreciate how frank I'm being, because I don't like being accused of theft."

"I do appreciate it," Verlaque said, nodding very slightly. "I asked if you knew Lopez or Formentin because yesterday Lopez was found murdered, in the museum."

"What?" Mlle Blay asked, dropping one of her gloves. "That can't be!"

"Why not?"

"It's not a thing that usually happens in downtown Aix to a museum director! How awful." She bent over with her hands on her knees, took in two or three deep breaths, then after a few seconds straightened her back.

"Yes," Verlaque said. "And Achille Formentin was also attacked that night, hit from behind on the head. He's in the ICU."

"Also in the museum?"

"Yes."

She shook her head. "It must be related to the break-in, don't you think?"

"Undoubtedly," Verlaque said. "Thank you for your time. If you remember anything else, would you mind calling me? You have my business card."

Verlaque and Marine climbed quickly into the car as Mlle Blay watched them back down the driveway. Once they turned onto the road she reached into her overalls and got out her cell phone.

"What do you think?" Verlaque asked his wife.

"I'm not sure," Marine said, staring straight ahead with her right hand poised on the dashboard to steady herself on the winding road. "I can't decide if she's being honest or outright lying. Or it could be a mix of the two."

"Meaning?"

"That she may be lying in order to protect someone," Marine

said. "I would imagine those thieves stick together, that there's some kind of code of ethics. Perhaps she knows who did it. But she would never tell you."

"No, she wouldn't. I agree."

"I'll call the restaurant, shall I?"

"We'll be there in ten minutes or so," Verlaque said. "Don't bother."

But due to the winding roads and switchbacks, it was thirty minutes later when they pulled into the parking lot of the restaurant. "This doesn't look good," Marine said. "All the spots are taken. There! At the end of the row on the right!"

"Beside the garbage cans," Verlaque said glumly. He stopped to let Marine out before he pulled into the narrow spot.

"I'll run in and see if they have a table," she said as she opened her door. "If they don't, we may go without lunch as we're in the middle of nowhere."

Verlaque parked the car, turned off the engine, grabbed his cigars, and got out. He walked quickly across the parking lot and almost ran straight into Marine, who was coming out of the front door. "I should have booked ahead," he said.

"Yes, they're full," Marine said. "But then I did this." She opened her coat and proudly thrust forward her baby bump. "And mentioned that you're a magistrate here on business, and they're setting us up in the private dining room."

"Wow!" he said, kissing her. "Thank you!"

"We're lucky the private room isn't booked," she went on. "The owner said it usually is. Here's the maître d'."

"Table for three!" Verlaque said, beaming, as they followed the frazzled maître d' through the busy dining room. "My wife's eating for two!" he went on, grinning at an elderly foursome who were eating in silence.

"Stop it!" Marine hissed, laughing, giving her husband an elbow.

They entered a small dining room that consisted of a polished oval table with eight chairs. The table was set for two people at the far end. "We really appreciate this, sir," Verlaque said. The maître d' nodded as he held out Marine's chair for her, gave them menus, and then quickly left.

"What's with all the corny clichés?" Marine asked, still laughing. "'My wife's eating for two'?"

"No one knows us here," he replied. "And I'm incredibly happy to be here, with you."

"Liar. You're incredibly happy to be eating lunch."

"That, too."

She snorted, quickly putting her hand up to her mouth.

Verlaque said, "Lucky we're on our own in here, with all the noise you're making!"

Marine looked around the room and smiled.

"It's a bit like the Musée Quentin-Savary in here," Verlaque said, tilting his head up toward the ceiling. "Wood beams, red walls, brass chandeliers. But we'd better look at the menu or we'll be thrown out for taking too long."

"I'm ravenous."

"You said that at breakfast."

"Yes, but then I stopped eating," Marine said, not looking up from the menu. "I'm getting the three-course discovery menu."

Verlaque said, "Here comes the waiter."

She glanced up and smiled. "I'll have the rabbit in gelatin, please," she said, throwing a look at Verlaque, who was grinning; she knew that he'd think this an old-fashioned dish. "Then the lobster with ginger and spring vegetables, and the cherry soup for dessert."

"*Très bien, madame*," the waiter said. "*Et monsieur?*"

"I'll have the sautéed shrimp in butter, then the roasted pheasant, and cheese instead of dessert."

"Of course," the waiter said, taking their menus. "And to drink?"

"It's just me drinking wine," Verlaque said. "So a glass of white, then a glass or two of red. Along with a large bottle of sparkling water."

"May I suggest a local organic chardonnay?"

"That would be great."

"And after, if we head up the Rhône Valley, perhaps a Saint-Joseph to accompany your pheasant, as it's stuffed with foie gras."

"Perfect, thank you."

"Foie-gras-stuffed pheasant?" Marine asked after the waiter left.

"Encased in puff pastry to keep the moisture in." Verlaque couldn't help but grin.

"Well, my lobster is sounding rather dull now," she said as she looked around the room.

The waiter returned with the sparkling water and poured some white wine into a glass for Verlaque. Verlaque swirled the wine around, sniffed, and took a sip. "It's excellent," he said.

"I'm glad you like it, sir."

"These paintings are lovely," Marine said, gesturing around the room with her hand.

"Family, madam," the waiter said. "Those are the two older generations. The woman over there"—he pointed to a painting of a woman dressed in a brilliant red Edwardian-style dress—"was the first to open the restaurant here. Her young husband was an accomplished cook and she had family money to invest, so she bought this place and the restaurant took off almost from day one. She was quite daring."

"I'll say she was," Marine said. "Good for her."

The waiter smiled and left. "Obviously having a family fortune helped," she said to Verlaque. "That's how she could afford to pay for portraits. Most early-nineteenth-century *aubergistes* wouldn't have had enough money to do that. Don't you think, Antoine?"

"The portraits," he said, his body half turned in the chair so that he could look at the paintings. "That might be it!"

"Pardon me?"

"Those hideous family portraits in Gilbert's apartment!"

Chapter Eighteen

Monday, April 30

When Verlaque walked into the office area, France Dubois quickly got out of her chair, standing up behind her desk. She did it partly out of respect; at her primary school the students had always stood up when *la maîtresse* entered the classroom, and in junior high, when the tradition had been dropped, she thought it unfortunate. She pointed to his office door with her pen. "The commissioner is waiting for you," she said.

"Thank you, France," Verlaque said, looking at his watch. "I'm later than usual. But I have brioches." He opened a paper bag marked MICHAUD and handed it to her.

"Thank you!" she said, awkwardly taking a sticky pastry between her thumb and index finger and setting it on her desk. She'd eaten a big breakfast, but she would try to eat a little of it later in the day, to be polite. She handed the bag back to him, as there were still four brioches in it. Could the two men eat that many?

Verlaque walked into his office and waved to Paulik, who was speaking on his cell phone. Verlaque turned on the espresso maker, set a cup under the nozzle, and stared at the lights on the machine, transfixed.

Paulik ended his conversation, hung up, and watched the judge watching the espresso machine. "It takes longer that way," he finally said.

Verlaque kept his eyes on the machine, which seemed to be taking unusually long to warm up. "Watch out or you won't get any brioches."

"Do you want the bad news first or the good news?"

Verlaque turned slowly around. "Please tell me you're joking."

"Patrice Roche, the young officer, finally got ahold of DJ Kool about the porcelain plate for sale, but let it slip that he was calling from Aix."

"So DJ hung up, right?"

"Yes. And now the phone number doesn't work; it must be a disposable cell. And the ad has been removed from the website. The webmaster of leboncoin is trying to help us gather more information about Kool."

"*Merde*," Verlaque said. The coffee machine finally made a little noise announcing it was ready and he turned around and made an espresso, then handed it to Paulik. He began making the second one. "What's the good news?"

"Raymond Policante has an alibi for the evening of the murder," Paulik said. "So we can eliminate him." He sat down and told the judge of his talk with Luis Sandoval. Verlaque listened, almost with the same rapture as Roche. "So I promised to try to keep his evening tryst with Policante quiet," Paulik said, finishing his story. "He's terrified the press will get ahold of it. He was shaking."

"I can understand why," Verlaque said. "Wow. Poor guy." Soccer had never been a sport he enjoyed watching—too many theatrics and egos—but even he had to admit that at times Luis Sandoval played like a god. Marseille was lucky to have him. His move to nearby Aix with his journalist wife, an Aix native who was as famous as her husband, had been front-page news and the pride of Aix's politicians. "So that's Policante's alibi," Verlaque said. "I don't see why either man would lie about it."

"Nor do I."

"Don't people recognize Sandoval?" Verlaque asked. "I always wondered why he lives downtown."

"He said, oddly, no," Paulik replied. "I asked him the same question as I walked him out of the building. He said that with a suit on and sunglasses, he can pretty much go unnoticed. A hat helps, too. His house is over by Les Thermes, in a sort of compound surrounded by high walls and a gate. It used to be a convent."

"I know that place."

"There's a three-car garage in there, and even a swimming pool. . . ."

"He told you that as well?"

Paulik laughed. "No. Patrice Roche told me. He read an article about it in *L'Équipe*. He was awestruck."

"And what's going on with the board members each having keys to the museum?" Verlaque asked. "For goodness' sake."

"Mme Devaux said it hadn't occurred to her to tell us, since none of them live in Aix, except for Gilbert, who of course has keys since he lives there."

"You're treating them like suspects?"

"Each one. The attacks took place on Thursday night between six and eight o'clock, according to Dr. Cohen, while they had some time off, after my meeting with them ended and before their dinner—about an hour, which would have been plenty of time. I have some officers going through the museum yet again, including the garden, just in case the murderer left in a hurry and quickly buried the weapon."

"Did you find Lopez's cell phone?" Verlaque sat down and took a sip of coffee, pushing the Michaud bag across the desk toward Paulik.

"No, unfortunately. But I can have an officer check his calls through the mobile network operator. That's one of the reasons I'm here, besides to mooch breakfast."

"Right, your officer will need a warrant," Verlaque said. He opened a desk drawer, pulled out a form, put on his reading glasses, and began to fill it in. "Help yourself to a brioche."

"Thanks," Paulik said, reaching into the bag. "How was the Ardèche?"

Verlaque kept writing. "We ate very well and managed to speak to Marie-Claire Blay, former art thief."

"I've heard of her . . ."

Verlaque looked up from his paperwork. "The Rembrandt in 1997."

"That's where I've heard of her. I take it she's retired?"

"Yes, she raises water buffalo," Verlaque said. "Makes a good living from it, or so she says."

"I have a cousin . . ."

Verlaque sighed dramatically, smiling.

". . . who is lactose intolerant but can drink water buffalo milk. She says it's delicious."

"To get back on the subject, Mlle Blay says she doesn't know Formentin or Lopez, but she has an uncanny knowledge of what was in the Musée Quentin-Savary."

"Just as a professional?"

Verlaque laughed. "Perhaps. She did have an interesting theory, although I'm not sure whether it was meant to help us or to throw us off. She suggested that one of the pieces in the collection could be worth millions—priceless, almost—and no one knows it."

"Except the thief," Paulik said, "which is why they took everything, to hide it."

"Yes. What do you think?"

Paulik winced. "The board members assured me that however much they love the collection, none of it is worth that much." He paused and then said, "Unless they're not as expert as they let on." He sat back, pleased. He quite liked this theory, as he believed that people who did not work the land, or in emergency services, or in the restaurant business, were just pencil pushers.

Verlaque tried not to grin, as he knew exactly what the commissioner was thinking. "Or they could have made an honest mistake and overlooked this one piece. Or they're lying."

Paulik grunted in agreement.

A knock on the door interrupted their conversation and each

man quickly set down his half-eaten brioche (the second one each) as if getting caught stealing or being indolent on the job. "Yes?" Verlaque called out, brushing crumbs off the desk.

France Dubois opened the door and took a few steps forward. "Please excuse me . . ."

"It's no problem, France," Verlaque said. "What is it?"

"Journalists have been calling."

"Up here?" Paulik asked. "The secretaries downstairs aren't supposed to put them through."

"Well, they've gotten through," she continued. "And I'm not sure how much longer I can put them off. One of them says he knows you, Judge. His name is José and he writes for *La Provence*."

Verlaque leaned forward. "Yes. He's in my cigar club, and we're meeting tonight. If he calls again, tell him that I'll fill him in tonight. Thank you, France."

She turned to go and then hesitated.

Verlaque asked, "What is it?"

"The deceased," she quietly said. "The murdered man. I saw that his name is Aurélien Lopez."

"That's right."

"Well, there's an Aurélien Lopez in my Chinese class, and he was absent from class on Thursday night."

"That's very interesting," Paulik said, turning to face her.

"It might not be the same man," France said. "He's in his early fifties, and I think he works in the arts in Marseille. He brags about it a bit."

"That's him, France," Verlaque said. "Did he say why he was learning Chinese?"

She shook her head. For all she knew, he had been there for

the same reasons she was: boredom, some vague interest in the culture . . . and perhaps he, too, had had a crush on the teacher, Isaac Bonnard.

Paulik asked, "Can you leave us your teacher's name and contact information?"

"Yes, of course," France said. "I'll send you both an email."

Verlaque added, "Good work on holding off the journalists. Has the television station France 24 called? You'll be able to show off your English."

"Yes, they have," she said in English with almost no accent. She beamed.

"Thank you," he replied, also in English.

"You're welcome," she said, leaving the office.

"Before I go downstairs and give hell to the secretaries at the front desk, do you think that Lopez was the thief?" Paulik asked, getting up. "Did he plan on selling the loot in China?"

"Could be," Verlaque said. "And poor Achille walked in when Lopez was arguing with someone. But whom? Achille told me that he visited the museum most evenings; some kind of penance, or pilgrimage."

"Maybe Lopez *knew* who the thief was. That's what they were fighting about. Lopez could have been extorting him."

"Or her," Verlaque said. "And I was so sure that the thief was Gilbert Quentin-Savary. But now I'm having doubts, even if one of the châteaux plates has appeared. What did the webmaster of leboncoin say about the situation?"

"Since the cell phone has been disconnected, it's difficult. Apparently lots of people who sell things on their site don't have their own computer, so they use a library computer, or a friend's, and all contact is via telephone. But what we do have are the messages between DJ Kool and potential buyers, which Roche has been working on, contacting the people who made offers on the plate."

"How many are there?"

"Only four, as DJ Kool for some reason listed the plate under the category 'Gardening' instead of the more obvious 'Tableware.'"

"So he's dim, or did that intentionally, perhaps wanting to keep it under the radar."

"In the meantime, what about the water buffalo farmer? What's her name, Marie-Claire Blay?"

"She didn't tell me the whole truth."

"I'll get more checks done on her."

Verlaque nodded. Mlle Blay had a clear interest in paintings; she'd once stolen them for a living, and she had proudly showed off her small Ziem to him and Marine. He decided not to share his theory of Gilbert Quentin-Savary's family portraits just yet; he'd seek advice from an expert before sidetracking Paulik and his officers.

Verlaque saw as he approached the Café Mazarin that Raymond Policante was already there, seated and reading a newspaper. He quickened his pace. "Thank you for meeting me on short notice," Verlaque said as he shook hands with Policante. Verlaque sat down opposite as Policante folded his newspaper and set it aside.

"It's no problem, Judge," Policante replied. "Besides, we board members are stuck here, aren't we? As if under house arrest. At least you've chosen a nice café terrace where we can meet."

"Not at all house arrest. You'll be able to return home tomorrow as soon as we've spoken to you all." He waved to the waiter,

Fréderic, who walked slowly toward them, cleaning and arranging chairs as he moved along the row of identical round marble-topped tables.

"*Salut*," Fréderic said with a sigh.

Verlaque smiled, enjoying Fréderic's game. "I'll have an espresso, please."

"Same," said Policante.

"As you wish," Fréderic said, walking away. He added an extra-long sigh that made even M Policante laugh.

"He'd make an excellent Parisian waiter," Policante remarked.

"He *is* Parisian," Verlaque said. "Do you mind if I smoke a cigar?"

"Not at all. We're on a terrace outside, after all."

Verlaque took out a long, thin Partagás 898, cut the end off, and slowly lit it. Policante looked on, fascinated. "I quite enjoy the process of cigars," he said. "The first sniff of the outer wrapper, the snip, the careful lighting . . ."

Verlaque continued lighting the cigar until it had an even burn. He did not look up at the antiques dealer. "But you've never smoked them?"

"Oh, heavens, no. But I'd be quite a fan of collecting the old-fashioned lighters, the beautiful wood humidors, those funny little leather carrying cases."

"What *do* you collect?" Verlaque asked as he sat back and smoked, now looking at Policante. "My grandmother, who was English and a painter herself, collected small-format paintings. She even had a Lucian Freud."

"Dreadful stuff! I hope it wasn't one of those awful nudes!"

"No," Verlaque said, laughing. "A potted plant."

"In fact, I do have a collection. Mostly paintings. All nineteenth century or earlier."

"Do you ever look at stuff on leboncoin?" Verlaque asked, trying not to wince.

"All the time. I'm addicted."

Verlaque turned to face the antiques dealer. "Do you look at the whole site or only in the painting category, for example?"

"Oh, I look at most of it, except for cars and power tools. You never know, some senile grandmother could list a treasure under an oddball category."

Policante's back straightened as Fréderic arrived with their espressos, setting the cups and the bill on the table. Policante paused, waiting for the waiter to leave, then asked, "The police are keeping quiet about Luis?" His eyes were pleading.

"Yes, don't worry," Verlaque said. Having the local and national press know about Policante's affair with the famous soccer player was the last thing he wanted. "For the moment we have no reason to disclose that information."

Policante let his shoulders fall, and he managed a small smile.

Verlaque continued, "What do you think of Gilbert Quentin-Savary's painting collection? The family portraits."

Policante was about to take a sip of his coffee but then put the cup back down, laughing. "That's hardly a *collection*!"

"Oh, I beg your pardon," Verlaque said. "My grandmother was the painting specialist, not me. It was just a long shot, a weird idea that someone put into my head."

"Now, dear Judge, you'll have to explain," Policante said. "Because I do like a mystery, and I'd rather be here, on this terrace, than back at the hotel."

"One of the police officers has a degree in fine arts," Verlaque said, lying, "and suggested that perhaps there's an item in the Quentin-Savary collection that the thief was after. An item that could be priceless but has gone unnoticed."

"Well, I can assure you that it's not one of those monstrous family portraits. Besides, those are hanging in Gilbert's apartment and were never downstairs in the museum."

"True," Verlaque said. "What about one of the paintings that *was* hanging downstairs?"

Policante glared at the judge. "Are you questioning my judgment and knowledge of nineteenth-century art?"

"Not at all," Verlaque said. "It's just that this kind of thing has happened before."

"Oh, you mean the Cézanne found in the attic, the Goya hiding behind a kitsch still life, that kind of thing?"

"Precisely."

"Not on my watch."

Verlaque said again, "I beg your pardon." He tried a different tack, thankful that he had the cigar with him, which now tasted of lovely Swiss milk chocolate mixed with something else that brought him childhood memories of Emmeline, his grandmother. Cedar. Her cedar closet, where she kept her fur coats and cashmere sweaters, each one carefully folded into a small box. "What about one of the other pieces in the museum's collection?" he asked. "Ceramics? Documents?"

Policante tilted his head toward the judge. "Not my domain. And those two . . ."

"Mlle Peronne and Professor Lagouanere?"

"Well, I shouldn't say anything, but . . ."

"Please, go on."

"Myriam didn't even get into the École du Louvre! She had to study abroad!"

Verlaque smiled, humoring him. He'd read her file and saw that she'd studied at Dartmouth College, which he believed was an Ivy League school. But he didn't bother correcting Policante, as he had obviously never heard of it. "And the professor?"

Policante leaned in closer, smelling heavily of Sauvage by Christian Dior. "A few years ago, he had to take a semester off. *A breakdown*. Ever since then, his judgment has been blurred; he's slow, and makes mistakes."

"I see," Verlaque said, liking Raymond Policante a bit less. "And M Lopez. Did you know him?"

Policante played with an empty sugar packet, folding and unfolding it. "Yes, of course. Lopez came to one of our board meetings, invited by Professor Lagouanere. Lopez envisioned combining his Musée Cavasino with the Quentin-Savary. He even had the backing of some high flyers in Marseille politics. But Achille was against it."

"And you?"

"I was also opposed. Marseille?" Policante gave an exaggerated shudder. "Can you imagine our beautiful things there? With all those . . ."

Verlaque raised his eyebrows. He tried to imagine what word would come next: immigrants? North Africans? Or prostitutes and sailors? Perhaps Policante had an outdated image of the city, something dating from the 1950s. He waited, but Policante didn't finish his sentence. "And the others?" Verlaque finally asked.

"Gilbert was against the idea," Policante replied. "Although I'm not sure why, as he's never been very interested in the museum."

"Do you know why Achille Formentin changed his mind? Lopez told the commissioner that M Formentin was for the idea in the beginning."

Policante nodded. "Achille admitted to me that he saw after their first few meetings that he would lose all of his power if their museums merged. It's easy to see who the more powerful personality is there."

"Lopez, of course," Verlaque said. "And the other board members?"

"The others were for it."

"Split right down the middle," Verlaque said, draining his coffee.

Chapter Nineteen

Monday, April 30

Marine was tired of drinking only juice or water, going for what seemed like endless visits to the doctor for checkups, and worrying about everything she ate; tired of people asking her about her pregnancy and if she knew the baby's sex; tired of the constant volunteering of information, especially at what age their children or grandchildren had begun sleeping through the night. And so she dreaded her appointment later that morning at the maternity clinic just north of Aix, a favorite birthing hospital for generations of Aixois, including her mother. Sylvie accompanied Marine, as Verlaque at the last minute had to cancel.

But the visit ended up being informative, reassuring, and even funny; at one point they overheard two women who had both recently given birth talk about their bowel movements. Marine doubled over with laughter and Sylvie took her by the arm and said, "There's so much I need to fill you in about childbirth. You need to prepare."

"Oh, I've been doing that," Marine, the good student, replied.

"No, I mean Antoine," Sylvie said. "He needs to prepare."

After the clinic visit, they ate lunch back in Aix at Sylvie's apartment. "I'll make you some killer eggs," she said, tying a vintage apron around her waist.

"Thank you," Marine said. She ate eggs for lunch at least four times a week, and was a little tired of them, but she stayed silent.

"Charlotte made us fresh salsa yesterday, so I'm going to add the rest of it to the fried eggs. Huevos rancheros!"

The eggs began to sound more interesting. "Charlotte still likes cooking, I take it?"

"More and more," Sylvie said of her thirteen-year-old. "Cooking suits her temperament. I wouldn't be surprised if she studied it full-time after high school."

"Lausanne," Marine suggested, referring to the famous culinary school.

Sylvie made the sign of money by rubbing her fingers back and forth against her thumb.

"Student loans?" Marine suggested, laughing.

"Do Swiss universities even give out loans? I'll have to get more creative financially. At least you and Antoine won't have to worry about that." Sylvie turned toward the stove and began cooking.

Marine thought about how easy it was for others to think

that money could solve all problems. It couldn't solve her husband's anger whenever his childhood came up or his awkwardness when having conversations about their own offspring, *the bump*. For some reason she couldn't explain, it had become easier recently with Antoine, talking about the baby and their future. She wasn't sure what had happened, but she was thankful for it.

She looked up from her teacup and saw that Sylvie had set the spatula down and was staring at her. "I'm sorry," Sylvie said. "I didn't mean to say that everything would be easy because you guys are well off."

Marine smiled. "Thank you. It's been tricky with Antoine, the whole baby thing, but he's coming around now. As of two days ago it seems like his whole attitude has changed and he's feeling positive, even excited, about the baby."

"He called me."

"What?"

"He was worried that the baby wasn't kicking enough," Sylvie said.

Marine's shoulders fell in relief.

"He was so worried," Sylvie went on, "that I could hardly make out what he was saying at first. He was mumbling like a madman. Is he better?"

"Yes. I thought he was just getting more used to the idea of being a parent, but now I see that he was hiding his anxieties from me. Thank you for reassuring him."

"I made up some phony facts to reassure him," Sylvie said. "But as soon as we got off the phone, I double-checked them in my old maternity books. What I told him was actually fairly accurate. Everyone's pregnancy is different, too, I told him."

"Thank you, dear friend."

Despite how busy he was—an emptied museum, and now two attacks, one of them fatal—Verlaque found himself walking slowly, strolling actually, through Aix's medieval streets on the way back to the Palais de Justice. His cigar was burning unevenly and he stepped aside to relight it, so as not to block the foot traffic behind him. With his back to a boutique he watched his fellow Aixois; the city seemed to be getting busier and busier and he was divided in his sentiments as to whether it was a positive or negative thing. It certainly was an animated town—no boarded-up shops as he had seen in other French provincial towns and on the news in North America and even in England. And for this—despite the tourist groups and the worsening traffic—he was grateful. He put his lighter back in his pocket and turned around, looking in the shop window. It was a store for children's clothes called Jacadi, a play on the children's game that Emmeline had called "Simon Says." Once even his grandfather Charles had gotten in on the game. Verlaque looked at the clothes, impossibly cute in their pastel colors, and he realized that he liked them because they were very solidly children's clothes, not mini-adult clothes in small sizes. He always thought it looked ridiculous when he saw babies in jeans and running shoes. He bent down to look at one of the price tags—of a tiny blue wool coat with a faux fur collar—and whistled.

"I'm only buying that stuff on sale," a voice behind him said.

He recognized the perfume and turned around, smiling. "*Cou-cou, chérie*," he said, kissing Marine. "It's a really cute coat," he continued, turning back to the shop window. "That collar . . ."

Marine laughed. "I knew you'd be a sucker for little girls' outfits."

"And she'll wear those proper leather shoes with the little straps and buttons instead of buckles, and certainly no Velcro . . ."

"Stride Rite," she said, moaning. "All my snooty female class-mates wore those when we were kids. Always navy blue. With cotton dresses that were smocked."

"What did your mother dress you up in?"

"Can't you guess?" Marine asked. "Monoprix on sale, or hand-me-downs from her colleagues' kids. The shoes I can't remember, but they sure weren't Stride Rites."

"Well, we won't be doing that—"

"And you see it didn't hurt me a bit," Marine cut in. She took her husband by the arm and they began to walk, without having to discuss it, north toward the Palais de Justice.

"That's true," he said. "You have excellent fashion sense despite your mother's lack of curiosity in the subject."

"But I'm in no way a fashionista," she argued. "I'm often torn about the fashion industry: one minute I adore it, with all its ex-travagance and creativity, and the next I hate it for its obvious conspicuous wealth and shallowness."

"You're not a fashion *victim*," Verlaque said. "I think that's the difference. And I know that you still buy clothes at Monoprix; I've seen the labels."

Marine laughed. "They hire cool designers now. Any news on the Lopez case?"

"I'm on my way to find out. Bruno suspects every one of the museum's board members, and I'm inclined to believe him. I just had coffee with one of them and he told me that they were split down the middle on whether or not to join the two museums. Apparently the Marseille politicians were very excited for this to happen, as the new museum would be in Marseille."

"Of course they'd be excited."

He slowed down. "Do you still have that girlfriend from high school? The one married to one of the Marseille mayor's top aides?"

"Oh, yes," Marine answered, snapping her fingers. "Béatrice. She's married to a lawyer, Daniel Louron. They keep asking us to come to dinner. Why? Do you want me to give her a ring and ask a few questions about Lopez?"

"No, no," Verlaque said quickly, looking at Marine's stomach. He was worried about her enthusiasm and really didn't want her to get involved in this case. "I just couldn't remember her husband's name. Was she a Stride Rite gal?"

"Oh, you bet she was."

Verlaque laughed and kissed her. "I have to get back to the office."

Marine said, "If I'm still awake when you get back from your cigar club, I'll tell you about the maternity clinic visit."

Verlaque slapped his forehead. "I'm so sorry! I forgot that was this morning!"

Marine kissed him. "It's okay," she said. "We'll catch up later."

"Where are you going?"

"I'm just going to wander and perhaps go to a bookstore," she said. "I'll see you tonight." They held hands for a moment before parting ways.

Marine took a detour and walked along the rue Fabrot until she came to a furniture store that advertised interior design services. She had always admired their windows, full of expensive and beautiful Scandinavian and Italian household objects. She breathed in and opened the door, walking to the back of the boutique, where a woman in her fifties with designer glasses sat behind an enormous Mac. "May I help you?" she asked.

Marine smiled and told her all about the baby and their apartment and house in the country, and the need for a new bedroom in both places. The woman smiled back and took notes, then suggested she visit both properties. They agreed on a date and shook hands. "Congratulations," she said. "We'd better get a move on if the baby's due to arrive in September."

Chapter Twenty

Monday, April 30

When Verlaque got back to his office, hiding the unlit cigar in his hand, he closed the door, threw open the windows, and lit up. It was a warm sunny day and he was happy he had run into Marine in the street. She looked radiant.

France Dubois had placed a pile of mail on his desk and he took out his paper knife, a gift from his father, and opened the first envelope. The stationery was from a tough prison east of Marseille; he quickly looked down at the signature and saw that it was from Kévin Malango, a petty thief he had helped Paulik incarcerate a few years previously. Malango was requesting a prison transfer to a medium-sized prison near Montpellier, citing the reason as being that his new girlfriend lived in Montpellier and had two children enrolled in school there. It always surprised

Verlaque that guys in prison could get a "new girlfriend," but it happened all the time. He sat back, smoking and thinking; it was more than likely that Malango wanted to leave because of the squalor in the Marseille prison and the girlfriend was fictitious. Verlaque then read through Malango's prison record, which was attached to his letter. It was impeccable, including a letter of recommendation signed by Malango's creative writing teacher, who came Tuesday nights to the prison. He signed the permission slip and set it aside for France to mail.

A knock on the door stopped him from opening the next envelope, which he could see was from a local lawyer. "*Entrez,*" Verlaque said.

"It's just me," Bruno Paulik said as he walked in. He could smell the cigar smoke, so he quickly shut the door behind him.

"France is all right about it," Verlaque said, holding his cigar up, "but some of the other employees are not."

"They haven't outlawed cigars in France yet."

"'Yet' being the key word. What's up?"

"I met this morning with the two other employees of Lopez's Musée Cavasino."

Verlaque sat back, relaxed and contented. This was one of his favorite moments, debriefing with Paulik. "Interesting?"

"No, unfortunately," Paulik replied. "They're students and each get paid five hundred euros a month on one of those government internships. Neither of them seemed to know Lopez very well, and neither has seen anything fishy going on, although one of them, Gilles Robert, said that lately Lopez had been nervous and edgy. The students gave us the keys to Lopez's rented storage space out by the airport. Three officers went earlier today and checked the contents along with the Cavasino inventory list; everything is in order."

"They didn't find a missing museum from the rue Mistral in there?"

Paulik laughed. "No, unfortunately."

"Did Lopez have family?"

"No, he was a loner. Both parents are deceased and he never married. One sister who has lived in Brittany for the past twenty years. We've contacted her."

"Did the interns have any idea why Lopez was edgy?"

"No, and both of them told me that Lopez didn't tell them very much about what was going on in the museum. They both felt that they were employed solely to man the gallery and stuff envelopes. Neither knew about Lopez's plans to merge with the Quentin-Savary, for example."

"That's a very different work mode than at the museum that Achille Formentin runs," Verlaque said. "Mme Devaux is very involved in the museum's business."

"Formentin is going to be okay, by the way," Paulik said. "He's just come out of his coma and isn't to be disturbed for another twenty-four hours. Then we can question him about what happened."

"Keep guarding his room," Verlaque said. "Have your officers found anything out of the ordinary in the museum?"

"No, besides there being a missing collection, nothing," Paulik said. "Nothing in the garden, either. And one of my officers spoke with the front-desk employees at the Hôtel Roi René. On the night of Lopez's murder, the hotel received a busload of tourists and it was mayhem."

"So they didn't notice whether any of the board members left the hotel?"

"No. So we can't verify the board members' statements. Plus the travel agency hadn't reserved enough rooms, so the hotel staff was running around trying to come up with three extra rooms on a full night. I'm going to question Mlle Peronne from the Sèvres museum in a few minutes. Care to join me?"

Verlaque looked at his watch. "Yes, sure. Is she coming here?"

"Yes, in twenty-five minutes."

"I'll finish my cigar and be right down."

Paulik left, closing the office door behind him. Verlaque picked up the next envelope and opened it, eager to get through the mail as something told him that very soon his days would get busier and more complicated. But for now, with a Cuban cigar in his hand, time had slowed down. He had colleagues he respected and enjoyed working with, an always interesting job, and a wife he adored—and soon, he would be a father.

Myriam Peronne sat upright across from Paulik and Verlaque, a thick purple dossier and a small leather purse at her side. "This may sound odd," she launched in before Verlaque had even sat down, "but I'm happy to be here." She put her hand on the purple file and said, "I've brought photographs of the ceramics in the Quentin-Savary collection. If I may show you something?"

"By all means," Paulik said, leaning forward.

She opened the file and pulled out a color photograph of a small plate, passing it along the desk to Verlaque and Paulik. "A dessert plate?" Verlaque asked. He glanced at Paulik, pleased with his knowledge of porcelainware. Paulik scowled.

"Yes, it's one of four in the collection from the Quentin-Savary," Mlle Peronne replied. "Here are the other three plates." She gave them the other photographs. "As you can see, two are pictured with views of Paris, one with a Tuscan landscape, and one with an—"

"Egyptian scene," Paulik cut in, looking sideways at Verlaque.

"Precisely, Commissioner," Mlle Peronne said. "The palm tree and the Pyramids in the distance."

"Judging from the identical green-and-gold trim on each plate, they're from the same collection," Verlaque said. "But there are only four?"

"Yes, they are part of a larger collection—one that would have been commissioned, with various scenes dictated by the person who commissioned the set."

"Are they signed by the painter?" Paulik asked.

"No, that's the odd part," Mlle Peronne said. "But they have the Sèvres mark."

"Are they valuable?" Verlaque asked.

"They haven't been thought so, because they aren't signed. They're beautiful and obviously old, early nineteenth century, but we've never been sure of their provenance, so they've been . . . undervalued."

Paulik and Verlaque exchanged looks. "Are you telling us you've discovered their history?" Verlaque asked.

"Yes, I'm almost sure," Mlle Peronne replied. "I'd been re-searching it before all of this happened . . . before the theft, I mean . . . but hadn't said anything, especially to Achille, as I didn't want to get anyone's hopes up before I was sure. Achille always said they were special, but I didn't believe him."

"We're all ears," Verlaque said. "Tell us the story."

Mlle Peronne began, "It was known as the Emperor's Personal Service."

"Napoleon?" Paulik asked.

"Yes. Napoleon decided in October of 1807 to commission a dinner service from Sèvres for the imperial table. The service consists of seventy-two flat plates, and Napoleon himself suggested images for more than half of them. At the time, the whole service came to a princely sum of over sixty-five thousand francs."

Paulik whistled. "That's insane."

"Yes, that's a lot of money, I would think," Verlaque said.

"In today's currency, that's anywhere from three hundred and fifty thousand to five hundred thousand euros," Mlle Peronne said. "I spoke with a Swedish researcher who spends his days doing historical monetary conversions."

"But wouldn't these four plates have been signed by the painter?" Verlaque asked. "For such an important collection?"

"Yes, and the others in the collection are signed. We have two at Sèvres, and there's one in the Louvre. Those are priceless."

"And the rest?" Verlaque asked.

"By the time of Napoleon's death, there were only fifty-four left, most of them at St. Helena. They were so precious to the emperor that he requested them to be passed on to his son in his will, along with his medal."

"What makes you think that these four plates belong to this famous collection?" Paulik asked.

"The green of the trim that the judge pointed out," Mlle Peronne answered. Verlaque resisted the temptation to look at Paulik.

She went on. "That green, a chrome green, had just been perfected at Sèvres by the chemist Vauquelin. The painters began work in January 1808, for the plates were to be used in April 1810 at the banquet marking the marriage of Napoleon and Marie-Louise."

"Which brings us back to the question of why they weren't signed," Verlaque said.

"I was going through our records at Sèvres, doing research for an upcoming catalog," Mlle Peronne said. "Erwan Broc'han painted the châteaux plates in the Quentin-Savary collection. He stopped working for two years beginning in March of 1808."

"Then picked it up again?" Paulik asked.

"Yes, in 1810."

"Was that unusual in those days?" Verlaque asked. "I always find it amazing that there's any information at all."

"You're right, except our records at Sèvres are very complete," Mlle Peronne said. "It was an extremely well-run business, and our records have always been kept safe from fires and wars and whatever else usually destroys these things."

"So why the gap?" Verlaque asked, sitting on the edge of his seat. "Do you know?"

"I think so, but I only just figured it out." She leaned forward. "I thought perhaps Broc'han had fallen ill, but I was just guessing, as no one keeps a record of that. It must have happened all the time back then. But then one of my brighter interns did some in-depth research and found Sèvres prison records for those dates. She found Broc'han's name listed as a felon. He was in jail."

"Why?" Verlaque asked. "Do we know?"

"Broc'han was Breton, remember. And an adamant one. He

had started a movement to protect the Breton language and culture back in his hometown of Pont-Aven but was immediately
arrested upon his return to Sèvres."

"So he was jailed for disobedience," Paulik said.

"Yes, for two years, beginning in March of 1808 and then released in March 1810—right when they would have been finishing
the set."

"Did an underling paint these four plates?" Verlaque asked.

"No, I think Erwan Broc'han did them. The draftsmanship is
too good; it's in his style, too. Let me explain further: Napoleon
had a keen eye for this kind of thing; he used to admire his dinnerware before eating off it. So, he would have noticed if an as-
sistant painted some of the plates. He would have refused them.
These were part of his personal service, loved until the day he died.
But many were lost."

"So why weren't these signed?" Paulik asked.

"Embarrassment on the part of the director of the Sèvres," she
answered. "Broc'han was a rebel Breton, but a brilliant artisan.
The Sèvres workshop included his pieces, as they may have
been the last of the plates to be finished, but wouldn't let him
sign them. The provincial uprising he attempted would have
been seen as a direct insult to Napoleon. They hoped that the
emperor might not notice the back of the plate, as he was much
more interested in the painted scenes, all taken from his famous
successful military campaigns."

"So you think that the thief wanted these four plates?" Paulik
asked. Verlaque listened, intrigued, but not convinced. Empty a
museum for four little dessert plates?

"Yes. I only wish I could have identified the plates sooner,"

Mlle Peronne said. "They are a tremendous coup for the Quentin-Savary."

Verlaque thought of Lopez. "Did you tell anyone about your research?"

"Not a soul," she answered. "I was even vague with my interns. I didn't want to jinx it."

Chapter Twenty-one

❧

Monday, April 30

Who besides Mlle Peronne could know about the value of those Napoleonic plates?" Paulik asked, setting his glass of wine down. "It doesn't make sense."

"I agree," Verlaque answered. "Unless there's a spy at the Musée de Sèvres."

Paulik choked a little on his wine.

"Highly unlikely, isn't it?" Verlaque said, smiling.

"And who would steal an entire museum collection just for four dessert plates?" Paulik continued. "Even if Napoleon did order them himself? Quite frankly, I found her story of Napoleon swooning over the porcelain before dinner a little off-putting. He was one of my boyhood heroes. I almost lost my appetite for lunch."

The waitress appeared carrying two steaming dishes. "The plates are hot, gentlemen. The chef is still cursing that you guys arrived for lunch well after 2:00 p.m."

Verlaque leaned down to smell the rabbit thigh covered in mustard and cream sauce. "And now?" he asked. "Are you still off your lunch?"

Paulik picked up a small cube of roasted potato and popped it into his mouth. "It was a temporary glitch." The judge and the commissioner spread their pressed linen napkins on their knees and began eating, both realizing how hungry they were. They ate in silence until Paulik's cell phone began to vibrate on the table. He picked it up, listened to the caller, looked at Verlaque with raised eyebrows a few times, and then hung up.

Verlaque set his knife and fork down. "What is it?"

"That was that young officer, Roche," Paulik said. "He's found something on the CCTV cameras near Aix-les-Bains from the Saturday night before the robbery."

"Go on."

"He says it's hard to make out, but it's a large white van with two people up front. And the driver looks like Gilbert Quentin-Savary."

An hour later, having skipped dessert, Verlaque and Paulik were sitting beside Patrice Roche at the Palais de Justice, staring at a computer screen. "This is as clear and big as I can make it," Roche said, his hand on the computer's mouse. "Any bigger and the image will be pixelated."

"It's already very blurry," Verlaque said. "It's quite hard to see the driver, but I agree with you, he does bear a resemblance to M Quentin-Savary."

"Yes, the same fluffy hair and beard," Paulik said, squinting. "Is that a woman or a man beside him?"

"Hard to tell," Roche said, leaning in toward the screen. "The passenger has long hair, but that doesn't mean much."

"And the van's plates?" Paulik asked.

"It was stolen a month ago. The owner is a plumber, clean record. He reported it right away. He ran into a *tabac* to buy some cigarettes and left the keys in the ignition."

"Good work, Roche," Paulik said.

"Where did this happen?" Verlaque asked.

"West of Lyon," Roche said. "Far from here, and far from Aix-les-Bains."

Paulik squinted and Roche moved the mouse so that the photograph slid down on the screen about an inch. "I see the license plate now," Paulik said. "And it's registered in 69. Lyon region."

Roche looked up at them and Verlaque saw the exhaustion in his eyes and the desire to have helped in some way. "It might be Gilbert," Verlaque said, "and he or his accomplice could have taken a bus or train to Lyon and then stolen the van." Roche's shoulders collapsed with relief, but Verlaque saw a look of doubt spread across the commissioner's face.

Professeur Lagouanere walked up the rue Clémenceau slowly, not because he was looking at store windows, in which he had no interest—who buys all of this lingerie?—but because his right leg was sore. Years ago he had had a skiing accident and pulled some ligaments, and his leg had never really recovered. He got out his map of downtown Aix, free at the hotel (he had taken two). He realized from the map that he missed a possible shortcut, through a small passage off the Cours Mirabeau, but it was too late to turn back now. He folded the map and put it back in his jacket pocket.

At the top of the street, at yet another sidewalk café—so the Aixois drink coffee all day, *and* buy lingerie, he mused—he turned right. Passing a large American clothing store, he frowned, not happy that international brands were taking over the storefronts of his beloved French cities, including his own Toulouse. He had always thought that the independent, strong-willed Toulousains would be impervious to such temptations—their city had been a Visigoth capital, after all—but he was wrong. Money can buy anything.

Tired, he sat down on the edge of a fountain and thought about the museum. He knew deep down that the thief or thieves wouldn't have been interested in any of the ancient documents—his domain—in the museum. But then there had been a murder. At breakfast that morning Raymond complained that they were being treated like murder suspects and this made Lagouanere laugh out loud, almost upsetting his teacup. Why on earth would any of them want to hurt, even kill, M Lopez? They didn't even know him! He'd come to only one of their meetings, the professor was fairly certain, in an attempt to win them over with his idea of joining the two museums. He sighed. He was very fed up with this whole scenario and wished he were back home surrounded by his comfortable possessions and eating one of his wife's hearty southwestern dishes. He hadn't seen duck on one single menu here in Aix.

He heard voices arguing, even over the sound of the fountain's gurgling water, and so he looked up, because he was naturally curious and because he thought he recognized one of the voices. Two people, one of them Mme Devaux, were standing about ten feet away from him. He was hidden by the fountain's central column but leaned to the left in order to be more out of sight. He then saw that the museum's secretary was with Mlle Peronne, his own fellow board member. Why were they arguing? Should he intervene? But before he could move, the two women parted company, Mlle Peronne almost walking right past him. She was frowning, looking down at the sidewalk, and didn't see him. Mme Devaux turned the other way and marched across the vast square, her old-fashioned purse swinging along beside her.

He got up slowly, relieved that he hadn't been seen. It could mean nothing. On the other hand, it could be of great importance to the investigation. But would the judge and his bald commissioner listen to him? He knew that Raymond, and especially Gilbert, thought he was a dotty old man, just because he sometimes forgot his proper nouns. His wife told him that it was a normal occurrence at their age, although she seemed to forget things less often than he did. He decided he'd tell the police about what he had just witnessed. He just hoped he could remember it.

Back in her living room, exhausted, Marine slept for an hour on the sofa. When she awoke, she thought about how lucky she was. The interior designer's business card was on the coffee table. The baby suddenly kicked and she sat up, enjoying its stirring. When the baby quieted down, she stood up and walked to the back of the apartment to the bathroom, where she brushed her teeth and washed her face, deciding she should do some work before dinner.

She was about to go up to the mezzanine to her office when she saw the Musée Quentin-Savary's charter papers sitting on the far end of the dining room table. Sitting down, she began flipping through the yellowed pages, consoling herself with the fact that it was nearly 6:00 p.m. so she didn't have enough time to dive into her own research. But it was the building plans that drew her attention, perhaps because she had just met with an interior designer and she was thinking about spaces.

Verlaque walked to his best friend Jean-Marc's apartment, relieved that this evening's cigar club was downtown. His back hurt—he didn't get enough exercise, Marine always said, although as a young man he had been *un grand sportif*—and hours of sitting in a chair every day didn't help. Hence he relished his daily walks across Aix.

Around him he saw constant reminders of their impending parenthood: children running through the streets, many of them on scooters, their parents racing behind them; mothers, mostly, pushing elaborate strollers, talking on their cell phones at the same time, which for some reason irritated him; shops selling expensive clothes for babies and older children. Who would buy all the baby gear? Both of them? Who had done all that preparation when he and his brother, Sébastien, were children? He couldn't imagine either of his parents being interested, and yet the brothers had always had the best of everything. Had they sent their servants out to buy the necessities?

He couldn't very well ask for advice from his cigar friends; many of them were a decade older than him and their kids were already in university. Their conversations revolved around their sons and daughters getting into Sciences Po Paris, or Aix's law school, or, for many of them, expensive private business colleges, as their kids hadn't had the grades to get accepted into France's free elite universities. Before he had met Marine, he and Jean-Marc had been the odd ones out during these conversations;

Verlaque was the eternal bachelor and Jean-Marc was gay. Jean-Marc was a lawyer and a doting uncle to a tribe of smart nieces and nephews who lived in and around Aix, so he might be able to offer some useful advice. Verlaque then realized that he was behind in his research on the best primary schools and vowed to get back on track first thing in the morning.

He reached Jean-Marc's building, an elegant hôtel in the rue Papassaudi, and buzzed. "Antoine?" Jean-Marc's voice came out of the speaker mounted onto the stone wall.

"How did you know?" Verlaque asked.

"You're always the first to arrive. Come on up."

Jean-Marc was waiting at his apartment door by the time Verlaque walked up the three flights of stairs, holding up a whisky bottle and two crystal glasses. They exchanged the *bises* and Verlaque immediately recognized the green-and-black label. "A Springbank?"

"Fifteen years old," Jean-Marc said, closing the door and ushering Verlaque into his sitting room. "My brother brought it back from Scotland with him."

"Please thank him. I've only seen the ten-year-old Springbank for sale in France."

They sat down on matching love seats across from each other. Verlaque was happy to see his old friend, who, unlike Verlaque, never seemed to age and always stayed trim. The coffee table was covered in cleaned cigar ashtrays with various cutters and lighters at the ready, as well as a small vase of peonies. "The peonies are a nice touch," Verlaque said.

"Oh, right, I should move those," Jean-Marc said, laughing, then he picked up the vase and set it on an Empire-era console.

"The vase is equally lovely."

"All right, all right, enough of your teasing or you won't get any Springbank."

"No, I really meant it," Verlaque said. "It's Chinese, right?"

"Yes, I bought it at a Drouot auction," Jean-Marc replied, turning it around so that Verlaque could see it better. "It cost more than the console it's sitting on." He poured out two small drams and handed one to Verlaque. "Cheers," he said, raising his glass.

"Cheers," Verlaque said, raising his and then smelling the peaty goodness.

"Speaking of ceramics," Jean-Marc said, "are there any developments? I thought I'd ask you now, before the rest of the gang arrives."

Verlaque laughed, knowing exactly what Jean-Marc meant. "Nothing, I'm afraid, and it's turned into a murder investigation."

"I heard. I asked around at the office, but none of my colleagues know this Lopez guy."

"Thanks for asking," Verlaque said, sitting back, cradling the glass in his hands. "We've been given a host of conflicting opinions and tips, including the latest one tonight by telephone from a senile professor who's on the museum's board of directors. This is the toughest case I've ever dealt with. To be honest, in the beginning I thought it would sort itself out—as if it was sort of a prank. But now it's getting more mysterious, and evil."

"You sure you haven't missed something obvious?"

"I only wish." Verlaque took a sip of whisky. "Do you know Gilbert Quentin-Savary?"

Jean-Marc shook his head. "Not personally, but I've heard he's a real piece of work."

Verlaque tried not to smile; it amused him when Jean-Marc, so elegant and well read, used popular idioms. He imagined he picked them up from his nieces and nephews. He was about to ask another question when the door buzzer rang and Jean-Marc bounced up off the sofa. In less than three minutes the small living room was crowded with eight large men and one demure woman, each jostling for a comfortable chair. "We'll have to take turns!" Jean-Marc huffed, walking toward the kitchen. "Some of us will have to make do with sitting on the dining room chairs, which are very comfortable, I can assure you!"

"And please give Virginie the best spot," Verlaque said.

"Thank you, Antoine," Virginie, who ran one of Aix's biggest pharmacies, said.

"Playing favorites," complained Fabrice, a wealthy plumber, as he squeezed himself into one of Jean-Marc's leather dining room chairs.

"That's right," Virginie said. "It's enough that I have to listen all night to your car talk. As the sole woman, I should at least be comfortable."

"My dining room chairs *are* comfortable!" Jean-Marc yelled from the kitchen, whose door was open.

"Virginie, you know just as much about cars as we do!" Fabrice said.

Virginie beamed. "Why, thank you." A conversation ensued comparing the merits of various late-model Porsches and Verlaque sat back, delighted to be among these oddball friends from various walks of life, the one thing linking them was their passion for Cuban cigars.

"Who brought the fifteen-year-old Springbank?" another

asked, taking the bottle and looking at it. Jean-Marc came out of the kitchen and looked at Verlaque, raising his eyes toward the ceiling. He had meant to put it back in the drinks cabinet before they all got there and serve them ten-year-old Laphroaig, perfectly acceptable.

"Antoine, would you mind serving the Springbank?" Jean-Marc asked.

"Not at all," Verlaque said.

"I'll hand out the cigars," Virginie said, opening a new box. "I bought these last week for us."

"Oliva?!" Fabrice exclaimed when he saw the box. "They're not Cuban!"

"That's right," Virginie answered, her voice flat and calm. "I thought we'd think outside the box for once."

Fabrice continued, "But not outside a Cuban box!" He sat back, bellowing with laughter at his pun.

"Shut up, Fabrice," Verlaque said, holding his stomach from laughing so much.

"Antoine?" a voice beside him whispered.

"José," Verlaque said, turning to his right. "I'm glad you could make it tonight. I know that your work schedule doesn't always allow for it."

"Tonight, I'm free," José said, "but I have to go back into the newspaper offices tomorrow. Your museum caper is causing quite a stir."

Verlaque groaned. He whispered back, "Do you have anything?"

José, who was the editor in chief of the local paper, *La Provence*, nodded and looked around to make sure that no one could hear him. All that could be heard was Fabrice loudly complaining about the cigars and Jean-Marc calling for help from the kitchen.

"Go on," Verlaque said, leaning toward José.

"One of our reporters has been digging around in the paper's archives since Aurélien Lopez was killed," he said. "And I thought you should have this." He passed Verlaque a folded piece of paper.

Verlaque opened it, looked at it, and quickly folded it back up, putting it in his jacket pocket. "A million thanks. You know who these people are, right? I assume you do."

José nodded. "On the right is Lopez and the woman he has his arm around is that art thief, Marie-Claire Blay."

Chapter Twenty-two

Monday, April 30

The wind had picked up by the time Bruno Paulik left the Palais de Justice just after 7:00 p.m. He'd stayed late to do paperwork and to debrief with his officers working on the case; they were slowly making their way through a list of people who knew Aurélien Lopez, but nothing of interest had so far been revealed about the museum director or his life. After leaving the prestigious École du Louvre art history program as a young man of twenty-four, he had gone into the antiques business and then the museum business, where he'd been ever since. He had spent most of his working career in Marseille, with a brief stint in Gordes, where he had run an antiques shop—before the Luberon was discovered and real estate prices went through the roof, Paulik guessed. The only bit of interesting news that one of his officers had picked up during routine interviews with neighbors was that

Lopez was behind in his property taxes, and also behind in the communal co-owner fees for the private driveway shared by himself and five other households. Had he been having financial problems? Or had he just been cheap?

Paulik pulled the collar of his jacket closer around his neck, wishing he had brought a scarf despite the fact that it was already spring. In April the weather could change drastically from day to day. He looked at his watch. He usually had a coffee or a beer while he waited for Léa to finish choir practice on Monday evenings. Monday was a slow day in Aix—most shops and restaurants were closed—but one of the cafés at the north end of the rue d'Italie was open. As it was cold out and he had lots of time, he decided to walk up the rue du Maréchal Joffre, which began at the café where he usually stopped. Achille Formentin's apartment was around the corner, and the keys to it were in his pocket.

He walked uphill, against the wind, as university students came downhill, laughing and walking arm in arm toward the Cours. Sooner rather than later Léa would be their age. He looked up at the buildings on one of what he had always considered Aix's duller streets, with few historic *hôtels particuliers* and a couple of concrete-block eyesores pretending to look like the famous sand-colored stone from nearby Rognes that had been built in the 1960s. Two of the shops made him sad: a large print shop and a piano store. Both were still open for business, but for how much longer? He couldn't remember the last time he and Hélène had received a printed birth announcement. The last *faire-part* they had received, for a wedding, was over the internet. But as he walked, he slowly began to change his opinion of the street. Its lack of restaurants, cafés, and shops probably meant that it was quiet, and it did, if he remembered correctly, have a lovely chapel up at the top right-hand side of the street. And the old print shop and piano store added to its charm.

He came to number 19 and continued on; the next building didn't have a number posted outside, but he assumed it was 21. Looking at the buzzers and name plates, he saw FORMENTIN on the third one down, so he got out the keys, choosing the biggest one, and let himself in the front door. Inside, the floor was tiled in flagstone and a baby carriage was parked in the corner. The officers who had gone through Formentin's apartment after he'd been attacked told Paulik that it was the door on the left on the third floor. He walked up the stairs, not sure why he was there; he could be in a café having a beer and reading *La Provence*. But something was nagging him to see the apartment for himself.

You could tell a lot about a person by seeing where they lived. His mother, now elderly, said that, but he knew she was referring to house cleaning, or the lack thereof, more than anything else. How people decorated their homes was of no interest to her; his parents were farmers in the Luberon, and hospitality and generosity were more important to them than having the latest trendy Berber carpets or stainless-steel appliances. He and his wife, Hélène, met somewhere between the two.

He got to the third floor and put the key in the lock, opening it slowly. He reached along the darkened wall and found a light switch and turned it on, hearing a slight rustling sound as he did so. Closing the door behind him, he walked in. *"Bonsoir?"* he said. *"Il y a quelqu'un ici?"* He looked down the hallway, which was lined in bookcases and had four doors leading off of it, all of them closed. A kitchen, whose door was open, was situated straight ahead at the end of the hall. He could see a set of small copper pots hanging above a large stove. So Achille was a gourmet. He started walking toward the kitchen—further detective work on Achille's eating habits—when he heard the noise again. "*Merde,*" he mumbled to himself, opening the first door on his right and quickly turning on the light. It was a large living room furnished in dainty antiques and Oriental carpets. It looked like an old lady's sitting room, but he supposed he shouldn't be sexist. He turned around and walked across the hall to find a bathroom, pink 1960s tiles with matching sink, toilet, bidet, and large bathtub. All was now silent, and he wondered if the noises had come from a neighboring apartment.

Opening the door beside the bathroom, he found a bedroom with a single bed and a desk and a chair—a guest room, he supposed. He crossed the hallway once more, opened the last door, and turned on the light to the master bedroom, which had a large wooden sleigh bed covered in an extremely fluffy duvet. On the bed was a small open suitcase packed with men's clothes, including a pressed pair of pajamas that looked to Paulik very expensive. Someone must have been preparing some clothes to take to the hospital for Achille and they hadn't, for some reason, finished.

He looked around, wondering once again what he had expected to find. He saw a few silver-framed photographs on the dresser; family, he imagined, and he remembered that Formentin's elderly mother lived in Aix. He was about to turn off the lights when something else caught his eye on the dresser: an old-fashioned woman's snakeskin handbag. He shrugged; maybe Achille was a cross-dresser. Not wanting to judge, he walked over to the dresser and opened the purse. It was full of the usual assortment of cosmetics, tissues, and keys. He pulled out a wallet, but before he could open it to look for an ID, he heard a noise coming from the closet, whose oak door was closed. "*Allez,*" he said loudly. "*Police!*" He braced himself for a fight—he was unarmed—and quickly opened the door.

"*C'est moi!*" a voice called out. "Please don't hurt me!" Out of the many coats and suits appeared a long thin hand, and then the face and upper body of a woman.

"Mme Devaux? What in the world?" Paulik asked, taking her hand and helping her step over a small suitcase and out of the closet. "Why on earth were you hiding?"

She wiped her forehead and straightened her back, becoming the elegant secretary once more. "I didn't know it was you," she said. "I've been packing. For M Formentin."

"I saw that," Paulik answered, turning to look again at the suitcase. "But you still haven't answered my question. Why didn't you answer when I called out the first time?"

She paused. "I was . . . frightened."

"But didn't you recognize my voice?"

"No."

Paulik nodded, realizing that she must have never expected anyone to show up and panicked when he had called out. But still, they'd met a few times; he'd even been in her apartment, which he now realized was almost a replica of Formentin's. He stood there, thinking, when he saw that she glanced at the suitcase twice. In his head he retraced his steps. He had walked into the apartment and run his hand along the wall . . . yes, to turn on the lights. He looked down at her again. "Why were you working in the dark? I had to turn on all of the lights when I came in."

"I turned them off when I heard you."

"You wouldn't have had time," he said. "This is a big apartment, and you were back here, in the bedroom."

He sat down on the edge of the bed and looked at his watch. He had a half hour before he needed to meet Léa. "Please tell me the truth, Mme Devaux. Over a week ago the museum was emptied of its contents, and now one museum director is dead and another is lying in the hospital. I can see that you were packing, but what else were you doing?"

She hesitated, wringing her hands, and then wiped her forehead again.

He pressed on. "You were also seen downtown today arguing with Mlle Peronne."

"Really? By whom?"

"It doesn't matter," he said, remembering the strange phone call from the professor. "Aix is a small place, as you know. Care to fill me in?"

She sat down in a cane-backed chair beside the dresser. "I was asking Mlle Peronne for advice. I came to the apartment earlier this afternoon to pack. Achille didn't know; I've had keys for his apartment for years, in case of an emergency, and to water his plants when he goes to Marrakesh a few times a year. I thought I'd better get him a change of clothes."

"That's very kind."

"But when I went into the living room, on the fireplace mantel were . . . four plates."

Paulik tried not to sigh, worried about the time and his meeting with Léa. Soon he'd be starting to confuse all of these plates. Couldn't they steal something else? "Plates?"

"Four porcelain plates from . . . from . . ."

"The museum?"

She nodded.

"I see," Paulik said, now understanding what had happened. "And they shouldn't be here, right?"

"No, not at all."

"You hadn't noticed them missing from the museum, before the robbery?"

"No, they're delicate, and quite rare, and so are packed away most of the time."

Paulik raised an eyebrow. "Rare, are they? How rare? Napoleonic?"

She looked at him in surprise. "Yes, I think they belong to a set commissioned by the emperor. How did you know?"

"Mlle Peronne told us they were in the collection. She's found proof that the plates were part of that famous set. Is that what you were arguing about today?"

She stared at him, obviously shocked.

"You were seen," he explained, "by the professor; he called me. He's very close to Mlle Peronne and was protecting her."

"I see," she answered, pursing her lips. "I told her I found the plates here. She said that I should tell you at once. You see, I had no idea these plates were part of the famous Napoleonic service. Myriam just told me."

"She was right. Were you going to?"

Mme Devaux bit her lip. "Yes, but not this evening. I was confused. She accused Achille of being the thief behind this whole operation! Can you imagine?"

"You don't think that he is . . ."

"No, of course not," she answered sternly.

He was fairly certain at this point that Mme Devaux had no idea of their historical and cultural importance, as recently uncovered by Mlle Peronne. And if that was the thief's reason for the robbery, as Mlle Peronne surmised, then they were out of luck, as the plates were here in this nondescript apartment on a quiet Aix street. Would the thief put two and two together and come looking for them? "Where are the plates now?" he asked. "I didn't see them when I came in, but I wasn't looking for them, either."

"I put them in a drawer," she said, motioning to the dresser.

Paulik nodded, realizing he'd have to run down the street to meet Léa on time. "Let's leave them there until tomorrow morning, and I'll walk you out. Do you need help with the suitcase?"

"No, I was finished," she replied. She walked over to the bed and zipped the suitcase shut. Paulik took it for her even though it wasn't heavy.

They walked out of the apartment together, Paulik taking a quick glance at the living room's mantelpiece and seeing the four empty plate stands. As he locked the front door, he turned to her and asked, "Mme Devaux, if M Formentin didn't empty the museum last week, then what was he doing with those four plates in his apartment?"

"Enjoying their beauty, I suppose. He'd never sell them or bring harm to them, I can assure you."

Chapter Twenty-three

Tuesday, May 1

And you're sure that Mme Devaux isn't our thief?" Verlaque asked. "Has her background been checked?"

"Yes, it's been checked, and no, I'm not sure," Paulik replied as he looked out the judge's office window. Down below a young man and woman walked arm in arm. They paused to kiss. An elderly woman, pulling a shopping cart behind her, passed next to them. Paulik guessed that she was on her way back from the market that was held every Tuesday, Thursday, and Saturday in the square facing the Palais de Justice. She smiled and stopped and the three of them began speaking. Paulik smiled and turned back around to face Verlaque. "But I had her give me the keys to Formentin's apartment just in case," he continued. "She's agreed to return to the museum today with an officer to see if anything is missing that possibly could have been used as the murder weapon. Dr. Cohen reports that it was heavy, possibly a hammer."

Verlaque winced and sat back, tired, feeling that perhaps he had drunk one too many scotches the night before. But he didn't regret it. He unfolded the photograph from *La Provence* and handed it to Paulik. The commissioner looked at it, read the caption, and frowned. "A museum director friends with an art thief?" he asked.

"Check, discreetly if you can, where she was during the weekend of the museum robbery and on the night of Lopez's murder."

Paulik said, "I'll get right on it. I'll keep the photograph for a while."

"Go ahead," Verlaque said. "That photo was taken more than fifteen years ago. According to the caption, Lopez wasn't yet a museum director, just an antiques dealer."

Paulik smiled. "*Mais oui.* Their being together now makes more sense." He looked at the photograph once more. "Think they were more than just friends?"

"Possibly," Verlaque said. He thought of the tall, husky Mlle Blay and couldn't guess her sexual orientation; at that exact moment Paulik was thinking the same thing of Lopez. "Don't leave yet, Bruno." Verlaque picked up the phone and called France Dubois; in a few seconds she appeared in the doorway. "France," he began, "Did Lopez talk much during the Chinese class? I mean, do you have any idea why he was there?"

"He asked a lot of questions," France said. "He was interested in Chinese art. I thought it had to do with his job."

"Yes, it may have been," Verlaque replied, uneasy. Why Chinese art?

"Oh, and he was fussy about numbers."

"Numbers?" Paulik asked.

"Yes," France replied. "He really wanted to get his pronunciation right, on numbers especially. Once he sat beside me and he kept practicing writing them out. It annoyed me as I could tell he wasn't listening to Isaac—I mean M Bonnard, our teacher."

"Thank you," Verlaque said. He couldn't wait to tell Marine this evening about the "Isaac" slip. They both adored France Dubois, but especially Marine.

"One more thing, Mlle Dubois," Paulik said. "Did you ever see M Lopez with anyone else, before or after class?"

She shook her head. "No. He seemed to be a loner; at least, he didn't mingle with the other students."

France left, taking with her a stack of signed letters and documents from Verlaque's desk. Verlaque stood up and went to the window. A light rain began to fall, just a drizzle, and a woman ran to her car, a shopping bag held over her head, as if it were a tsunami. He smiled, then turned to Paulik and asked, "Was Lopez planning on selling art to the Chinese?"

"That's certainly what it sounds like," Paulik replied.

"Is he our museum thief?" Verlaque asked, vaguely embarrassed that he kept asking Paulik the same question, each time with a different suspect. "And was he found out?"

Paulik nodded. "I'll put more officers on Lopez's trail, find out what he was doing before he died. If he did organize the theft, he may have had meetings with accomplices."

"And his phone?"

"Last time I heard we were still waiting for France Telecom."

Verlaque groaned, knowing how inept they were. "I'll call Mlle Blay and see how soon she can get here."

"I'm off for another meeting with Dr. Cohen and then a trip

to Marseille to see what I can dig up regarding Lopez. I'll keep you posted," Paulik said, walking to the door. "Ciao."

"Ciao, Bruno." Verlaque sat down and opened a file, pulling out a business card with a drawing of a buffalo on it. He dialed the number.

"*La Ferme de Marie-Claire,*" a voice answered.

"Mlle Blay?"

"*Oui, c'est moi.*"

"Antoine Verlaque here," he said. "We met a few days ago, with my wife . . ."

"Oh, yes," she replied flatly. "What can I do for you, Judge?"

Verlaque realized that he had called her too quickly, before he had rehearsed the conversation in his head. He thought of the woman down in the street, running in the rain, and how ridiculous she'd looked. And that, for some inexplicable reason, made him think of Gilbert Quentin-Savary and his dour-looking ancestors. "I'm calling with a favor to ask," he said.

By the time that Verlaque got to the Parc Jourdan, the professor was already there, sitting on the bench facing the bust of Émile Zola, where they'd agreed to meet. Verlaque was relieved that the professor had made it there on his own, as the park was only a few hundred meters south of the Hôtel Roi René. Verlaque wanted to meet somewhere without the chance of running into the other board members, whom he presumed would head up into the old town for a stroll instead of in this newer part of Aix.

Verlaque sat down next to him and smiled. "Good afternoon, Professor Lagouanere," he said.

"Hello, Judge," the professor answered. He continued to stare ahead, at the statue. "My favorite writer—always has been and always will be. You know that the imaginary town of Plassans in Zola's novels is Aix."

"Yes, I did. But not until I moved here and reread the books. Now it's obvious that our rue d'Italie is the rue de Nice in his Plassans stories."

"And of course his novel *L'Oeuvre* is all about Cézanne."

"The story of a failed painter," Verlaque said, crossing his legs and leaning back, enjoying the spring sun on his face. "And hence the end of their friendship. I can't blame Cézanne for being angry, as he was anything but a failed painter." For that reason, he had a hard time reading Zola, knowing how the writer had betrayed his childhood best friend. But he kept his opinion to himself. "You telephoned the commissioner," he continued, "with the information that you witnessed Mlle Peronne and Mme Devaux arguing . . ."

"Oh, that's why you wanted to meet me," the professor said, turning his body slightly so that he could see Verlaque's face. "I wondered why."

"Why did you feel their argument was so important?"

"Mlle Peronne is a great friend and a fine person," the professor began. "I was defending her, as it upset me to see her in such an awkward situation. And I've never trusted Faustine Devaux."

"Oh?"

"One of the benefits of being a senile old man—and I know that's what I am—is that you can just sit back and observe."

Verlaque smiled and nodded.

The professor continued, "I saw that Faustine ran the museum, not Achille. He didn't have a chance with her around. She's possessive about the museum and its objects. She's the one who changed Achille's mind about that idea of Lopez's to join the two museums. Before that, the merger was almost a done deal."

"As you and Mlle Peronne were for it."

"Of course," he replied. "We badly need the money. The museum is quite destitute, you see."

"Then it's odd that Gilbert Quentin-Savary was against the merger."

"Yes, it does make you wonder, doesn't it? But he never really cared about the museum, anyway. Perhaps he wanted it to go under and be done with it."

A soccer ball landed at their feet. Verlaque picked it up and threw it to a ten-year-old boy, who caught it and yelled thanks. "That kid could grow up to be the next Cézanne," Verlaque said of the boy. "Or Zola."

"Perhaps," the professor said, not hiding the doubt in his voice. "Do you have children, Judge?"

"My wife is expecting our first."

"We have three," the professor said. "They're all very well, happily employed and each one married, which I'm told by friends I should be happy about, but even at my age you never stop worrying about them."

As Verlaque walked back to the office, his head was a jumble of images of Aix, Cézanne, Zola, the professor, and the kid with the soccer ball. He was waiting for the foot traffic to pass through a narrow passageway when he almost came face-to-face with Faustine Devaux, who was just exiting the passage. "Mme Devaux," Verlaque said, seeing it as a sign. "Do you have a minute or two?"

She looked nervous and a tiny bit annoyed. "Yes, I suppose so," she answered.

They both looked toward the Cours and saw a concrete bench that was miraculously empty. Verlaque gestured toward it and she followed, turning her nose up at the pizza stand that was behind the famed Deux Garçons café. They sat down facing the Cours and watched the passersby in silence until he said, "I understand you encouraged Achille Formentin to rebuff Aurélien Lopez's project of the museum merger."

"I assume one of the board members told you that," she replied, her lips pursed. "I won't bother guessing who. Yes, Achille has trouble making big decisions and the merger would have been such a disastrous project."

"Why so?"

She looked at him incredulously. "Why, for Aix, of course. The Quentin-Savary must stay here. Forgive me, Judge, but I can't understand why you'd think otherwise."

"For one, because there was no money left?"

She waved her hand in the air—not unlike the queen of England, mused Verlaque. "We could have come up with a solution," she said. "I was . . ."

"You were working on such a solution?"

She nodded. "The morning I found . . . the bodies . . . I went to the museum to get some documents."

"I remember that first morning that we met, just after the theft was discovered," Verlaque said. "You looked toward the stairs, as if worried about something."

"Yes. I've been hiding the documents from Achille. Please don't think ill of me. It's just that I've worked with him for years, and I know he'd panic if he saw how dire our financial state is. The board members are aware of it, to some extent. But I thought I had a solution."

"A way to raise funds?" Verlaque asked.

"Yes, but I need more time to work out my idea." She looked at him with her dark brown eyes. "Would it be all right if I told you later?"

He decided to take a chance, seeing the earnestness in her eyes. Either that or she was a great actress. "All right," he said, shaking her hand. "Thanks for the chat."

Once back at the Palais de Justice, Verlaque made his way to a large meeting room on the second floor where Paulik was about to bring everyone up-to-date on the case. The room was already full of officers, some in uniform and some, like Flamant, Schoelcher, and Goulin, dressed in civilian clothes. Everyone's eyes were fixed on Paulik.

"I'll begin with our news on Aix-les-Bains," Paulik said. He pointed to a color photograph of Gilbert. "Gilbert Quentin-Savary has a weekend house in a village near Les Bains and claims he was there the entire weekend of the museum break-in. We've had another conversation with his maid, Gisèle Borgia, who claims that Gilbert's white Volvo station wagon was parked in front of the house most of the weekend. She saw him arrive in the car on Friday afternoon around four o'clock, as he told us, and she saw him again on Saturday morning, buying bread in the village. The Volvo was parked on the main street. She again saw him sometime on Sunday, but can't remember when."

"No sign of the white van?" asked one of the officers.

"No," Paulik said. "But as you know, white vans are a dime a dozen."

"And Gilbert Quentin-Savary hasn't rented a garage or warehouse in the area?" Verlaque asked.

"No, neither here nor in the other Aix," Paulik replied. "Two of the board members have asked their clients if they've heard anything about some new porcelain on the market, or a Ziem painting of Venice, but there's been radio silence all around." He pointed to the photographs of the other three board members. "On the night of Lopez's murder and Achille Formentin's attack," he said, "Mlle Peronne and Professor Lagouanere were together, in his room, then walked to the restaurant together, arriving at eight o'clock. The restaurant's manager has confirmed that. He also confirmed that Gilbert arrived thirty minutes after, and Raymond Policante fifteen minutes after that. Gilbert has no alibi— he was at home, paying bills, he says. Policante was having an affair with someone here in Aix, and I've spoken to that person already. They're married, so for the moment it's between me, that person, and Officer Roche, who was in the room as well." Paulik looked at Roche and thought to himself, *Well, here's a good test for a junior officer. Can you stay quiet about the famous soccer player?*

"What about the secretary?" Sophie Goulin asked. "She was very shaken up, but what was she doing there at the museum? And is she a suspect in either the murder or the theft?"

"Mme Devaux was in Aix at the time of the museum theft, but she was mostly alone, at home. It's not much of an alibi, but I honestly can't see someone her age doing it, which includes the murder and attempted murder. From all accounts she loved the museum and admired Achille Formentin, so we have no motive."

Verlaque stayed quiet; he'd ask Faustine Devaux more questions later.

"And now the porcelain," Paulik said. "Someone has a plate that they're trying to sell over the internet, and we believe it's one of the châteaux plates from the museum's collection."

"Chenonceau," Patrice Roche added.

Paulik nodded as a way of saying thanks. "There's also a valuable dessert set commissioned by Napoleon, and the Quentin-Savary had four plates belonging to that collection. I've just found them and they are now here in the safe."

"Where were they?" Flamant asked.

"In Achille Formentin's apartment."

"Is that normal?"

"It's a little odd, I agree," Paulik replied. "Once M Formentin is feeling better, we'll question him about that. The third set of porcelain in this case is from the eighteenth century and is covered in Brazilian flora and fauna, and was stolen from Mme Montbarbon's Cours Mirabeau apartment two weeks before the museum theft. Those still haven't turned up."

"The two cases are related, right?" an officer asked.

"I honestly don't know," Paulik said. "So get out there and try to connect the dots. Look for connections between the Montbarbon and Quentin-Savary families. Look for connections between the museum's board members, its staff, Aurélien Lopez, and our retired art thief, Marie-Claire Blay. The Ziem painting. And let's go over the museum's inventory again—Goulin and Schoelcher, I'll put you in charge of that. Ask as many experts as you can about the collection in case we've missed something."

Chapter Twenty-four

❧

Tuesday, May 1

Philomène Joubert walked as quickly as her legs would take her. She'd never been inside Mme de Montbarbon's luxuriously decorated (so everyone said) apartment and was tickled by the invitation. In fact, she reflected, she'd never been in any apartment on the Cours Mirabeau. She and her husband didn't belong to those circles. Nonetheless, she knew that her constant volunteer work at Saint Jean-de-Malte and her position as the choir leader helped open certain doors that would otherwise have been closed.

She rang the buzzer at number 8, hoping she was the first to arrive. Solange Picard answered, sounding breathless, and buzzed her in, telling Philomène to come up to the first floor. Of course, Philomène reflected, it would be on the first floor, *l'étage noble*. She took the stairs two at a time.

"Good evening, Philomène," Solange said when they met at the magnificently carved doors. "Come in!" They exchanged the *bises* and Philomène quickly handed over her basket, filled with homemade provisions: olive tapenade, both green and black; tiny toasts for the tapenade, made from stale bread as she refused to buy them already toasted at the *boulangerie*; a garlicky spread that she made with old bits of chèvre; and a selection of small fruit tarts, all from blackberries that she had foraged and frozen, ready to use when she needed them. Solange hung up Philomène's coat and told her to make herself at home in the next room while she took the food into the kitchen at the back of the apartment.

Philomène had time to look around and was not disappointed. The apartment was laid out in an enfilade formation: one large room led into another, and another, as far as the eye could see, all connected by lovely polished terra-cotta floors. The floors smelled lovely, like honey. She wondered what kind of product Solange used. Philomène took her time, walking past furniture that looked old and delicate, trying not to step on the large silk area rugs that were patterned with pale pink roses. Paintings graced the walls, some portraits and some landscapes, all in gold frames and many spot-lit with little brass lamps, which, she imagined, helped to increase what must be an already very expensive electricity bill.

The next room was only a bit smaller than the first. It was full of the same type of delicate furnishings, including a small round table at which three bridge chairs and a deck of cards were set. A fire was lit in the fireplace. *On the first day of May?* thought Philomène. It *had* rained today, but only a tiny bit. She stood in the middle of the room and then she shivered, as if on cue. Perhaps the fire made sense: these big apartments were drafty, and she noticed that the windows were the original single-paned kind. She walked over to the fireplace and looked at the brownish landscape painting that hung above it: a few cows gathered around a sad little marsh that was dotted with spindly white trees. Poplars, she thought.

The doorbell rang and she could hear Solange instructing the next guest up the stairs. Philomène smiled, wondering if Florence Bonnet could take the stairs two at a time as she had done. Of all the people in their choir who were the same age as Philomène, the only one who was as fit was Florence. She turned away from the painting just as the two women walked into the room. "You two make yourselves comfortable," Solange said, "while I take these cheeses into the kitchen. Thank you, Florence."

Philomène saw the bag, from a grocery-store chain, and smiled. Florence Bonnet might be in good shape, but she was a notoriously bad cook. Philomène wondered if she could refuse to eat the tasteless rubbery cheese, perhaps feigning a diet, but people her age didn't diet. She'd just have to take a few pieces, to be polite.

"You're admiring the Corot?" Florence asked as she marched over to the fireplace and put on her reading glasses to take a better look. "A lesser work, I'm afraid."

"Um, indeed," Philomène answered. "Looks like it was painted up in Picardy, where the only things that grow are beets."

Florence laughed and Philomène no longer felt guilty that she had failed to see the importance of the painting. *Well, art should be like that*, she thought, almost saying it aloud. *Either you like it or you don't.* Her husband often said the same thing about wine, but secretly she knew that he bought according to price, scouring the shelves for the cheaper bottles that had won a lesser prize at small wine fairs.

"Well, now that we are all here, we can sit down and start playing," Solange said as she came back into the room. "I can't tell you what a pleasure it is to play belote with you. My husband doesn't care for cards."

"Mine doesn't, either," Florence said. "And I don't think I've ever played in such a wonderful setting."

"We have Mme de Montbarbon to thank for that," Solange said.

They sat down, after a slight squabble over the chairs; Philomène and Florence insisted that Solange, whom they both thought too thin, sit closest to the fire. "Before Madame died, she told me to come whenever I liked and check on things."

"She wouldn't mind us being here?" Philomène asked. "In the evening?"

"Oh, no," Solange replied. "Plus, she was a great card player."

"And her son?" Florence asked. "When is he coming home?"

"Not in the near future," Solange said. "He didn't even come at Christmas."

"Perhaps he owns a business that's very busy over the *holidays*," Philomène said, careful not to say Christmas, as she had read in *Madame Figaro* that it was no longer politically correct.

Florence snorted. "Like a candy shop? One doesn't emigrate all the way to Australia to sell licorices."

Solange said, "At any rate, once his maman died he should have been on the first plane back, to pay his respects."

"I agree," Philomène said.

"Are we going to play sometime this evening?" Florence asked, with mounting frustration in her voice. "Let's cut for dealer."

They drew cards, each one thankful that they didn't have to speak of Mme de Montbarbon or her son any longer. Philomène drew the lowest card, so she began shuffling and dealing out.

"I'll just pop into the kitchen and bring out some drinks," Solange said. "Then after a few rounds we'll break for something to eat." She scurried away. By the time the cards were dealt, she was back carrying a tray with three small wineglasses and a bottle of golden-colored Muscadet sweet wine. She set the tray on a small side table and poured out three glasses. "To Mme de Montbarbon," she said, holding her glass up above the table. They toasted.

Philomène said, "Solange, is there any news on the break-in?"

"No, it's a complete mystery."

"The robbers only took porcelain, right?" Florence asked. She quickly added, "I read it in the paper." She didn't want them to think that she had firsthand news from her son-in-law. That wouldn't be appropriate. Although with the last case she had been a big help to Antoine Verlaque, even if he hadn't said so in so many words.

"And they didn't bother with these fine paintings," Solange said, gesturing to the Corot.

"Jewels?" Philomène asked, hoping for some detailed descriptions.

Solange shook her head. "Mme de Montbarbon didn't care for them. Any jewels of value she willed to her granddaughters. I saw her give them to her son during his last visit."

"That's very odd," Philomène agreed. "I wonder if . . ."

"Are we playing cards or aren't we?" Florence asked.

"Oh, so you have a good hand?" Philomène teased, feeling brazen. Perhaps it was the wine.

"She's bluffing," Solange said.

"*Mais alors!*" Florence exclaimed. She leaned forward, ready to squash them with her near-perfect cards, when a loud thump sounded from far off in the apartment.

Philomène looked at Solange. "Does the apartment always make strange noises?" Her apartment—about the same age but of course not as grand—did, especially at night.

"No, not usually," Solange said. The sound came again. She got up slowly.

"Careful, Solange," Florence said. "We'll come with you."

"It's probably nothing," Solange said, realizing that she was whispering.

"Who has a cell phone?" Philomène whispered. "I left mine at home."

"Mine's in the kitchen," Solange said. She then realized that once again she had left the kitchen window open a tiny bit, to air out the room. "And I'm not sure that the landline works here anymore."

"I have mine in my purse," Florence said. "But let's not jump to any conclusions. We don't want to bother the police because of a little noise."

The others nodded, knowing that Florence knew about police matters, given that her son-in-law was Aix's magistrate. "It may be a cat," Solange said. "I left the kitchen window open, I'm afraid."

"Oh, for heaven's sake," said Florence. "Let's go."

Philomène turned around and picked up the fire poker.

They walked in single file slowly through the grand salon and out into a hallway. All was silent. Solange pointed to a closed door. "The kitchen," she whispered. She quickly opened the door. As she did, Florence and Philomène jumped inside the kitchen *as if they were the police*, Solange would tell her husband later that evening. They looked around the room and saw that the window was now fully open. Below it, on the wall, were fresh scuff marks.

Solange reached to her left and plucked a small key, one of many, off a key rack in the shape of a fish. She had given the key rack to Mme de Montbarbon as a gift, and had been proud to see it used and hanging in the kitchen. She held up the key. Philomène gave her a thumbs-up.

"Where are the bedrooms?" Florence whispered.

"Back down another hallway," Solange said.

"They've come back for the jewels," Philomène said. She gripped the fire poker.

"But I told you, there are no jewels here," Solange protested.

"My phone," Florence said. "It's back in the games room."

"You didn't bring it?" hissed Solange.

"You go and call the police," Philomène said. "And Solange and I will tackle them."

Solange looked at Philomène in shock, but then slowly nodded in agreement. It had been her idea to come here this evening, and she couldn't back out like a chicken now. She had to see it through. "Good plan," she said.

Florence grabbed their arms and said, "Good luck!" She left, and Philomène and Solange walked the other way, Solange opening a door onto a long dark hallway. She motioned to the light switch and looked at Philomène, who shook her head. They walked on toward the master bedroom, feeling their way along the cold walls, Solange leading the way. They heard a scuffle and voices coming from one of the rooms, stopped, looked at each other, now accustomed to the darkness, and carried on. Solange held the key up in the air in front of her, as if it were guiding them. A magic key. She just hoped she had picked the right one.

They inched down the hallway and came to the last door on the right. Another thump sounded from inside the room. Solange looked at Philomène, who nodded, and she quickly inserted the key into the lock, turning it once to the right to lock it. She was thankful that these old apartments always had doors that could be locked from inside or out; her own did as well.

"We've got you trapped!" Philomène cried out.

"*Putain!*" a male voice cried out.

"*Merde!*" shouted another.

Philomène shook her head in disgust. Just the kind of cuss words she was expecting to hear. She added, "The police are on their way!"

One of the thieves tried turning the doorknob, but it wouldn't budge.

"And we're heavily armed!" Philomène cried, holding up the poker. "I forgot to tell you that!"

Florence, who was now standing beside them, added, "My son-in-law will throw you both in the slammer!" She looked at the other two women, pleased. The men were now pounding on the door, trying to break it down. The women instinctively moved back, cowering together with their backs against the wall.

Solange said, "I think I'm going to faint."

"Don't quit on us now," Philomène said.

Just when the door was starting to come off its hinges, the doorbell rang. Florence ran up the hall and returned with two police officers. She was disappointed; she had specifically demanded for the magistrate or the commissioner, and instead here were a woman and a young man who looked like he had just graduated from the police academy. "Thank God!" Solange said. Philomène had to hold Solange back from hugging the officers.

"Police!" the female officer cried out in such a strong and affirmative voice that Florence was forced to take a step back. Her ears were sensitive to loud noises.

"Go into the living room, *please*, ladies," the young male officer instructed.

The three women walked as quickly as they could up the hall and through the grand salon until they found the games room and collapsed into armchairs by the fire, which by now had gone out. They could hear the two young thieves complaining loudly and the officers yelling out demands, and then the footsteps of all four of them as they left the apartment. The front door slammed. The women looked at one another in puzzlement and wonder. Was it all over? Weren't they going to be debriefed? They had so many important details to add.

Florence slowly got up and poured them each a full glass of Muscadet. It was warm now, but none of them noticed or cared. They sat, drinking and staring at the embers in the fireplace. Philomène was disappointed that they hadn't eaten her treats, but she was relieved that she wouldn't have to eat the supermarket cheese. Solange remembered that she should go and close the kitchen window, but she was too tired. Surely no one else would break in now. Florence looked at the painting, sad that it wasn't a different Corot, one of his views of Rome, for example.

"*Bonsoir, mesdames*," Bruno Paulik said as he walked into the room. Florence saw from the clock on the mantel that only ten minutes had gone by since the police left with the thieves; it seemed much longer. They looked up at Paulik, too tired to stand to properly greet him. He smiled and gestured for them to stay seated, pulling up one of the bridge chairs. "I was in the vicinity and got a call from headquarters."

Florence managed a smile that her demands had been met. Paulik looked at the women and saw that Philomène had a fire poker in her right hand. Philomène saw his gaze and set the poker down on the floor. "I'm glad you didn't have to use that, Madame Joubert." He remembered having met Philomène downtown a few times. She was usually nosing around one of their investigations, and she lived in the same building as France Dubois.

"The same thieves?" Solange asked, her voice cracking. "As the other break-in here?"

"Indeed," Paulik answered. "The same two young men who broke in here a few weeks ago. Well done, ladies. They quickly confessed in the police car, in exchange for information; I do believe they're somehow connected with the museum theft. When I know more, tomorrow, no doubt, I'll tell you all I know. You'll have to come in and give statements, too, but that can also wait until tomorrow."

"Thank you, Commissioner," Philomène said, slightly slurring her words. Paulik saw the empty Muscadet bottle and tried not to grin.

"Should we say tomorrow morning eleven o'clock at the Palais de Justice?" he asked.

"Sure," Florence said.

Paulik looked down and studied his hands, collecting himself, worried they could see him grinning. He stood up. "I have a car outside, ready to drive you all home." The women began to protest, which he had expected they would, being the excellent sort of women they were. But he was firm and they silently followed him out of the apartment and into the car.

Chapter Twenty-five

Tuesday, May 1

At the same time that Philomène Joubert was looking at the Corot, Marine Bonnet and Antoine Verlaque were driving along the Corniche Kennedy. Marine held firmly in her hands a small piece of paper with an address jotted down on it. She looked out of the window to her right, where the Mediterranean was spread out, flat as a sheet of glass. Verlaque drove, making comments from time to time about the ineptitude of other drivers. The traffic soon brought them to a stop, as it often did in Marseille, especially on the scenic coastal road. They sat in silence, watching people walk, jog, run, bicycle along the Corniche's winding sidewalk before the sun set. "We're getting close," she said, looking at the buildings to her left. "It's number 219. I'll drive home if you want. Béatrice and Daniel will have good wines."

"Surely you can have a bit of champagne?" Verlaque suggested.

Marine shook her head. "Nah. I don't feel like it. It doesn't feel right. . . . It's hard to explain." She broke into a wide smile. "It's so exciting, Antoine! A little person will soon be with us, sharing our life."

"Here we are, 219!" Verlaque said, turning the car into a steep narrow driveway squeezed between a pharmacy and a bar. He realized he had cut off Marine's enthusiastic exclamation and had a lump in his throat. The driveway got steeper as they inched along. Thick stone walls almost brushed the sides of his car and he felt his stomach muscles tightening.

"This is gorgeous," Marine said, craning her neck so that she could just barely see the tops of the stone walls, graced now and then with flowering plants. They turned a corner and the drive got even steeper and narrower until they came to an opening. Marine said, "Stop here, at this small parking lot. Béatrice said to park here."

Verlaque pulled the car next to a new BMW. A two-car garage, its doors closed, stood at the far end. They got out of the car, Marine reaching for her purse and their gift from the back seat. Verlaque looked up and saw another steep hill, dotted with olive and cypress trees. Steps zigzagged up the hill, through the gardens. "Did Béatrice mention the steps?" he asked.

Marine smiled, taking his arm. "Yes, but she also told me about the elevator."

"An elevator? Excellent!" Verlaque's mood immediately improved. He'd heard stories about these grand Corniche homes, many with private elevators. At the top of the hill, where the view was best, there was rarely room to park or to turn cars around. Every available square foot was given to the house, with a few feet left over for the inevitable swimming pool.

"There's the elevator," Marine said, pointing. "Around the corner, out of the view."

"How nice."

"Stop it, Antoine. You were the one who wanted this dinner to happen."

"I'll be good, I promise."

A few minutes later they were inside *chez les Louron*. Verlaque's immediate impression was one of disappointment; the outside of the house had been promising, Italianate in style, painted a soft pink, with arches forming a loggia that overlooked a small manicured garden. But inside it was cold. Too much gray and the furniture too new. Everything matched. He tried to smile, as Marine did naturally, and accepted the glass of champagne that Daniel Louron handed him. "A Reserve 2003," Daniel said. "Harder and harder to find."

"*Merci*," Verlaque replied. Béatrice found Marine a glass of juice and Daniel served the other two guests more champagne. Verlaque looked around the vast high-ceilinged living room, which was furnished with two huge sofas in white and black leather and glass tables dotted around the room. The room was so big that it looked like the Lourons had had trouble furnishing it. He didn't like the art on the walls, the sort of garish-colored abstracts purchased over the internet.

Verlaque and Marine sat down awkwardly; the sofas were spread so far apart that it was difficult to hear one another. How he wished he was at home alone with Marine or squashed into

Jean-Marc's apartment with his cigar friends. He was told that the other couple, a husband and wife both in their mid-fifties, worked for the new mayor with Daniel Louron. They were the ones who had arrived in the BMW. Béatrice floated around, quickly serving people aperitifs. She seemed uneasy, or even unhappy, to Verlaque.

"Do you also work at the mayor's office?" Verlaque asked Béatrice, taking advantage of the fact that she had sat down beside him for a few minutes.

"No," she replied. "I, too, am a lawyer, but I have a private practice on the rue Paradis." Before he could ask anything else, she quickly said, "Marine was the girl we all admired in school." She looked over at Marine and smiled sweetly.

"I can imagine. She's a wonderful person."

"How lucky you both are," Béatrice began, but then shot to her feet when she saw her husband looking at her. "Dinner's ready," she announced. "Bring your champagne glasses, as there will be, knowing Daniel, more at the end of the meal."

They were ushered into a large dining room, also furnished in black leather and glass. Béatrice directed them to their assigned places. A large oil painting of a stylized naked woman graced the far wall and Verlaque was relieved that he didn't have to look at it. He was placed beside the wife of the other couple, whom he learned was the communications director for the city. For the life of him he couldn't remember her name, although they had just been introduced.

Pouring the woman a glass of water, Verlaque said, "The celebration of Marseille as the European City of Culture certainly was a huge success."

"Thank you, although that was before my time, with the previous mayor," she replied, leaning back so that Béatrice could place before her a small plate of avocado and shrimp—a dish Verlaque detested as it reminded him of his mother, who couldn't cook.

"Oh, I see," said Verlaque. "Where were you before?"

She named a large Parisian publicity company with offices at the top of the Champs-Élysées. He knew it well; on the ground floor were a quite good Michelin-starred restaurant and a fine cigar shop. "Do you miss Paris?"

"Not at all! Marseille has the sea . . ." She made a sweeping gesture with her hand toward the large windows, where, somewhere below them, was the Mediterranean.

Verlaque smiled politely, knowing that living in Marseille with a lot of money was a very different life than most Marseillais experienced. He decided he might as well keep asking her questions, as he knew that she wasn't interested in him. "And what's in store for Marseille in the near future?"

"We are excited about the Mucem and the idea of promoting Marseille as a place to visit as a tourist."

"Yes, the new museum is gorgeous," Verlaque agreed. "It was sorely needed. But there are other, smaller museums in the city . . ."

But his attempt to get her talking about the Musée Cavasino was cut short by Daniel Louron, who interrupted to say, "Antoine, try a bit of this white Bordeaux with the avocado."

"It's hard to find?" Verlaque asked.

"Indeed it is, but I know the winemaker."

The BMW wife began a conversation with Daniel about their sailboats and the docking fees, so Verlaque busied himself with the shrimp, which hadn't been deveined. It turned his stomach. He didn't like the wine, either—too sharp and mineral, as if he were drinking from a tin can. He much preferred the rich round whites from Burgundy.

To his relief, there was a lull in the sailboat conversation, and Marine and Béatrice began telling stories of their adventures as young schoolgirls. In no time, Marine had all of them laughing over a story about the school's librarian, a nun whom they secretly called Sister Bulldog. Bulldog wouldn't allow any talking in the school's library, but she loved to share slightly risqué jokes with her fellow nuns, which the girls could all hear as Bulldog was hard of hearing and spoke too loudly. Verlaque smiled, proud that Marine had managed to break some of the ice in the cold room.

"Where did you go to school, Antoine?" Daniel asked.

"Boarding school, outside of Paris."

"Oh, that's so sad," Béatrice blurted out. "I'm sorry," she quickly said, putting her hand up to her mouth.

"Not at all," Verlaque said. "No worries." He liked Béatrice Louron, with her Mme Bovary sadness. "It wasn't that bad. I made friends, played lots of rugby, and on the whole the teachers were top-notch."

The BMW couple began complaining about Marseille's public schools—they had three children—and Verlaque saw Béatrice's face cloud over as she attempted to listen. Verlaque asked Daniel about the wine, feigning his enjoyment of it. Marine politely listened to the school debate; their child wouldn't be attending school in Marseille, but it could help her understand the national educational system. And she knew that Antoine was already fretting about schools. He hadn't said so out loud, but he asked friends and acquaintances about the best schools in Aix whenever he got the chance. She watched Daniel trying to impress Antoine with his wine knowledge. Daniel was intimidated, and impressed, by having a magistrate at his table, and it showed.

"Marine, would you mind coming into the kitchen with me?" Béatrice whispered.

"Not at all," Marine said, quickly setting her napkin aside and getting up.

"I'm afraid your husband isn't enjoying himself," Béatrice said once the women were in the immaculate kitchen.

"It's not that," Marine lied. "It's just that Antoine has a lot on his mind right now. A museum that's been robbed of its contents and now a murder."

"Oh, yes, I know about that. I've been waiting for the police to come to my office to ask questions."

"Pardon me? Did you know Aurélien Lopez?"

"He was a client," Béatrice said, putting on extra-large oven mittens in the shape of lambs, which Marine thought funny combined with Béatrice's very expensive little black dress and Cartier watch. Béatrice pulled a hot dish out of the oven and set it down on a trivet. "Gratin dauphinois," she explained. "My grandmother's recipe." She stared at Marine and sighed. "How lucky you are, Marine."

Marine looked confused. "We're all fortunate . . ."

"No, I mean your baby. We've been trying for years, and Daniel doesn't want to adopt."

"I'm so sorry," Marine said, putting her hand on Béatrice's shoulder.

Béatrice shook her head and body and smiled in a theatrical

kind of way. "Enough of my woes, especially when one of my clients has been murdered."

"Did Lopez say anything to you? Was he worried about something?"

"Money," Béatrice replied. "Aurélien was being sued by the city. He'd built an addition onto his house in Pointe Rouge without permits, thinking he could get away with it."

"Don't most people? Get away with it, I mean."

"Of course they do," Béatrice said, smiling. "This is Marseille." She lowered her voice and went on. "But Aurélien was vocal about his dislike of the current mayor."

"Ah, that wouldn't help."

"Not at all." Béatrice froze as Daniel walked into the kitchen and picked up two already-opened bottles of red wine that were sitting on the counter. "Don't let Béatrice get you down, Marine," he said, throwing his wife a parting glance.

Marine wanted to say "On the contrary," but she thought it best to stay silent. Sometimes no reply was just as powerful. Once Daniel was gone she said, "I would have assumed Lopez was on good terms with the mayor. I read about the joint museum project with our Musée Quentin-Savary in Aix. With the promise of a harborside location."

"Ah, that was the previous mayor. This one doesn't care for the idea. Too complicated dealing with the Aix snobs, he says. No offense."

Marine laughed. "None taken. I know that's what the Marseillais think of us."

"But the real reason the offer is off is that this mayor has given that location to someone else," Béatrice said. "The sailing club."

"Poor Lopez, then."

"Yes, it's very sad, especially since his money problems had just been resolved."

"Oh?"

"He told me that he was coming into some money—a lot—that would take care of his debts." Béatrice picked up the gratin. "Would you mind following with the roast beef?"

"Not at all," Marine said. She quickly asked, "Do you know where Lopez's new fortune came from?"

Béatrice said, "Yes, he did tell me. He had just sold some antique porcelain given to him by an aunt." She turned around to face Marine as she opened the swinging kitchen door with her hip and said, "Crazy, eh?"

Chapter Twenty-six

✦

Wednesday, May 2

Verlaque and Paulik met for coffee in Verlaque's office at 9:00 a.m., but it wasn't until thirty minutes after that that the coffee got made. Paulik had his boss spellbound over the "caper"—as Verlaque's mother-in-law had referred to it—the previous evening. Verlaque sat behind his desk, unable to move, aware of the fact that at times his mouth was hanging open, something he detested. "My evening at a pretentious party in Marseille is nothing in comparison. Dull, even," he said when Paulik had finished. Verlaque went on to describe the party, and the information that Marine had obtained from Béatrice Louron, but even as he was speaking he couldn't stop thinking about the three elderly women and how terribly wrong things could have gone. He got up to make the coffee. "When did the thieves confess?" he asked, changing the subject back to the fumbled robbery. "Back here?"

"No way," Paulik said, laughing. "In the car. They're just young punks from Jas de Bouffan. They're still in high school. Lopez hired them by hanging around outside the grocery store. I'm having Lopez's house and warehouse searched again."

"Can your officers keep all the ceramics straight? The plates taken from Mme Montbarbon's apartment had Brazilian flora and fauna on them," Verlaque said.

"Yes, I've had to put up a chart with drawings in the squad room. The Brazilian plates from the Montbarbon estate; the Napoleon plates that Achille was coveting, that we now know are worth a fortune; and all of the plates missing from the museum itself, namely the châteaux set and the fruit set. Schoelcher did the drawings with some colored markers."

"He did? A man of many talents."

Paulik asked, "Could Lopez have solved his debt simply by selling the Brazilian plates?"

"I doubt it. And so I think Lopez was connected to the museum break-in," Verlaque said as he made two espressos, "which is why he told his lawyer that he'd come into a lot of money. He might not have physically done it, but he was involved. He was murdered for it. But by whom?"

"A greedy partner in crime?" Paulik suggested. "Who wanted everything for himself?"

"Or herself?" Verlaque said. "That's all I can come up with, too." He carried the coffee cups across the room and handed one to Paulik, taking the other with him as he sat down behind his desk. "Or was he killed for love?"

"Always a popular motive for murder. But I don't think that Lopez had a love interest. He was a loner."

"None of his neighbors had ever seen him with a woman or a man?"

"No. They told my officers that he came home alone every evening."

"Too bad Lopez didn't have long hair."

"I beg your pardon?" Paulik asked.

"That CCTV footage."

"Oh, right. Gilbert at the wheel. His accomplice." Paulik set his cup down and looked at the judge. "And Mlle Blay?"

Verlaque looked at his watch. "She should be here soon."

"No, I mean, does she have long hair?"

"Yes, she does." He got up and walked around his desk. "I think we both need more coffee."

"Yeah, we're a bit foggy. I was rounding up senior citizens and you were stuck at that dreadful Marseillais party. Funny how the Marseillais can be so snooty, when they're always saying that about us."

"I think we still win," Verlaque said. He didn't imagine that Paulik, who lived in the countryside, his old house surrounded by vines, was ever invited to such horribly stiff parties in Aix. Hélène, Paulik's wife, was a winemaker and their parties were always fun. No snootiness at all.

Paulik's phone beeped and he pulled it out of his pocket, reading the message. "That was from Sophie Goulin," he said, putting the phone back into his pocket. "She's confirmed Marie-Claire Blay's alibi for the weekend of the museum theft. Completely sound."

Verlaque looked up, surprised. "It was checked before, right? She was a notorious art thief."

"Yes, but I didn't have the details," said Paulik, annoyed at himself that he hadn't prodded Goulin more. He added, "Two other well-known art thieves are still in prison, and the third is ill, at home in Switzerland."

"Switzerland. Figures. He must have done well. So where was Mlle Blay that weekend?"

"Le Salon de L'agriculture."

"The big agricultural fair in Paris?"

"Yes. Blay was there all weekend; she had a stand with some of her prize buffalo. Officer Goulin checked out her hotel, too, near the Porte de Versailles, where the fair was held. She was there three nights."

"I went once, with my grandparents," Verlaque said, sitting down. "The cows were so impressive. Huge."

"And the crowds."

"Yes, but it was a friendly crowd. It didn't bother me, whereas it does in an airport or even in a museum." He smiled, thinking of Charles and Emmeline, and how much they had done for him and Sébastien. "We had to pull my grandfather away from the food hall." He was about to ask Paulik something about the cows when his phone buzzed. "*Oui, France?*" he answered. There was a pause. "*Merci,*" he said, hanging up. "Mlle Blay is here," he told Paulik.

Both men got to their feet as France Dubois opened the door and Marie-Claire Blay walked in, looking much different than she had on her farm in the Ardèche. Her long hair was pulled up into a bun and she wore red lipstick that matched her linen jacket and a series of long necklaces made out of multicolored glass beads. She walked across the room and shook their hands as if she were on a job interview. Verlaque introduced her to Paulik and she sat down beside him. "Coffee?" Verlaque asked.

"No, thank you," she answered. "I drank a thermos of the stuff in the car."

"We were just talking about the agriculture fair in Paris," Paulik said.

"I was there this year," Mlle Blay said.

"We know," he said, looking at Verlaque.

She didn't flinch, or she hid it well. "There was a record turnout," she said. "Including two presidential hopefuls and their entourages."

"Listen," Verlaque said. "I wasn't entirely truthful on the phone with you."

"*Ah, bon?*"

"I asked you here under false pretenses," he admitted. "But I *would* like you to look at those paintings in Gilbert Quentin-Savary's apartment that I told you about on the telephone . . ."

"But now that I have a solid alibi, I'm in the clear?"

Verlaque smiled. "Something like that."

She shifted slightly in her chair. "In the car, with all that coffee, I decided there's something I should tell you, too."

Paulik wondered if she had decided to be honest in the car, as she said, or just now, helped by the fact that they had checked her alibi and told her so.

"It's about Aurélien Lopez," she said. "I knew him."

Verlaque pushed the newspaper photo across the desk to her in response. She picked it up and looked at it. "That's why you called me here."

"Yes."

"I remember that evening," she said. "It was at an antiques dealer's party."

"You were friends?"

"Yes, we were." She then saw Verlaque's right eyebrow rise and she laughed. "Just friends, mind you. I don't think that Aurélien was interested in sex with anyone. And I prefer women."

"Had you any recent contact with Lopez?" Paulik asked.

"Yes, that's what I wanted to tell you. He called me up a few months ago out of the blue. He had a project, one that he needed my help with."

"Stealing?" Verlaque asked.

"Of course. But I told him I was finished with all that." She looked at Verlaque, and then at Paulik, and said, "Which is absolutely true. I'm so happy where I am right now. In all aspects of my life. So I told him no way."

"Do you know what kind of heist Lopez had in mind?" Paulik asked.

"Yes and no," Mlle Blay replied. "I know the address, because he blurted it out straightaway as he wanted me to check it out or be impressed. I grabbed a pen and jotted it down. It's at number 16 rue Mistral."

"Musée Quentin-Savary," Verlaque said.

She shrugged. "And I don't know what Aurélien was after, but he did say 'it' once or twice."

"As if he was after only one object?"

"Yes. So not the entire museum," she said. "But I may have misunderstood or he may have changed his mind. But he did say that the object was priceless."

Verlaque sat back and asked, "So not the Ziem painting."

"He told me about that painting of Venice, as I'm a big Ziem fan," she said. "He didn't care for it and even thought it might be a fake. So, no, he wasn't interested in the Ziem painting."

"And Lopez never mentioned the museum by name?"

"No."

"Could he have been referring to an apartment at that address? Gilbert's apartment, for example?"

"He may have," she replied. "He hated Gilbert, by the way. But what could Gilbert possibly have worth stealing?"

"I was hoping you could tell us," Verlaque said. "If we took you to Gilbert's apartment."

"We also have some small-time thieves whom we caught last night," Paulik said, trying to get the image of Philomène Joubert holding a poker out of his head, "and they confessed that Lopez hired them to rob the apartment of a dying noblewoman here in Aix. They stole a set of Sèvres porcelain."

"Porcelain isn't my specialty, but Aurélien loved it."

"But paintings you do know," Verlaque said.

"Does Gilbert own a valuable painting?" she asked. "I can't imagine he would. He was always complaining about his meager—as he called it—inheritance. That's one of the things that infuriated Aurélien, who came from a mining family in Picardy and worked his way up in the museum world. But I think I see your train of thought: that the museum was emptied just to get at one object, perhaps not even in the museum but *chez* Gilbert. I'd be happy to help. It's the least I can do."

"The thing is, I don't want Gilbert to know," Verlaque said.

Both Paulik and Blay looked at him, surprised. "Why not?" she asked.

"I have my reasons, even if now I'm fairly certain that Lopez was behind everything."

"I doubt he was," Mlle Blay said. "Aurélien may have had your noblewoman's home robbed, but an entire museum? I don't see him capable of it. He was a nervous colt. Have you found anything in his house or office linking him to the crime?"

Verlaque shifted, half wishing Mlle Blay worked with them full time. "No. Not yet."

"And how am I supposed to get into Gilbert's apartment?" Verlaque raised an eyebrow and she laughed. "Right, okay. I get it. I suppose it will be easier than an art gallery or museum. It will be like old times."

"You won't even have to break in," Verlaque said. "We have a key for his apartment. The museum's secretary gave it to us; it was at the museum in case of an emergency."

"Do you want *me* to get Gilbert away from his apartment tonight?" Paulik asked.

"I was hoping you could," Verlaque said. "Invent a board meeting or something."

Chapter Twenty-seven

Wednesday, May 2

Verlaque preferred to walk to the hospital. It was faster: in the time it took him to get his car out of the underground garage and drive around the hospital parking lot looking for an available spot he could be there on foot. Plus by walking he could rationalize the second helping of the lamb dinner that Marine had promised for that evening.

As he crossed the ring road and headed north up the avenue Pasteur, he thought about the questions he would ask Achille Formentin, who was now awake and slowly recovering: Did he always make it a habit of taking pieces from the museum back to his apartment? And how well was he acquainted with Aurélien Lopez?

Fifteen minutes later Verlaque was being let into Achille

Formentin's hospital room, after having said hello to the police officer who was sitting outside the room looking surprisingly alert despite his boring task. What Verlaque didn't know was that the nurses had taken a liking to Officer Lapointe's boyish good looks and polite manners, and were supplying him not only with bottomless cups of coffee but also sugary treats, either made at home or purchased at a nearby patisserie.

"Good afternoon, M Formentin," Verlaque said when he saw Achille half sitting up, resting on several pillows.

"*Juge*," Formentin mumbled as he struggled to sit up a few more inches.

Verlaque motioned with his hand for him not to bother, and he pulled up a chair beside the bed. "How are you feeling?"

"A giant headache."

Verlaque smiled. "You were lucky, nevertheless."

"So I'm told."

"Do you remember anything from that night?"

Formentin closed his eyes. "Nothing."

"Do you remember why you were there?" Verlaque asked.

"I go at night, ever since the robbery, just to check on things. That must have been why I was there."

"Check on things? Nothing was in the museum."

Formentin shifted, trying to get comfortable. He took a sip of water before replying to Verlaque's comment. "She was hiding something. . . ."

"Mme Devaux?"

"Yes." Formentin paused, then continued, "Upstairs, in the office. A file she was working on. I went to find it."

"Why didn't you just question her about it?"

Formentin blushed and closed his eyes.

Verlaque, worried that Formentin was quickly tiring, changed the direction of his questions. "So you don't remember seeing anyone there that night?"

"No. I remember waking up here. That's all."

On his walk to the hospital Verlaque had tried to figure out how to ask the next question, but he now realized there was no easy way to do so. "M Formentin," he slowly began, "we know that from time to time you borrow certain pieces from the museum to use in your home . . ."

Formentin winced, either from the pain or the realization that he'd been found out, or both. He said, "I don't use them, I look at them."

"Very well," Verlaque said. "It's not anything that's worrying me at the moment. But given that you enjoy certain pieces so much, I do have to ask you if you are certain that you in no way took part in the emptying of the museum."

Now the museum director stared at the judge in horror. "Absolutely not!"

A nurse walked in and came to Formentin's side, checking the monitor. She caught Verlaque's eye and held up a hand with her fingers spread out, signaling that he had five more minutes. When she left, Verlaque waited a minute, hoping Formentin would reflect on his questions.

Verlaque finally asked, "And you don't know who did organize the theft or why?"

Formentin shook his head.

"Before you were hit, do you remember anything?" Verlaque pressed. "Something unusual or out of place?"

Formentin sighed and sank back into the pillows. "Everything gone," he mumbled.

"Yes . . ."

"Even the flowers . . ."

Verlaque leaned forward. "Even the flowers, M Formentin?"

But Formentin had closed his eyes and Verlaque could hear the slow rhythmic breathing of someone asleep.

By the time Verlaque returned home, it was almost 7:00 p.m. Before going upstairs, he went down into the basement and opened their cellar with a small key that he now carried in his wallet to prevent having to go up and down from their fourth-floor apartment more than once. He turned on the light and stepped inside, reaching to his right to pull out a bottle from a rack that held well over one hundred bottles. Marine had helped him organize the wine cellar, beginning by buying used stainless-steel wine racks and hand-writing tags to identify wine regions. Both were a big improvement over the stacks of cardboard boxes that had stored the wine before her arrival in Verlaque's life. He turned the bottle over in his hand and saw that it was exactly the one he had been thinking of: a red Châteauneuf-du-Pape from 2001.

When he got up to the third floor he could already smell food cooking, and as he got closer to their door the smell got stronger. "*Bonsoir!*" he called out as he opened the door and stepped into their apartment. There was a bouquet of fresh lilacs on the console in the entryway, but their fragrance was temporarily overpowered. "The lamb smells amazing!" he said.

"I'm in the kitchen!" Marine answered.

"Oh, you come carrying wine!" a woman's voice rang out as Verlaque walked into the kitchen. "I hope you have more."

"Rebecca!" Verlaque said, seeing his father's partner. He set the bottle down and crossed the room, giving her a quick hug and the *bises*. "What a surprise . . ."

"I hope it's a good one," he heard his father say. Verlaque swung around as his father entered the room.

"*Mais oui!*" Verlaque insisted.

"Rebecca telephoned me a few days ago," Marine quickly explained. "We thought we'd surprise you." She looked at Verlaque and gave him a quick wink, acknowledging that although her husband detested surprises, she hoped he would allow this one.

"Our visit is a little out of the blue," Rebecca said. "We've rented a car and are taking the ferry to Sardinia tomorrow, from Toulon."

"The joys of retirement," M Verlaque said. Verlaque smiled and looked at his father, who had been retired from the family business for as long as Verlaque could remember, after having sold it to a multinational company in the early eighties. It was the longest retirement on record.

Rebecca crossed the room and put her arm through Marine's. "Let's go into the living room and I'll show you what I brought you from Paris."

Once the women had left, Verlaque busied himself with getting out a bottle of champagne from the small wine fridge.

"Can I help?" M Verlaque asked.

"The champagne flutes are in the cupboard right behind you," Verlaque said. "Thank you. Oh, and I'll grab some juice for Marine."

"Surely she can have a glass of champagne," M Verlaque said. "Your mother drank a little bit during her two pregnancies."

"I'm sure she did," Verlaque replied flatly. She and her needs had always come first, above the boys, above her husband, above everything else. Wanting to change the subject, he said, "You're looking well."

"Thank you," his father replied. "I feel good. Of course, dating a woman thirty years younger helps." He laughed awkwardly.

The laugh hadn't been necessary as they both knew that Rebecca Schultz was nothing like a young trophy wife, nor was she taking advantage of an older man's wealth and prestige. "When does Rebecca have to go back to Yale?" Verlaque asked.

"Ah, she's teaching during the fall semester," his father answered. "That's why we're getting some last-minute trips in."

"Won't you go, too?"

"Perhaps for a few weeks," M Verlaque replied. "But I like Paris, and to be honest a break will be good for us."

"Is anything wrong?" Verlaque asked, now alarmed. Rebecca brought out qualities—good ones—in the elder Verlaque that his son had never seen but always wished for.

"No, no, just, you know, absence makes the heart grow fonder kind of thing. We've been inseparable since that Cézanne case you had three years ago."

Verlaque nodded. Rebecca had been an invaluable aid as a Cézanne scholar during that case. He smiled, remembering the evening when he and his father had been crammed into the back of his father's chauffeured car, chasing a maniacal motorcycle driver through Paris, with Rebecca squeezed between them. The same Rebecca—who, had she not been an art historian, could probably have made millions modeling—had then fallen for his grumpy father.

"I think you're right, Father," Verlaque said. "You'll both be fine. The semester will fly by."

"And by Christmas we'll have a new family member." Verlaque thought he saw tears forming in the corners of his father's eyes.

"Let's join the ladies," Verlaque said, taking the champagne and juice as his father carried four flutes upside down by their stems.

In the living room Verlaque saw two bags from Tartine et Chocolat, the luxury children's clothing store. He tried not to cringe.

Rebecca saw his look and said, "Don't worry, Antoine, I didn't buy too many baby clothes. Yet."

They laughed as Verlaque opened the champagne. Marine unwrapped the gifts, which included a small cashmere blanket, the tiniest knit cap Verlaque had ever seen, and a pale yellow sweater. "All in gender-neutral colors," Rebecca said as Marine and Verlaque thanked her profusely. "Since we don't know the sex."

"It's a girl," Verlaque said, pouring out the champagne.

"What?" his father cried.

"Antoine's just guessing," Marine said, laughing. She threw her husband a confused look. This was the first time he had mentioned the baby's sex. Up until now he had just been obsessing about their education.

"How are things in quiet Aix?" Rebecca asked as Verlaque handed her a glass of champagne.

"Not so quiet, actually," he replied. "A small museum has been emptied of its contents, its director is in the hospital after having been attacked, and another museum director from Marseille was murdered in the now-empty museum."

Rebecca and the senior Verlaque stared at each other in disbelief. "What were the thieves after?" M Verlaque asked.

"We don't know yet. The museum owns nineteenth-century manuscripts, porcelain, and some rather unfashionable murky paintings that have been valued at almost nothing. And yet they took everything."

"They were after something," Rebecca said.

Verlaque nodded. "Something possibly priceless."

"You're probably well aware of that," Rebecca said. "I'm sorry."

Verlaque looked at Rebecca and suddenly realized he had a nineteenth-century painting expert right in front of him. "I do have a hunch," he said. "It has to do with a collection of dismal portraits that are hanging in the apartment of the last remaining member of the museum's founding family, a guy named Gilbert. I thought that perhaps one of them might be worth something . . . a lot, actually."

"Which one?" Rebecca asked, leaning forward.

"That's the problem," Verlaque said. "None of them stood out."

"You weren't there to look at those portraits," Marine said. "So naturally you didn't pay much attention to them."

Verlaque tried to smile at his wife's kindness. He continued, "For whatever reason, I think that Gilbert emptied the museum, perhaps to get ahold of a rather nice Ziem painting. But then after, completely by chance, he found out about the value of one of his own portraits." He paused, took a sip of wine while all eyes were on him, and then said, "It was Lopez who connected the dots, which was why he was killed. Lopez wanted to steal the portrait, and Gilbert found out about it, so Gilbert killed him." He thought of Mlle Blay; that's why Lopez had contacted her. To steal one of Gilbert's portraits, which may have been a Rembrandt for all he knew.

"Not a bad theory," his father said.

"Are the portraits late nineteenth century?" Rebecca asked, her eyes shining.

"No, earlier," Verlaque said.

"Not my territory," she said, disappointed. "Sorry." She finished her champagne and set down the glass.

"More?" Verlaque asked.

"No, thank you," she said. "I'll wait until dinner. Antoine, your theory reminds me of a story. Decades ago, a colleague at Yale had a surprise encounter with a Jackson Pollock painting in an old man's garage somewhere in Texas."

"The old man didn't know he had a Pollock?" Marine asked.

"Exactly," Rebecca said. "He had called an antiques dealer to help empty out his house as he was moving to a retirement home. The antiques dealer saw a signed basketball poster from the 1970s that he was really excited about, so he called in an expert to value it. The expert brought his summer student along—my colleague, who's now a renowned modernist—and they both saw the Pollock leaning up in the back of the garage behind the garbage cans. The old guy had won it in a poker game."

"It would have been hard to miss," Marine said, laughing. "Sorry, Antoine. I didn't mean to suggest you've missed something obvious."

Verlaque tried to laugh. "No offense taken. I'd recognize a

Pollock, too. But I'm afraid what we're looking for must be much smaller, if it is indeed one item."

That night, Verlaque dreamed that he was in their cellar, looking for another bottle of Châteauneuf-du-Pape, when he found an enormous Jackson Pollock painting hidden behind some plastic crates that contained Marine's old lecture notes. He struggled with the canvas, about four feet wide, finally managing to lift it up over the crates but knocking over a wine rack in the process. Five or six broken bottles lay at his feet, dark red wine streaming out of them onto the rough concrete floor. The painting was dirty and unsigned. He managed to carry it all the way to the Palais de Justice, passing Aixois in the street who jumped aside when they saw him, whispering among themselves. Once at work he gathered everyone around and proudly revealed his dusty treasure. But his colleagues looked at him with varying expressions of disbelief, pity, and embarrassment. Turning around, he saw that the painting was nothing more than a canvas whose surface had been splattered with a few colors of garish neon-colored paint. It had none of the finesse or rhythm of a Pollock. Plastered diagonally across the top left-hand corner was a foot-long red sticker and he blinked, puzzled as to how he could have missed seeing something so obvious. It read: PRICE SLASHED! LIQUIDATION SALE! 9,99 €!

Chapter Twenty-eight

Thursday, May 3

In a small office Patrice Roche sat staring at the screenshot of the stolen château plate and dialed the third number on the list. The webmaster from leboncoin had managed to get him the cell phone numbers of the four people who had contacted DJ Kool. The first two had given him no information; neither of them had been interested enough in the plate to follow up on the seller's refusal, by message, to lower the price. Neither had spoken with DJ Kool. Roche had been trying to speak to buyers three and four for ages now, without success, so he jumped when on the fifth ring someone answered. The voice on the other end of the phone was of an elderly woman whom he could barely hear. Twice he asked her to speak louder, before understanding that she lived in the countryside near Pau. "Did you speak to the seller on the telephone?" Roche asked.

"Who?"

"The seller," Roche continued, "the person selling the plate."

"Such a beautiful plate, wasn't it?"

"Yes, madame, it is. Tell me more about the seller. Man or woman?"

"A man," she said, her voice wobbling. "But it could have been a woman . . ."

"I beg your pardon?" Roche asked, rubbing his forehead.

"They had a soft voice. Very nice sounding it was."

"Where do they live?" Roche asked, realizing that he was almost yelling.

"Oh, they didn't say."

"Weren't you interested in buying the plate? Didn't you ask?"

"Now you've no need to speak so harshly with me, young man."

"What I mean is, how would you get the plate if, say, by chance, they lived far from Pau?"

"They could ship it."

Roche could hear her whispering to something and he realized it was a cat. Suddenly a purring sounded in the telephone. "Did he say anything at all? Anything that might tell you who he was or where he lived?" he asked. "He must have said something . . ."

"I have to go now," she said, her voice getting fainter. "I just don't understand why you have so many questions . . ."

"It's because I'm a police officer!" Roche yelled into the phone.

"I don't care if you're François Mitterrand come back from the dead!"

Roche heard the call end. He sat back, opened a box of aspirin, and took one with a huge gulp of water. He decided to give up on the old woman and try to call number four again. He dialed and was once again rewarded with an answer.

"*Oui?*" a male voice asked.

This time Roche got right to the point, explaining that he was a police officer from Aix-en-Provence trying to track down the stolen objects from a local museum.

"Oh, I see," the voice said. He paused, and for a moment Roche wondered if he, too, had hung up on him. But after a few seconds he gave Roche his name and address, in Geneva.

Roche quickly wrote down the information. "But your cell phone is a French number," he said.

"I have a chalet in Megève," the man explained. "This is the phone I use when I'm in France. I have a large antiques shop in Geneva and a very, very small apartment."

Roche pumped his fist in the air. "An antiques shop?"

"Yes, which is why I'll answer your questions as truthfully as I can. I recognized the plate right away; it's worth much more than a thousand euros. I didn't tell the seller that, of course."

"You spoke to the seller?"

"Not only did I speak to him," the antiques dealer said. "I met him."

The day flew by, but not in the way that Verlaque wanted it to. He spent most of the day in court or speaking to journalists. By 6:00 p.m. his normally deep voice was hoarse and, oddly, high-pitched. He dreaded how he had sounded, and looked, on national television. He remembered reading an article in *Le Monde* about one of his favorite actors who had walked out of a television interview, refusing to watch a five-second clip of his last film. "Can you imagine anything more dreadful," he had asked the *Le Monde* journalist a few days later, "pretending to be someone else and then watching yourself doing just that?"

France Dubois heard her boss trying to clear his throat and brought him a pot of his favorite tea, a smoky lapsang souchong. "All of France seems to be fascinated with the garbage-can case," she said as she set the teapot down on an old law textbook that had been relegated to the task of trivet. "My aunt even called me from northern France, which she never does."

Verlaque wearily looked up at France and tried to make out if she was at all saddened over the fact that she rarely heard from her only living relative. But he saw nothing revealing in the pale gray eyes of his over-qualified secretary as she stood at the foot of his desk. No, she was much too proud to be asking for pity, he thought. But at the same time she had let him know that she never heard from her aunt. He found that interesting.

"Would you like anything else?" she asked.

"No, thank you, France," he said. "A million thank-yous for making my favorite tea."

"How did it go?" Bruno Paulik asked as he walked in.

"I'll get another mug," France said, turning around and leaving the office.

"What kind of tea is it?"

"Souchong," said Verlaque.

Paulik wrinkled his nose in disgust. "Don't bother, France! But thanks. I'll make myself an espresso."

"All right," she said from the doorway. "I'm off to my Chinese class. Good evening."

"Have fun," Paulik said.

"Do you know," Verlaque said, his throat somewhat soothed by the tea, "I don't know a single word in Chinese."

"I know a couple of words," Paulik replied, "thanks to a kids' book we used to read Léa. So how was it today? Was the delivery guy charged?"

"No," Verlaque said. "I didn't see how someone could be charged with manslaughter for being lazy or exhausted, as was his case."

Paulik made a grumbling sound.

"I know," Verlaque said. "There's going to be hell to pay, especially with the press and general public." He ran his fingers through his hair. "How could this case have taken ahold of the country's imagination?"

Paulik said, "A delivery guy, who should have retired long ago but who desperately needs the money, skips his last delivery because he'll be late back to the warehouse and be docked a late fine, throws a small cardboard box in a garbage can. A lonely old Marseille widow who spends all day looking out of her window sees him do this, hears that there's some weight to the box, and after he's gone goes outside and grabs it out of the garbage, opens it, and finds a bag of dark red blood labeled for La Timone Hospital. She calls the police. How could that story *not* go viral?"

Verlaque winced.

Paulik put a demitasse under the nozzle of the espresso maker and continued speaking as the coffee slowly ran into the cup. "The blood, the rarest AB negative, was meant to help save a teenager who'd been shot in a drug war. He doesn't get the blood in time and dies."

"Since when is blood, a rare one at that, sent by a local delivery company?" Verlaque asked. "It's bad enough that we no longer go to bookstores or clothing shops, preferring to sit on our fat arses and order the stuff online, but *blood*? Why wasn't it sent in an ambulance?"

Paulik sipped his coffee and waited.

Verlaque went on. "Because the ambulance drivers were on strike!"

"You see?" Paulik asked. "This case has so many things going for it: retirement unfairness, drug wars, lonely old widows, and an inevitable French strike. I'm surprised the case hasn't had international attention."

"Don't say that too loudly."

"To make matters worse, Mlle Blay didn't find any treasures in Gilbert's apartment last night."

"The paintings?"

"Just as awful as you said," Paulik said. "She was impressed with your judgment."

Verlaque got up and opened a window. Paulik grinned, knowing the judge was going to smoke a cigar. Verlaque walked across the room, opened one of the glass doors to his bookcase, and selected a cigar out of a shiny walnut humidor. "Care for a drink?"

Paulik looked at his watch. "Sure, why not?"

"I have a Springbank here. I'm blazing outside my Islay comfort zone."

"Why? Where's it made?"

"In Argyll, just across the sound."

Paulik smiled. "Poor Roche is stuck in an office trying to contact those people who messaged our DJ Kool about the porcelain plate. Let's hope he soon has some answers."

"Like a name. The seller is in Paris, right?"

Paulik said, "The webmaster told Roche that he registered as a Paris client, but the location is easy to fabricate."

"Let's start looking for him in Aix-les-Bains and assume he has long hair."

"Even though Gilbert Quentin-Savary has an alibi and a collection of crappy paintings?"

"Yes," Verlaque said. "Where else could we start?"

"All right. I'll make a few phone calls to our colleagues up in Aix. The other Aix."

Verlaque took a sip of whisky and leaned back against the edge of the windowsill. He was finally beginning to feel normal. "I had about six and a half minutes with Achille Formentin yesterday."

"So what was he doing in the museum that night?"

"Trying to find out what Mme Devaux was up to."

"Did you tell him?"

"No. He was fading quickly. He blushed when I mentioned her name."

Paulik said, "Is he in love with her?"

Verlaque thought about the commissioner's comment. He had meant it as a joke, but what if Paulik was on to something? It would certainly shed some light on the case. Or confuse it even further. "And he said he took those plates home, quote, just to look at them, close quote. He mumbled some nonsense about everything being cleared out of the museum, including the flowers."

"Poor guy. Well, thanks for the drink. I'm off." Paulik got up and set his empty glass on Verlaque's desk.

"See you tomorrow," Verlaque said.

"I'm making dinner this evening," Verlaque said as he walked through their apartment door, kissing Marine and rubbing her stomach.

"That's good because I'm too tired."

He held up a bag from their favorite butcher. "Pepper steaks? You need the iron."

"You're probably right," Marine said as she walked toward the kitchen. "I'll pull up a stool and watch."

"How did the writing go today?" Verlaque asked. He unwrapped two thick marbled steaks and began rubbing them with coarse pepper.

Marine yawned. "When I embarked upon this dual biography of Sartre and de Beauvoir, I had no idea how long it would take."

"Good thing your publishers knew about that ahead of time and extended your contract without you having to ask for it."

"Yes, biographies take a notoriously long time to research and write. Some guy who wrote a biography on Flaubert took ten years."

Verlaque whistled. "Our kid would almost be in junior high school by then."

Marine laughed. "You are obsessed with our unborn child's education."

"Isn't that normal?"

"Yes, actually, it's a good thing to obsess about." She caressed her husband's leg with her foot.

Verlaque lit a gas burner and set a large frying pan on top before reaching over and opening a bottle of red wine that he had also bought on his way home.

"In answer to your question, the writing went well today," Marine said, picking an olive from a small bowl and popping it into her mouth. "I've advanced to 1944, when Sartre and eight resistance journalists got an all-paid trip to the United States to report on the American war effort."

"Oh, yeah," Verlaque said. "Sartre was oddly thrilled over that invitation, wasn't he?"

Marine laughed. "He told a colleague, 'Heck! I'll *run* over there!'"

Verlaque laughed, trying to imagine the short, pudgy philosopher running *anywhere*. He threw a generous amount of kosher salt into the frying pan, then added a tiny bit of olive oil and put in the two steaks.

Marine asked, "How did your day go?"

"All right," he said, sighing. He didn't bother telling her about his day in court. "I'm starting to dream about this museum case. Missing the details."

"That's normal. There's a whole museum missing. That's a lot of details."

"Yes, but I'm haunted that there's only one detail that's the key to this whole thing." He poured himself a glass of wine and took a sip. "It's just an average Côtes du Rhône," he said.

"Oh, so I'm not missing much, is that it?" Marine laughed and grabbed the bottle. "It's a Saint-Joseph!"

"I'm sorry." Verlaque grinned as he flipped the steaks and opened a cupboard, getting out a bottle of cheap cognac and a box of matches.

"I'll toss a salad," Marine said. "I think there's dressing left over from last night."

"Two more minutes and we're ready," he said as he cut two pieces of butter and placed a dab on each of the steaks. He then poured in some cognac and lit a match, throwing it into the pan and jumping back as the flames leaped up.

Marine squealed in delight. "I always love that bit!"

"Yes, and it always scares me. I'd make a terrible pyromaniac."

Marine wrapped her arms around his waist and kissed him. "But you do make a great pepper steak. Mmm, I can taste the wine on your lips." Verlaque kissed her back, running his hand through her curly hair.

"The steaks!" he suddenly shouted, turning toward the stove and lifting each steak out with a long fork. He set them on two plates and poured the flambéed cognac jus over them. "Could we eat on the terrace this evening? It's quite mild."

"Yes, let's."

"You just bring up the plates," he said. "I'll do the rest of the trips."

"I won't argue."

By the time Verlaque joined his wife on their rooftop terrace with the wine, water, glasses, and salad, the table was already set and lit by several candles. Marine stood at the edge of the terrace, looking at the cathedral's lit octagonal tower. "Do you think our child will love this view as much as we do?"

"Of course they will," Verlaque said, standing behind her with his arms around her stomach. "*Because* we do."

Marine turned around and kissed him. "You're right. The child will learn by our example."

"And by not being allowed video games."

"Completely agree. Even if they are ostracized by their peers . . . especially the boys."

Verlaque said, "The child will have to grow a thick skin."

"And now the steak is getting cold."

Thirty minutes later Marine leaned back and picked the last leaf of arugula off her plate and put it in her mouth. "I think that was the best steak I've ever had."

"Pan-fried pepper steak was my specialty back in my bachelor days."

She nodded, not caring to hear more about Antoine Verlaque's Parisian bachelor days, when he dated minor European nobility and the odd model here and there. "Don't forget we're invited to the Pauliks' tomorrow night for dinner," she said. "Hélène sent me a text message reminding me."

"Okay, thanks. I had forgotten." Then Verlaque looked at his watch and jumped up.

"What is it?" Marine asked.

"That antiques show is just starting on television! You know the one, where they go across France and people show up trying to get Granny's silver tea service evaluated by the antiques experts."

She laughed. "You're like an old woman watching that garbage! You don't even have any knickknacks."

"Yeah, but it's a riot. And besides, my grandparents' Normandy house is full of stuff, possibly some of it worth thousands."

"Thousands of pains in the rear end is more like it," Marine said, stacking their empty plates and carrying them down the stairs. "There's something to be said for having socialist parents who didn't buy anything for our house."

Verlaque nodded, resisting the urge to point out that Marine's parents did buy things for the house; unfortunately, they ordered all of their dull furnishings out of the Camif catalog, where civil servants had a discount. He turned on the television, rubbed his hands together, and sat down on the small sofa in their mezzanine.

From the living room Marine could hear the theme music to the show and her husband's laughter. "You realize that you're watching reality television!" she called up the stairs.

"It's funny and informative!"

"And that's just after saying you won't allow your future child to play video games."

"They're violent and addictive!"

"Oh, if it's funny, it's permitted," Marine said to herself, amused. She shrugged. "I'm okay with that." She sat down in her favorite armchair, kicked off her shoes, and picked up David Lodge's latest novel.

Chapter Twenty-nine

❧

Friday, May 4

Good morning, France," Verlaque said as he walked into the office. "Could you do me a favor?"

France Dubois looked up from her computer. "Sure."

"Oh, sorry, provided you're not too busy . . ."

"No, I'm just fending off journalists who keep trying to speak to you about the garbage-can case."

Verlaque winced. "Do you have to call it that?"

France giggled. "Sorry, it's what the press is calling it."

"You'd think they could come up with a more appropriate name."

"Like the Case of the Missing Blood?" she asked.

"Right! Or the Mysterious Discarded Parcel," he suggested. "They sound like Agatha Christie titles, don't they?"

"Yes. I devoured her books when I was young."

"Me, too." He smiled and headed to his office, amused by all of the hidden mysteries behind the demure France Dubois.

"*Monsieur le juge!*" France called out. "You haven't told me what my task is."

Verlaque reappeared in the doorway. "Sorry. Could you look up that antiques show that airs on France 3 and research the subjects of their past episodes—let's say, going back six months before the museum break-in?"

"Sure thing, as long as I don't have to watch it," she replied, turning around to face her computer. "Such garbage."

"You think so?" he asked innocently.

She made a snorting noise and then asked, "Am I looking for anything in particular?"

"That's the problem," he said. "No. Or let's just say I'll know it when I see it. At least, I hope so. Please jot down each evening's topic, because as I understand it each episode has a theme—by era, as in Empire, or Art Deco, or by subject, like classic cars." He coughed. "That's what I've heard, anyway."

She focused her eyes on her computer screen, trying to hide her grin. "I'll get right on it."

The setting sun shone on the south side of the mountain, changing its normally bright white limestone into a soft pink. Both driver and passenger smiled as their car inched up the gravel driveway that led to the Pauliks' stone farmhouse. "I love it here," Marine said. "This long narrow drive lined with olive trees . . ."

"And Mont Sainte-Victoire looming over us," Verlaque added, lowering his head so that he could see the mountain through the windshield. "Somehow, that gnarly white mountain isn't oppressive at this pink hour."

"No, it's protective."

"And there's where Valère's house was," Verlaque said, now looking to his right, past Marine. "It wasn't so long ago he was being chased by ghosts around the Bastide Blanche."

"There's a bulldozer. Do you see it?" Marine said, squinting and pointing.

"Yes, that architect from Marseille who designed the new museum bought the land. What's his name?"

"Are you serious? Rudy Ricciotti? I love his buildings. It will be strange to have a concrete flat-roofed house here, among the vines, but he'll make it work."

"And the Pauliks will welcome him and his strange contemporary house," Verlaque said, slowing the car down and parking it beside Hélène's bright red tractor. "They get along with everyone."

"Oh, here's Léa now!" Marine exclaimed. Léa ran out of the door and to their car, her arms open. Marine thought how lovely it was to have a junior high school student who still wasn't afraid to show her emotions.

"Hello, you two!" Léa shouted against the wind. "It's crazy in the house!"

"What's happening?" Marine asked, bending down to give Léa the *bises*. Verlaque walked around the car and did the same.

"What's up, kiddo?" he asked. "How's our favorite singer?"

"I'm fine, thank you. But Papa's trying to fix our computer printer 'cause I have a report due on Monday, and he's already sworn twice, and Maman's cake isn't rising." She grinned, as if it was the funniest thing in the world.

"Well," Verlaque said, putting his arm around Léa's shoulders as they walked to the house, "we have a nice bottle of champagne with us. That always helps things."

"Oh, yes, Maman says that about champagne, too." She turned to Marine and asked, "How's the baby?"

"Kicking away," Marine answered, smiling. "Do you have any name ideas? For a girl, for example?" she added, glancing at her husband.

"Maria."

Verlaque looked at Marine, puzzled. "Oh," she said. "Maria Callas."

"Who else?" Léa asked as she opened the door and motioned for her guests to enter the house before her.

"Welcome to our nightmare!" Bruno Paulik called out from the living room. They could see only his wide shoulders and back, hunched over a printer.

Hélène brushed flour off her apron and walked across the room, giving Marine and Verlaque the *bises*. "I'm sure Léa gave you a full report," she said.

"Sorry about the cake," Verlaque said.

"I forgot to add baking powder. Can you believe it?"

"These things happen."

"But how could I miss such an important detail?"

Verlaque felt the hairs on his forearms rise.

Hélène went on. "I had to pack up a rush delivery of wine to California late this afternoon. To a restaurant in Berkeley. Chez Panisse. Have you heard of it?"

"Have I heard of it?" Verlaque asked. "Of course! My father took my brother and me there once when we were in our early teens. He was on a business trip to San Francisco. We giggled at the hippie waitstaff and Sébastien refused to eat the salad as it had flowers in it."

"I think it's quite posh now," she said. Verlaque agreed that it must be. He looked across the room to where Marine was leaning over to look at the printer with Paulik. She lifted up the lid and clicked the ink cartridges into place. The machine made a lurching sound, then began printing.

"You're a genius!" Paulik shouted, jumping up and hugging Marine.

Léa clapped her hands together. She quickly sat down and began typing on the computer's keyboard.

"I didn't own a toolbox until I met Marine," Verlaque said. "She brought her own."

"You don't even know where I keep it," Marine said, laughing.

"Sure I do," he replied, and then paused. "Under the kitchen sink." He hoped he sounded sure of himself.

"Wrong!"

"Let's open this champagne," Hélène said, winking at Verlaque. She turned the bottle around in her hands. "A Krug blanc de blancs! Antoine and Marine, you guys are too generous."

"Antoine is," Marine said, putting her arm around his waist.

The computer printer made a thumping noise and began printing. "Oh, no!" Léa cried out as she pulled the sheet of paper out of the printer.

"Now what?" Paulik called over to his daughter.

"There's no more yellow ink!"

Paulik raised his eyes to the ceiling. "Do you have to print in color?" he asked.

"In my day," Hélène began, giggling, lowering her voice, "on the farm in the Luberon . . ."

"Yes, I do!" Lea answered.

"Well, my goodness!" Paulik said to his wife and guests. "These kids have everything now, and the teachers expect their reports printed as if they were documents published by the EU."

"We have to go to the mall!" Léa called out.

"No, Léa, we have company," Hélène said, firmly but quietly. "Tomorrow's Saturday. You can get it then."

"I have choir practice all day! I wanted to finish the museum report tonight!"

"Léa, you have to be flexible," Paulik said.

Hélène whispered to Marine, "She's a bit of a maniac sometimes. You should see how neat and tidy her desk is."

"Mine was, too," Marine said, glancing in Lea's direction. "So I understand."

Verlaque carried his champagne glass over to the computer. "Have a sip, kiddo. It's a blanc de blancs, which means it's made only with Chardonnay grapes."

Léa took the glass and had a sip, then looked up at Verlaque, wide-eyed. She broke out into a wide grin and helped herself to another sip.

"What's the yellow for?" Verlaque asked, taking the printout from her.

"For the beautiful Chinese vase," Léa said, calmer now. "There's a dragon carved into it—that's why I think it's Chinese."

Verlaque smiled, and Paulik walked over to his side. "I'm sorry

I got angry, Léa," he said. "I'll go get more ink tomorrow while you're at choir."

"Thank you, Papa. I'm sorry, too."

"Wait a minute," Verlaque said. "What Chinese vase?" He showed the printout to Paulik, who looked at it and said, "There isn't any Far Eastern art in the Quentin-Savary collection. Where did this come from?"

Léa sighed. "Papa, I just saw the whole collection before it disappeared, and that vase was there. I know because it was on a windowsill and Eddy almost knocked it over."

"On a windowsill?" Paulik asked. "It wasn't in the collection, then."

"No, I don't think it was," said Léa, "as I looked for a label but there wasn't one."

"Léa, can we look at your other photographs?" Verlaque asked.

Léa unplugged her smartphone from its charger and began scrolling through her photographs. "I took a shot of a fig plate for Mélanie, as she loves figs," she said, holding her phone up to Verlaque and Paulik. She scrolled to the next image. "And then I took a few of the Chinese vase, which is why we need yellow, Papa. The pale green color was so beautiful. And the porcelain was so thin, you could see through it."

"It's called celadon glazing," Marine called from across the room.

Verlaque looked at Paulik, who asked his daughter, "Léa, could we put these photos up on the computer screen?"

"Okay," she said. She plugged her phone into the back of the computer and typed a few commands on the keyboard.

Verlaque stared at the screen, mesmerized and a bit woozy from hunger. "The flowers!" he said.

Paulik leaned over to look. "There are fresh flowers in the vase . . ."

"As if the vase were just decoration."

"That's what it is," Paulik said, pointing to the image. "It's sitting on a windowsill with white lilies in it."

"My coat!" Verlaque said. He quickly walked across the room to where his wool coat was hanging on a coat rack. "France Dubois did some research for me earlier today, and I was in such a rush to leave the office that I just folded the printout and put it in my pocket. She said she was quite pleased with her findings."

Taking the paper out of his coat pocket, Verlaque scanned it. France had highlighted an episode with a pink marker. "Here we go!" he said. "The theme of the antiques road show on April 5 was ancient China!" He paused. "And Lopez was in France's Chinese class." He looked back at the printout and read France's scribbled notes at the end. *Very easy search, Judge. I only had to go back three weeks. ;)*

"He saw the television program," Paulik suggested.

"That's why he was recently interested in learning Chinese numbers, just like France told us."

"In order to sell it to the Chinese," Paulik said.

"How many other people may have seen that program?" Marine asked. "I hear that show is very popular." She glanced at her husband, who smiled sheepishly at her.

"You're right, Marine," Verlaque said, kicking himself for having missed that particular episode. "Any of the board members, for example, might have watched it and then recognized the vase."

"I'm confused," Hélène said. "How did the vase from the museum get on that show?"

"I agree, it doesn't make sense," Verlaque answered, "as the television show aired weeks before the museum theft. So although the theme of that episode was China, our vase must not be on it." But the image of the vase continued to bother him, as if he knew it from somewhere. He said so to Paulik, and then glanced over at Léa, aware of the fact that they shouldn't be speaking of the case in front of her.

"I'm not listening," Léa said, keeping her eyes fixed on the opened page of a book.

"On the other hand, there has to be a link to this television show, as the clues about China have been in front of us the whole time," Verlaque said, draining his champagne and realizing that he hadn't properly tasted it. "France's Chinese classes, a Chinese vase with flowers in it . . . Achille mumbling about the flowers, meaning they stole even the decorative pieces, the cheap vases that Mme Devaux would have proudly put fresh flowers into . . ."

"Mme Devaux . . . ," Paulik repeated. He looked at Léa and asked, "When your little pal Eddy . . ."

"He's not my pal," Léa corrected.

"Oh, sorry," Paulik said. "When Eddy almost knocked over the vase, was M Formentin upset?"

"Not really," Léa answered. "Just more irritated at being interrupted."

"So he didn't know its value," Marine said.

"Can we send that photo to Mlle Peronne at the Musée de Sèvres?" Verlaque asked, looking at Paulik. "Do we trust her? If anyone would have known about the vase's value, it's her."

"I do trust her. She has solid alibis for the break-in and for Lopez's murder," Paulik said. "But I don't think she knows the vase's value. She's been a board member for ten years and would have seen it countless times. She, too, overlooked it."

"Perhaps because it wasn't under glass," Marine suggested.

"You're right," Verlaque said. "It didn't attract any attention. For all we know, it may have been kept in the cellar until very recently. Let's send a photo to Mlle Peronne. If she can't identify it, perhaps a museum colleague can."

"Léa," Paulik began, "could you please . . ."

"I'm on it," Léa said, picking up her cell phone. "I'll forward you the photo, Papa."

"Léa, I thought you weren't listening," Hélène said.

"No offense, but sometimes the four of you talk about really boring stuff," Léa explained. "But not tonight!"

Chapter Thirty

❧

Saturday, May 5

By 8:45 the next morning Verlaque was sitting behind his desk, staring at his telephone, waiting for it to ring. At 9:00 Paulik walked into the office, carrying a bag from Michaud. "I thought we'd switch from brioches," he said to the judge as he set the bag on the desk, "so I got almond and plain croissants."

"Good decision, thanks," Verlaque said, reaching into the bag. "Maybe the change in breakfast will strengthen our brain cells. I'm still reeling over the fact that a jade-colored vase is worth killing for, even if it's old."

Paulik said, "If indeed the vase is our desired object."

Verlaque mumbled in agreement and pulled out a plain croissant, then quickly put it back, before Paulik could see, and selected an almond one. "I'm expecting phone calls from Mlle Peronne," he said, "and France 3, as they produce the antique show."

"It's Saturday," Paulik said, stifling a yawn, "so we may have a long wait."

As if to prove the commissioner wrong, the telephone rang. Verlaque quickly set his croissant down and picked up the phone. "*Juge Verlaque*," he said. He listened and said, "*Ah, oui, bonjour.*" He set his hand over the mouthpiece and whispered to Paulik, "France 3." He then put the telephone on speaker mode and said into the receiver, "I need a copy of your show that was aired on April 5. Please. With whom am I speaking?"

"Gaston," the employee said.

"You'll find it easily, Gaston," Verlaque said. "The episode was all about Chinese art."

"I'm looking it up as we speak. Okay, I found it. It's no longer available to watch for free online, so I'll have to get you a link and email that to you. Give me a day or two."

"Not right away?"

"I'm all alone here today and I'm just an intern. I need permission; it's only on our internal network."

Verlaque said, "Get it to us as quickly as you can, and I promise to speak to your superiors about what a stellar job you've done."

"Thanks! Consider it done."

Verlaque continued, "Wait. I have a better idea. Can you watch it now and tell us what's going on while you're watching it?"

"Sure, there's nothing to do here today," Gaston said. "This sounds way more exciting. So what am I looking for?"

"What we're looking for is any kind of green-glazed Chinese vase."

"As in celadon?"

Verlaque rolled his eyes and Paulik grinned. "Yes, celadon."

"I'm on it! But first I'll grab something to eat."

"Thanks, Gaston," Verlaque said, sighing. He hung up the phone and said to Paulik, "We lucked out getting a bored intern."

"Maybe we'll have the same luck at the Musée de Sèvres."

"I'd rather speak to an expert in Far Eastern ceramics than another intern."

The telephone rang again and Verlaque almost jumped out of his chair. He quickly picked up the receiver and set it on speaker mode. "Antoine Verlaque, Aix-en-Provence."

"Hello." A male voice sounded on the other end. "This is Jean-Michel Bureau at the Musée de Sèvres. I'm actually *not* at the museum as it's a *Saturday*."

"Yes, and I do apologize," Verlaque said.

"Mlle Peronne sent me the blurry photograph and told me of its importance in your investigation."

Verlaque looked at Paulik, who was frowning in defense of his daughter's photography skills. "Can you make anything out of it?" Verlaque asked.

"It *is* rather blurry," Bureau said. "At a glance, it's rather hard to tell if it's a precious work of art or something my brother-in-law might buy at Maisons du Monde."

"Anything you can tell us about the vase is paramount to this investigation."

"Yes, that's why I called you right away," Bureau said. "But I'm not at home now. Could you describe the vase in more detail?"

"Dragon!" Paulik whispered. "Tell him about the dragon."

"There is a dragon on it," Verlaque said, wincing, as he knew he wasn't using the proper term.

Jean-Michel Bureau snickered. "Ah, yes, a dragon."

"They're common in Chinese art, I realize . . ."

"Yes, indeed. Do you have any idea of its date?"

"No, unfortunately."

"Or markings? Underneath . . ."

"No, we don't know if it has markings. All we have is this photo."

"Listen, I'm in Le Bon Marché food emporium right now, doing some shopping," Bureau said, perhaps feeling sorry for the Aixois. "When I get home, I'll transfer this photo to my computer to get a better and larger look at it." He paused, and they could hear the noise of items being dropped into his handheld wire shopping basket. "Hmm. On second thought, there is a . . . could it be . . . ?"

"Yes?" Verlaque asked, leaning in toward the phone.

"No, ignore my comment. It's too early to guess. I'll be home in an hour."

"Thank you so much," Verlaque said, frustrated. "We'll wait for your call. You may have better luck reaching me on my cell phone."

"All right, I have that number. Goodbye."

Verlaque hung up, then stood and began pacing the room. "I've seen that damn vase before."

"At Maisons du Monde?"

"Very funny."

"Do you really think you've seen it recently?" Paulik asked. "How is that possible? You only visited Solange Picard's apartment, and Gilbert's. If either of them is guilty, they wouldn't advertise the fact by displaying the vase in their home."

"You're right. It could have been any vase. I'm not exactly a specialist."

Paulik also got up and began walking around the room, in the opposite direction. "Mme Devaux," he said slowly.

Verlaque stopped pacing and looked across the room. "She's the person who put the flowers in the vase, that's almost for sure."

"And she'd be the kind of person to watch that show. All alone in her fussy apartment."

Verlaque shook his head. "But she'd never be able to empty a museum over a weekend."

"With help?"

"Could she murder someone and almost kill her own boss?"

Paulik winced. "No, I don't see it."

"On the other hand," Verlaque said, now walking the other way, "what about our housekeeper and her husband? I didn't ask to meet him, which was stupid, now that I think of it."

"Solange Picard?"

"Yes. She told me that Mme de Montbarbon was very generous in her will and now she is retiring and going to travel the world with her husband."

"To sell the vase," Paulik said, pointing his finger at Verlaque. "Or they're traveling with the earnings of the already-sold vase."

"Besides, old nobility never leaves a generous bequest to the staff. They'd sooner leave their fortune to some animal shelter than human beings who've slaved for them for decades. I should have seen through that one."

Paulik asked, "Do you think you saw the vase in her apartment?"

"I remember books, only books, and a very cute small kitchen," Verlaque answered, sitting down. Thinking of the books and the well-equipped homey kitchen, he felt guilty. "I'm drawing a blank. I don't think I saw it there."

"On a bookshelf at her place?"

Verlaque closed his eyes and shook his head back and forth. "Forget what I said. Solange Picard wouldn't have keys to get into the museum. So who killed Lopez?"

The phone rang and Verlaque picked up the receiver and said hello.

"It's Gaston! Ready to report, sir!"

"Have you started the video?" Verlaque asked.

"Yes, I just started it. They're in Paris, in some posh apartment, looking at an old fan."

"A fan?"

"Yeah, like ladies use when it's too hot. It's painted. I'll fast-forward."

"Thanks."

After a few seconds Gaston said, "Okay, now they're in a village and a schoolteacher is showing them an old Chinese calligraphy book she found in their library. It's not that old, they're saying; 1980s. She looks disappointed. Too bad."

"Okay, keep going."

Gaston whistled lightly as he ran through the footage. "I'm at the twenty-minute mark, so we're nearing the end of the show. Here we go. Now we're in the Aubrac, in a château. Totally Middle Ages. Nice!"

"A château sounds promising," Paulik whispered.

"They're being walked through various living rooms by some bogus guy dressed up in a three-piece suit," Gaston said, and then realized he might have offended the officers on the other end of the line. "Oh, sorry."

"Neither of us is wearing a three-piece suit, Gaston," Verlaque said. "Don't worry."

"His name is Remi de Solignac. He's opening a cabinet," Gaston said. "And pointing to a celadon vase!"

"Dragons?"

"Wait a second," Gaston said. "I'm watching the show on normal speed now. Can you hear it? I've turned on the speakerphone."

"Yes, we can hear," Verlaque said. "Thanks."

"This belonged to my grandparents," a pompous voice said. "It came from China. Eighteenth century, the Qing dynasty. That's all we know. My grandmother especially loved the delicately carved dragon."

"That's the three-piece suit talking," Gaston said quickly.

The vase owner continued, "We know it's valuable, but just not how much. We'd like to sell it as the château needs various repairs."

"That's what we're here for," a female presenter said in an enthusiastic voice. "And we've invited along Mme Claude Bosquet of the Far Eastern department of Sotheby's Paris, along with M Piers Sumner-Smith of the same department at Christie's in London."

"They're looking at it," Gaston reported. He whistled a bit more. "She's picked it up and turned it upside down. She's now showing the vase's underside to the English dude. She's smiling."

"The seal and mark are intact," Mme Bosquet said. "It's from the Qianlong period."

"This kind of opportunity comes once in a lifetime," an English voice said in lightly accented French. "This vase is a dragon jar from the reign of the sixth Qing emperor, eighteenth century. The delicate carving of the dragon, and the waves, has never been equaled in Chinese art. The vase has even been written about in various Chinese texts."

Mme Bosquet from Sotheby's joined in. "I never thought I'd see this vase," she said. "And the incredible thing is, we know this vase arrived in France in a pair."

Verlaque threw his fists into the air as Paulik yelled out in excitement.

"So I'm correct in assuming there were two of these?" the presenter excitedly asked.

"That's right," Mme Bosquet said. "Although the second is most likely lost or was broken long ago."

"Could you give our viewers an idea of this vase's value?" the presenter asked, her voice now so high that it could have shattered the vase itself.

Verlaque leaned forward and Paulik jumped up and began to pace the room.

"I'll give you a low estimate," Mme Bosquet said, "and say five million American dollars."

"Did you hear that, viewers?" the presenter asked. "Our vase's owner is quite speechless!"

"The castle dude's gonna pass out," Gaston interjected. "He loosened his tie."

"I'd increase that estimate," M Sumner-Smith said, "given the vase's fame in ancient Chinese history . . . to eight million American dollars."

"The show is almost over," Gaston said. "The host is shaking their hands and the credits are rolling."

"Could our vase possibly be the twin?" Verlaque asked Paulik with his hand over the receiver.

"She's back!" Gaston said. "It's an epilogue."

"Dear viewers," they heard the presenter say. "A few weeks

after we filmed this episode, that very vase went to Sotheby's in Paris and was auctioned off. The buyer—an anonymous telephone bidder from the Far East—paid . . . wait for it! . . . twelve million American dollars. That's a record for a Qing monochrome porcelain vase, or for any vase I would think! See you next Thursday at this same time, when we'll be visiting three different village flea markets, each one with an incredible find!"

"Twelve million dollars for a vase!" Gaston repeated. "What a waste of money!"

"Thank you so much, Gaston," Verlaque said. "You've been a huge help."

"Don't forget your promise."

"I won't," Verlaque said. "Goodbye." He hung up and grabbed his jacket off the back of his chair. "Two vases. That's how one appeared on the show while the other one sat safe and sound in the museum. Let's go pay the Picards, and then Mme Devaux, a visit. Mme Devaux had daily contact with that vase and may have seen the television show, and, coincidentally, Mme Picard has just come into a lot of money."

"They could have done it together," Paulik added. "Mme Devaux had the keys; Mme Picard, the husband who could do the heavy stuff."

Ten minutes later they were outside the Picards' building on the rue Manuel. "She's not answering her cell phone," Verlaque said, hanging up his own. Luckily the front door opened and an old man stepped out, a very small dog on a leash beside him. Paulik held the front door for the man and his dog.

"*Merci,*" the old man said with a grunt.

"We're visiting the Picards," Paulik said by way of an explanation. The old man didn't seem to care one way or another what two strangers were doing going into the building. The dog barked excitedly and pulled him ahead along the sidewalk.

Paulik and Verlaque walked in and ascended the stairs to the second floor. Paulik rang the Picards' doorbell, but there was no answer. After waiting a few seconds, he pounded loudly on the door. Still no one came. He tried one more time and the door across the hall quickly opened.

"What is the meaning of this?" a middle-aged woman asked. "Can't you take a hint? They're not home!"

Paulik introduced himself and showed her his identification.

"You're the police? What's wrong?" she asked. "Is someone ill? They've just left on holiday . . ."

"Where?" Paulik asked.

"Venice."

Paulik looked at Verlaque with a frown.

"What's wrong with going on vacation?" the woman asked. "Solange was put through plenty of stress after that break-in at Mme de Montbarbon's, which I'm sure you know."

"The vase," Verlaque said, looking at the Picards' door.

"What vase?" she asked.

"Let's get into the apartment," Verlaque mumbled to Paulik, ignoring her.

"Oh, no, you don't," the neighbor continued. "You need a warrant."

"No, I don't," Verlaque said, showing her his identification card.

"Examining magistrates don't need a warrant?" she asked, reading it.

"No, madame, they don't," he answered. "Would you mind helping us out a bit then?"

"If it stops you two from bursting into Solange's apartment without her permission, then yes."

"M Picard," he said. "Can you tell us anything about him?"

"Jean-Paul?" she asked. "He's as pure as the driven snow. He spends his spare time working with disadvantaged kids in Jas de Bouffan. He's slowed down since his car accident, though. He lost an arm."

Paulik and Verlaque exchanged irate looks. Jean-Paul Picard would have had a hard time emptying out a museum and hitting two people over the head. "Does he have longish hair?" Paulik asked, making chopping gestures with his hands below his shoulders.

She laughed, holding onto the door frame. "He's as bald as you are. They left me the name of their hotel in Venice in case of an emergency. Someone fleeing the law wouldn't have done that, would they? I'll go and get it for you." They heard her laughing as she walked into the depths of her apartment.

She returned a few seconds later with a slip of paper and handed it to Verlaque. He recognized the hotel's name as a three-star hotel near the lagoon. He'd passed by it many times walking to his favorite restaurant in Castello. It certainly wasn't the Danieli or the Cipriani, where he usually stayed. It was the sort of modest, clean hotel that the humble hardworking Picards would have chosen; even though they had suddenly come into money, they would be reticent to spend it. He thought of Solange Picard and her neat book-filled apartment and the madeleines. "Thank you," he said to her irate neighbor. "And we are sorry to have disturbed you."

"Never mind," she said, closing the door. "It beats vacuuming."

"We were wrong in suspecting them, which is a relief to me," Paulik said as they left the building and went out into the sunny street.

They walked in silence, turning down the rue Chastel and into the giant Place Verdun. Here, Verlaque stopped and looked across the square at the classical columns of the Palais de Justice. The sun shone, magically brightening the building into a brilliant white instead of the dirty, needs-a-paint-job white that it actually was. He said, "The light. On the vase."

"Like Léa said? Almost translucent?"

"Yes. I just remembered where I saw the vase. Okay, I'm not sure it's our dragon vase, but it was definitely a greenish-colored Oriental-style vase."

Paulik shot the judge a doubtful look.

Verlaque went on, "It was the first time I visited Gilbert. There were bouquets of flowers all around the apartment. I even complimented him on the flowers as I was leaving. I was being cheeky, as he had just raced back to Aix but had had time to buy flowers."

"But we already had this conversation. Do you think he'd steal a priceless vase and then leave it out for all to see?" Paulik asked as they continued to walk across the square.

"Yes, I do," Verlaque said. "As if to taunt us, the pretentious rat that he is. This case is all about flowers. Remember Achille Formentin's words to me, before he fell asleep?"

"But any of us could have seen the antiques show," Paulik said. "Although Gilbert probably assumed you don't watch that kind of stuff." His cell phone rang and he reached into his jacket and got it out. "Paulik," he answered. "Hello, Roche. What did you find?"

As Paulik listened, he nodded and then began to pick up his pace. Verlaque followed him, dodging some tourists taking photographs of the square and a teenager on a skateboard. Paulik hung up just as they reached the front doors of the Palais de Justice. "Roche wants to see us, right away. I told him to come to your office."

Five minutes later, Patrice Roche walked in to Verlaque's office, smiling from ear to ear and carrying a small laptop computer. "Leboncoin has come through!" he said.

"Do you need to set up your computer somewhere?" Paulik asked.

"Yes."

"You can put it here," Verlaque said, quickly walking out from behind his desk, "on the round meeting table."

Roche put his computer down and opened it up while Verlaque and Paulik pulled out chairs and sat down on either side of him. Roche said, "Luckily I took a screenshot of the plate when I saw it on leboncoin because in the time it took me to text you about it, it was already gone, wiped off the site."

"That's when you got in touch with their webmaster, right?" Paulik asked.

"Exactly. Here's the ad as it appeared, with the château plate in a somewhat blurry and off-center photo." Roche pointed to the bottom of the ad. "And here's where the conversations appear between the seller and people writing with questions about the plate, which the webmaster was able to send to me. I have it saved here, on another page." He swiped with his mouse and opened a page, revealing a long list of conversations, then sighed. "It took me a while to get ahold of everyone, even if only four people contacted DJ Kool. People are just so lousy about answering their telephones, or returning phone calls, even if it's a police officer on the other end." He shook his head to emphasize his disappointment.

"So did it sell? Did anyone speak to DJ Kool?" Paulik asked, trying to hide his impatience. "Or even meet him or her?"

"Yes, a Swiss antiques dealer. They met halfway, at a gas station café. Guess where the seller is from?"

"Aix-les-Bains?" Verlaque asked. "Please say Aix-les-Bains."

Roche grinned. "He did better than that: he told the antiques dealer he lived in a village called Allènes."

Paulik whistled. "Where the Quentin-Savary country house is located."

Roche went on. "The antiques dealer felt sorry for him as he looked like he hadn't eaten or bathed in days. He bought him a hot lunch, so he got the seller's life story out of it."

"So? Who is this person? Name?" Paulik asked.

Roche said, "The Swiss antiques guy didn't get a name and he paid in cash, seven hundred euros. Maybe that's why he bought the seller lunch. He didn't notice if the seller had a car, as he left quickly, the plate in a plastic bag."

"So all we know is that the Swiss guy was able to argue the price down three hundred euros," Verlaque said.

"We know more than that," Roche said, thrilled to have kept them both waiting. "The seller is a drug user, judging by his battered forearms and his admission of it over lunch. He wouldn't tell the Swiss guy where or how he got the plate, and to tell you the truth, I don't think our antiques dealer was too interested in the plate's provenance. But we do know that the seller's in his twenties, is from Allènes, so probably knows Gilbert, he's thin and has long hair."

"The CCTV image!" Paulik said. "The passenger beside Gilbert . . ."

"And it's blue," Roche added.

"Blue?"

"His hair."

Paulik's cell phone rang. Looking at the number he did a fist pump and quickly answered. Paulik listened, nodded a few times, thanked them, and hung up, smiling.

"You forgot to do another fist pump," Verlaque said. Roche looked on, trying to hide his grin.

"That was the police in Aix-les-Bains," Paulik said. "They've found our blue-haired drug addict. He's a local and known to the police."

"Back to Aix-les-Bains," Verlaque said. "Or more specifically, Allènes. Where Gilbert spends his weekends. Where is the guy now?"

"In custody," Paulik replied. "He was caught trying to sell another one of those château plates at a local flea market. An antiques dealer reported him instead of buying the plate himself."

"That's very honorable."

"Well, apparently the antiques dealer spent time in jail for buying and selling stolen goods, so he was earning brownie points. We've been lucky twice today."

"Third time's the charm."

Chapter Thirty-one

≈

Saturday, May 5

Gilbert Quentin-Savary is our main suspect for the murder of Aurélien Lopez, the attack on Achille Formentin, and the robbery of the Musée Quentin-Savary," Bruno Paulik announced to the team of officers standing around him. "We are going to call Quentin-Savary in for questioning," he continued, nodding toward Antoine Verlaque, who was standing beside him, "and while he is here with the judge and myself, six of you will go to 16 rue Mistral and search high and low, including in Gilbert Quentin-Savary's apartment, for this." He pointed a remote control at a screen and a photograph of the celadon vase appeared. He clicked once more and details of its wave patterns and stylized dragon appeared. "I don't have to tell you to be careful and to use gloves. The vase has been temporarily identified by an expert at the Musée de Sèvres, who just called Judge Verlaque a few minutes ago. Judge Verlaque saw this vase in Gilbert's apartment at the beginning of this case. We've been in touch with someone in the Aubrac, Remi de Solignac, who owns the twin to this vase, which just sold for twelve million dollars. He told us that his father and Gilbert's father were good friends. He remembered their many whisky-soaked card games, where heavy betting went on. Remi would watch, hidden, from behind the door."

"Did the elder Quentin-Savary win the vase in a card game?" Officer Goulin asked.

"That's what we're assuming for the moment," Paulik replied. "Although he obviously wasn't aware of its value. Perhaps Remi de Solignac's father didn't tell him, and was hoping to win it back one day. Or he himself didn't know of the twin vases' real value."

"So we're just supposed to carry it in our arms if we find it?" an older officer asked from the back of the room.

Paulik calmly replied, hiding his irritation, "Each of you will take a small duffel bag that's filled with bubble wrap to carry it back here in; the duffel bags are on the long table by the door."

"And if we don't find the vase?" another officer asked.

"Hurry back here and we go to plan B," Paulik said. "Which is drilling Quentin-Savary until he tells us where the vase is hidden."

"Is there a chance the vase is already gone?" Sophie Goulin asked. "As in sold?"

"Yes," Paulik answered. "But we've been watching Gilbert, and he hasn't made any unusual movements since the museum robbery, so we believe he still has it."

Verlaque reached into his pocket and pulled out his cell phone. "Go ahead and call him now," Paulik said. Verlaque dialed the number that France Dubois had written down for him and walked out of the room. The police officers gathered by the door and Paulik handed out the duffel bags to six of them. "Roche, since you've been our contact with Aix-les-Bains, please stay here," he said.

The young officer's shoulders collapsed in disappointment.

"I'd also like you to be present while we drill M Quentin-Savary," Paulik added.

"Yes, sir!" Roche said, perking up again.

Verlaque walked back into the room and held up his cell phone. "He'll be here in twenty minutes," he said. Then he whispered to Paulik, "He's doing us a favor, he says. We're 'lucky he's free.' That's a quote."

"I really hope we nab him," Paulik whispered back to Verlaque, "if only because he's so pretentious."

Roche spent ten minutes before the interview started trying to find the green tea that Gilbert had demanded. He knew that Gilbert should be served the awful plain tea that came out of the vending machine, but he wanted to impress their number one suspect, even destabilize him a bit. After searching in vain through the drawers of several small communal kitchens—empty of people, as it was a Saturday—it was a security guard who gave Roche a sachet of green tea.

Gilbert Quentin-Savary sat in the examining room, his legs crossed and his fingers interlocked across his knees, humming. Roche set the tea down in front of him and Gilbert blew on it, not looking at the young officer, not thanking him.

"Thank you, Officer Roche," Verlaque said.

"You're welcome, Judge Verlaque," Roche said in his most

polite voice. He sat down and readied himself to turn on the tape recorder. Finally Bruno Paulik walked in, intentionally five minutes late and intentionally unapologetic. He sat down, nodding to Roche to begin taping.

"Fire away," Gilbert said, swinging his head back and forth as if a symphony that only he could hear was playing.

"Interview with prime suspect Gilbert Quentin-Savary, Aix-en-Provence," Paulik said.

"I'm flattered," Gilbert said. "But you've—"

"You should be flattered," Paulik cut in. "You're sitting in the seat of many illustrious criminals."

"Pfff," Gilbert scoffed.

"Do you know this person?" Paulik asked, pushing a color photograph across the table.

Gilbert barely looked down at the photograph, which showed a man in his twenties with long, greasy blue hair and tattoos up and down his long thin arms. "Yes," he said, pushing it back toward Paulik in disgust. "I mean, I don't know him personally, but I've seen him around our village near Aix-les-Bains. He's a local junkie, or should I say *the* local junkie."

"Do you know his name?" Paulik asked.

"Haven't got a clue."

"That's funny, because André Sabouret knows you," Paulik said. "He claims that you hired him to help empty out the museum on the long weekend over Easter."

Gilbert made a hissing noise that turned into a laugh. "I was at the country house all that weekend, as my maid can testify."

"Well, you see, Gilbert, your maid, Gisèle Borgia, has just changed her story," Verlaque said.

Gilbert glared at him. "How could she? She was there. She saw me all weekend."

"Let's say she has been more specific in her story," Paulik said. "Although she originally said that she saw you around that weekend, after our colleagues in Aix-les-Bains visited her yesterday, she admitted that she only saw you when you arrived on Friday, on Saturday morning, and then perhaps on Sunday late afternoon. It would have been easy for you to have been seen by her—intentionally—in the late morning when returning from Aix, or later in the evening before heading out, leaving lots of time for you to get to and from Aix more than once."

"This Aix," Verlaque added. "Not that one."

"Either would work, actually," Paulik said, looking at Verlaque.

"Would it?" he asked nonchalantly, looking back at the commissioner. "I think you're right. But then you're always right, isn't he, Roche?"

"Yes, Judge, in my experience," Roche said, staring at Gilbert.

"I would ask for a lawyer to be present, given your odd comedy routine and the three-against-one ratio," Gilbert said, "but I have nothing to hide. You're going by the hearsay of a heroin junkie and an almost-senile maid."

"And CCTV cameras," Paulik added.

Gilbert shifted slightly in his chair. His tea stayed untouched, which annoyed Roche.

"You are the perfect suspect, in a way," Verlaque said. "It was so obvious you were guilty that it took us longer than usual to realize it. Although the commissioner thought so right away."

"He's always right," Roche said.

Gilbert said, "Don't make me laugh."

"You have keys to the entire building," Verlaque continued, "an intimate knowledge of the collection, and, more important, how to get it in and out of the museum, and any number of places to hide it near Aix-les-Bains. Plus, you want and need money, as I'm sure your vacationing accountant can attest to."

"She has," Paulik said, nodding. "I spoke to her yesterday as she sat by a pool in Guadeloupe."

"Really?" Verlaque asked in an affected voice. "Why would anyone go to the Caribbean at this time of year?"

"Beats me," Paulik said.

"You're lying about my accountant," Gilbert seethed. "Besides, she wouldn't divulge anything. That's private information."

"She also handles the museum's accounts," Paulik said, "so she was willing to bend a few rules for us." His phone buzzed and he saw that it was a text message from Sophie Goulin. *Nothing so far.*

Verlaque passed another photograph across the table, this one of the dragon vase. Gilbert looked at it and scoffed. "I hate Far Eastern art," he said.

"Me, too," Verlaque said. "I'm more of a mid-century-modern guy myself. Nevertheless, what do you make of this vase?"

"Absolutely nothing."

"You've never seen it before?" Verlaque pressed.

"No."

"Because I saw it in your apartment."

"Prove it!"

"Stop arguing, you two," Paulik said. "You sound like twelve-year-olds." He silently apologized to Léa and looked at his watch. "I'm hungry," he announced.

"Where are we going for dinner?" Roche asked. His superiors looked at him in suppressed shock.

Paulik said, "Well, since it's dinnertime and we should be eating with our families right now, we're going to let you go home, M Quentin-Savary."

Gilbert stood up and pushed his chair in under the table. "You have no choice, since you have nothing on me."

"Until our favorite junkie arrives here tomorrow morning to identify you," Paulik said. "So please come back here at 10:00 a.m. sharp."

"You're bluffing once again," Gilbert said. "But I'll be back tomorrow, just to prove you wrong." He walked across the room and opened the door. "I'll see myself out."

"No, there's an officer standing outside the door to accompany you to the front door," Paulik said. "See you tomorrow!"

Gilbert slammed the door. Paulik showed Verlaque and Roche Goulin's text message and they said "*Merde*" in unison. "*Where* are we *eating*?" Paulik asked, looking at Roche.

Roche smiled and shrugged his shoulders.

"I thought you played along wonderfully," Verlaque said, gently slapping Roche on the shoulder. "And now I am going to go home and have dinner with my wife." He stood up and turned to Paulik and asked, "Is the junkie really coming here tomorrow morning?"

"Yes, but at noon, not ten," Paulik replied.

"And did you really speak to the accountant? The one sitting by the pool?"

"Not exactly, no," Paulik replied. "I called her *cabinet* yesterday afternoon and the secretary told me she was in Guadeloupe. All of the partners had already left for the day, so I'll call back on Monday."

Verlaque said, "There's something I'd like to check on at the museum. Do you have the keys on you?"

Paulik reached into his pocket and pulled out a set of keys. "They're all there," he said, giving them to Verlaque. "And did you *really* see the vase at Gilbert's?"

"Of course I did," Verlaque said. "On a windowsill, just like at the museum, with fresh flowers in it." He closed his eyes, then continued, "It was in a fussy, overly feminine setting . . ."

Paulik looked at his boss. "That could be the Picards', or Mme Devaux's, or even Achille's apartment."

Verlaque shook his finger at Paulik. "Now, now," he said. "I've never been inside Achille's, or Mme Devaux's, apartment. And we've just cleared the Picards. Right?"

Paulik rubbed his eyes with his hands and sighed. "You're right. I was in their apartments, not you." He looked up at Verlaque, who was standing by the door. "Did I see that vase? And tell you about it?"

"Now you're paranoid."

"I'm going out for a beer." Paulik looked at Roche. "There may even be a hamburger involved. Care to join me? My treat."

"Yes, sir!"

Verlaque walked down the rue Clemenceau on his way to the *tabac* to buy a cigar when he saw, in the street ahead of him, Gilbert, sauntering along and pausing to look in shop windows now and again. Verlaque slowed down and did the same. Just before the *tabac*, Gilbert turned left and walked into the side door of the

Café Mazarin. Verlaque could see through the Mazarin's windows that Gilbert had sat down and was ordering a drink.

He felt the museum keys in his pocket. He had planned to just walk around the museum's empty rooms, to try to make sense of this puzzling story. But seeing Gilbert occupied, he changed his mind. A group of tourists passed along Verlaque's left, between him and the café, and he took advantage of their mass to walk beside them, hidden from Gilbert's view. He'd buy the cigar later.

Crossing the Cours Mirabeau, he called Marine on his cell phone. "I'm on my way to Gilbert's," he said just after he apologized for being late. "Gilbert's having a drink at the Mazarin like he doesn't have a care in the world. He knows we're on to him, so he's hidden the vase, no doubt. Paulik sent a bunch of officers to search his apartment, but they didn't find anything."

"*Cheri*," Marine began calmly, "I don't think he'd hide it in his own apartment."

Verlaque said, "But don't you see? He's such a jerk that he would. He had it out there, for all of us to see."

"Not now he wouldn't."

"In the museum?"

"Nor would he hide it in the museum."

"No, unlikely, as the police are still in and out of there."

"Don't forget that at one time the Quentin-Savary family lived in that entire building," Marine went on. "Gilbert knows that building. What about the second-floor apartment? Back in the day, the family bedrooms would have been on that floor."

"The chocolate seller . . ." Verlaque reached the museum and quickly let himself in the main door of the building, not the museum's front door. He turned on the hall lights. "I'm walking up the stairs," he said. He got to the second floor and rang the doorbell, waiting. "He's not here. I feel a bit bad going into this guy's apartment, plus the police have already searched it."

"They must have missed something," Marine said. "But you should tell Bruno what you're doing."

"He's taken some rookie officer out for a beer."

"Call him anyway."

"Okay," Verlaque said. "Let me know if you have any good ideas where this vase could be hidden."

"I'll get the plans out."

"You have the plans?"

"Yes," she answered. "They were with the museum's charter. Remember?"

"Thanks," Verlaque said. "My phone's running out of battery. See you later." He hung up and dialed Paulik's number, but it went to voice mail. Verlaque left a quick message saying he was at 16 rue Mistral. On the third try he found the correct key to the apartment door and opened it and walked in.

He turned the light switch on and saw that he was in a neatly furnished but dull living room where the predominant colors were gray and black and all of the furniture had been purchased on the same day at the same store. He scanned the room but saw no possible hiding spots; it was sparsely furnished, and there were no cupboards or bookshelves that could hide an object. He walked across the living room and turned the lights off, conscious of the fact that Gilbert could come up the stairs at any time and see the light under the door.

The kitchen, in the middle of the apartment, offered better possibilities. Verlaque opened the cupboards and moved cereal boxes and some big pots and pans around but found nothing. The next room was an office, as neat and tidy as the first two rooms. Besides a filing cabinet, which was full of color-coded files, there were no good places to hide a priceless vase. In the bathroom, the next room, Verlaque checked the shower and the washing machine. Nothing.

Back out in the hall he passed a linen closet whose five shelves held a few spare sheets and towels and a small suitcase. He took the suitcase out and opened it; it was empty. Lifting the stacks of towels out of the closet, he peered into the depths of the shelves, but there was nothing. He put the towels back and closed the closet door.

The salesman's bedroom was very big. Verlaque imagined that originally, as Marine had suggested, it would have been two rooms. A king-sized bed took up much of the space, and another desk sat against the far wall. There wasn't a dresser or a commode, but when Verlaque opened a set of double doors he understood why: there was a very big walk-in closet. An iron and ironing board were set up, and various gray and navy blue suits and pressed white shirts hung neatly on the racks. As he looked around the closet, gently moving things around, he thought about why this apartment, with its big, grand rooms, would attract a single, well-off businessman. It was very much the sort of apartment he had been looking for when he first arrived in Aix, before Marine.

As if on cue, his phone rang. "*Allô*, Marine," he said. "I'm in the world's biggest walk-in closet."

"What walk-in closet?" she asked.

"Off the master bedroom, at the back of the apartment, facing the gardens."

"Oh, that's the third bedroom on the plan."

"Three? Not two? There's a big master bedroom here and a small bedroom he uses as an office."

"Your giant walk-in closet must have been a bedroom."

"But there's no window," Verlaque said, moving aside the suits once again to be sure.

"There is one on the plan. It would be on the south side of the apartment, next to the bathroom."

"That's where I am."

"And there's a small closet in the hallway," she continued, "probably for linens."

"Yep."

"So the bedroom begins behind that linen closet."

Verlaque looked around, trying to make sense of the space.

"The window is directly parallel to the closet," she said. "Right behind it."

"No window."

"It may have been boarded up. Some tax thing."

"Right, they were taxed on the number of windows," he said. "Listen, I'm almost out of battery . . ."

"Are you sure you're in the right room?"

"Wait a minute," Verlaque said as he shone his cell phone flashlight against the far wall, where he thought the window was supposed to be. A long mirror hung on the wall, and running around the entire mirror was a wood frame about six inches from the mirror itself. Verlaque said goodbye to Marine just as his phone died, so he put his phone back in his pocket. Lifting the mirror up and off the wall, he leaned it against some suit jackets to his left and pushed on the wall where the mirror had been. A door clicked open.

"Ooh la la," Verlaque whispered. He held up his cigar lighter and shone it around another room almost as big as the walk-in closet and, straight in front of him, a window whose shutters, he imagined, had been closed for decades.

The shelves, which ran about two feet wide along two sides of the room, were full of ceramics. "That's how you emptied the museum so quickly," he muttered. "But you couldn't fit everything in here, hardly." He shone his lighter up and down the shelves until he came to an object that looked about the right size and shape to be the vase, wrapped in bubble wrap and sealed with packing tape. Finding the edge of the packing tape, he picked at it with his thumbnail, but a noise farther back in the apartment caused him to switch off his lighter. The light switch for the walk-in closet was to the right of the bedroom door, so he took three long strides to the door and switched the overhead light off as well. He could hear someone walking and the sound of wheels on the wooden floors. He was about to close the closet door when the bedroom door opened. Gilbert stood in the doorway, a large suitcase at his side.

Verlaque smiled meekly. "I think I found one of your hiding spots," he said. "Are you off somewhere?"

Gilbert didn't return the smile. He reached into his jacket pocket and pulled out a small gun. "Get back in the closet, all the way into the smaller one."

"I've called the commissioner already," Verlaque said, putting his hands in the air. All he could think of was Marine and the baby. He focused on Gilbert's face and tried not to look at the gun.

"Liar."

"I found the twin celadon vase," Verlaque said. "Your father won it in a card game. You told me he gambled the first time we met. How did you find out it was so valuable?"

"I've always been curious about it."

"Oh, come on. I'm entitled to the true story now. Plus I love that show. So did Aurélien Lopez, I would guess."

Gilbert sighed. "Lopez saw the same program, unfortunately, and had a hunch it might be in our collection. He knew about my father's friendship with old man de Solignac, as we had spoken about it before; Lopez sold antiques for the family ages ago. Anyway, I had already emptied the museum and brought the vase up to my place when I made the somewhat stupid mistake of inviting him up to look at the hideous family portraits."

"And Lopez recognized the vase right away."

"Yes," Gilbert said. Verlaque expected him to wince, but instead Gilbert grinned. "Lopez almost fell over when he saw the vase, filled with a lovely bouquet of lilies. He pretended not to know its value." Gilbert laughed and went on. "He offered to buy it from me then, but I refused."

"Lopez didn't give up."

"He kept calling, saying it must have been me who emptied out the museum. He even came to Aix, threatening to call the police if I didn't share the proceeds of the sale of the vase with him. I didn't want him in my apartment, so I arranged an excuse for us to meet in the museum offices. And then stupid Achille walked in."

"Who trusted you," Verlaque said. "Or was afraid of you."

"Get in the closet!"

"The police will be here any minute," Verlaque said.

"Like I believe you."

Suddenly, the apartment's front door opened and someone walked in, followed by a thud, as if they had set something heavy on the floor. "I told you the police were on their way," Verlaque said, smiling but perplexed about how Paulik could have come so quickly. Gilbert turned slowly toward the bedroom door, still keeping the gun on Verlaque.

Footsteps came toward the bedroom; a light was turned on in the hallway. But then they heard wheels; the same sound that Gilbert's suitcase had made. The door opened. A tall, thin man whom Verlaque had never seen before stood before them, a briefcase in his hand. He dropped the briefcase on the floor and screamed, "What's going on?!"

Gilbert showed him the gun. "Sit down on the bed and shut up," he barked.

"Oh my God, oh my God," the salesman muttered as he sat down on the edge of the bed and held onto his knees, which, Verlaque could see even from the depths of the walk-in closet, were shaking.

"I'm Judge Antoine Verlaque," he said, giving the salesman a quick wave.

"Shut up!" Gilbert yelled, gesturing with the gun. "Go back into the closet!"

"My wife knows all about the closet," Verlaque lied. "She has the original house plans. They were with the museum's charter."

"What's going on here?" the salesman cried out again.

"Okay, neighbor, follow the judge into the closet," Gilbert

said, turning toward the bed. Verlaque saw Gilbert slowly relax his right hand and the gun point toward the floor. He lurched forward, throwing all of his weight at Gilbert, causing him to stumble forward and drop the gun.

"The gun!" Verlaque called to the salesman, who stayed seated, his body swaying back and forth, his mouth gaping. Finally his eyes closed and he fell back onto the bed. "Thanks!" Verlaque managed to call out sarcastically before he was pinned to the floor by Gilbert, who had somehow struggled to his feet, his foot pressing down on Verlaque's right hand. Gilbert bent down and dug his left knee into Verlaque's back, pinning him to the floor. Verlaque could now see the gun, which had slid under the bed, but it was too far away to grab.

Gilbert pressed harder with his knee. Verlaque opened his mouth, took in as much air as he could, and swung his left arm up over his head, grabbing Gilbert's right ankle and pulling him down.

As Gilbert fell, the front door opened again and multiple feet pounded into the apartment. "Quentin-Savary!" he heard Paulik call out, and at once several police officers were in the room. All Verlaque could see was a scurry of black boots and then a foul-mouthed Gilbert was taken away.

Verlaque slid his body about a foot closer to the bed. He reached for the gun and gingerly picked it up, half afraid it would go off in his now-throbbing hand. The salesman began to mumble and Officers Roche and Goulin went to him. "He fainted," Verlaque explained. Paulik kneeled down beside him. "You can have this," Verlaque went on, handing him the gun. "I certainly don't want it."

"Do you want me to help you to your feet?" Paulik asked. He handed the gun to another officer, then put a hand on Verlaque's upper arm.

"I think I'll sit on the floor for a bit," Verlaque said, panting. "There's a secret closet . . ."

"Marine called and told me," Paulik said. "Roche and I were just leaving the bar when she called. She was worried and knew your cell phone was dead."

"Can you call her and tell her I'm fine?" Verlaque asked, trying not to complain about the pain.

Paulik nodded and called Marine while Verlaque sat on the floor, his back resting against the bed. He could hear Paulik reassuring Marine, and Patrice Roche and Sophie Goulin doing the same to the bewildered salesman. "Japan . . . Singapore . . . four weeks," the salesman mumbled. "Just got home . . ."

"You were a great help," Verlaque said to the salesman. Roche glanced at Goulin, who had to look away toward the window to hide her grin.

Paulik hung up his cell phone and came back to kneel next to Verlaque. "I told Marine I'd take you to Emergency for a quick checkup and that she is *not* to come but to stay at home and wait for you there," he said. "She promised to call her friend Sylvie to keep her company."

"Thank you," Verlaque said, managing a smile. "You know Marine well . . ."

"Is the twin celadon vase here?"

Verlaque motioned with his head to the walk-in closet. Paulik looked at Officer Flamant, who understood his cue and went in. "Bubble-wrapped, on the floor," Verlaque called out.

Flamant came back with the object in his hands.

"Unwrap it on the bed," Paulik said. The chocolate salesman was led away by a compassionate Roche, who listened politely to his version of the events.

They watched in silence as Flamant carefully peeled back the bubble wrap until a large pale green vase was revealed. He held it up, turning it so that they could see all of its sides. Still no one spoke, until another officer, very young, walked into the room.

"Twelve million for *that*?" he asked.

Chapter Thirty-two

❧

Monday, May 7

Marine and Verlaque left the doctor's office arm in arm. "Everything's on schedule," Verlaque said, pulling her toward him as they walked up the rue Espariat.

"It's a relief," Marine replied.

Verlaque smiled and kissed her. "That's normal. It's your first."

Marine smiled back and said nothing of her husband's panicked phone call to Sylvie. Plus, did he think they would have more than one child? "It's also a relief to have this museum case wrapped up," she said.

"Yes, I was getting more gray hairs over it. Our kid would think she had a grandpa-dad."

"A grandpa-dad? What's that?"

"My brother made it up when we were kids; we knew quite a few in our parents' crowd. Those men who start second families when they're in their late fifties or early sixties."

She laughed as they turned a corner. "You're hardly that. When is Gilbert's trial?"

"As soon as possible. Which means in a few months. They're busy going through the rented garage he had near Aix-les-Bains. The contents need to be documented, and only then will they be able to be returned to the museum. Most of the smaller objects were stored in that secret closet you found on the plans, including the murder weapon. A hammer."

Verlaque stayed silent about Gilbert's gun; he had given Marine the barest of details about their altercation in the salesman's apartment, and she had somehow understood not to ask too many questions. The gun in question ended up being a relic that had belonged to Gilbert's father but was still in working condition. Gilbert's plan had been to lock Verlaque in the closet, which would have given him enough time to get to the airport and board a plane for Brazil. But the salesman had arrived. And then Paulik.

"And his accomplice in the theft?" Marine asked.

"In a prison hospital," Verlaque said. "On a drug withdrawal program. He's cooperating, so he will be given a reduced sentence. I'm going to write a recommendation letter to that effect next week. Gilbert paid him in drugs for his help in emptying the museum; when they were doing just that, he slipped two château plates into his coat."

"Why?" Marine asked. She stopped walking.

"Why what?"

"Why do all of that? What was Gilbert's motive?"

"Millions of dollars," Verlaque answered.

"Yes, I know that part. But why empty the museum? Why didn't Gilbert just grab the Chinese vase and run?"

"Mme Devaux."

Marine looked at her husband. "You'll have to be more specific."

Verlaque smiled. "Do you remember Léa's photograph? The vase had fresh lilies in it. In fact, every week it had fresh flowers. The flower shop on the rue d'Italie confirms it: the museum had an account with them, and Mme Devaux picked up the flowers every Tuesday morning. The flower shop owner said that Gilbert often bought flowers there as well, and that on more than one occasion he and Mme Devaux fought over the same bouquet. The florist takes pride in her arranged bouquets, as you know."

"I do, I love that shop," Marine said, and then suddenly tightened her grip on Verlaque's hand. "Oh! I'm being slow today. Had Gilbert taken *only* the vase, she would have noticed! He knew how much she loved cut flowers, and that it was routine for her to refresh the flowers in that vase."

"And Gilbert couldn't legally sell the vase, as it belonged to the museum foundation, not to him. We can only guess why Gilbert's father added it to the collection instead of getting rid of it. We finally found it hand-written in an old inventory under 'gifts' with just the date and, oddly, Gilbert's mother's name. Perhaps she took the vase from him in punishment for his gambling. There isn't a photo, not even a proper description, which is why Paulik's officers missed it. In recent computerized lists, the vase was left out. Forgotten."

"Ah, yes, Gilbert would have assumed that the vase was properly listed in the inventory," Marine said. "But why did he have the vase in his apartment for all to see, even you?"

"I honestly think he liked playing cat and mouse with us," Verlaque said. "Plus, he assumed I didn't watch the antiques show."

Marine laughed. "Well, you didn't see that one episode. But was he really *that* bored?"

"Yes, and he really was that egotistical."

"And why was he bothering Mme de Montbarbon? My mother wants to know."

"Before he figured out what the celadon vase was worth, he had his eye on the Ziem painting," Verlaque replied. "That's what we figure, anyway. We'll know more as the days progress and Gilbert decides how much he wants to help us. He needed money, and he knew that his family portraits were worthless. The Ziem was at least worth a quarter of a million euros. That's better than nothing." He paused and added a thought that had just come into his head. "By emptying the museum not only could he hide the vase among all the other museum objects, but he could also throw off any suspicions people like Mme Picard may have had of him; she had overheard him harassing Mme de Montbarbon about the Ziem."

Marine drew herself closer to Verlaque. "And Mme Picard would have told Philomène, who would have told my mother . . ."

Verlaque grimaced. "Heaven forbid . . . those three . . ."

"So Gilbert found out about the vase's worth by watching that show," Marine said. "And so did Lopez. So you could say that the antique show was responsible for his murder."

"Touché," Verlaque replied. "And Lopez harassed Gilbert over it, which was his mistake."

"And what about Achille? What will he do until the museum reopens?"

"Take a long vacation," Verlaque said. "Mme Devaux has arranged everything."

"Ah, yes, the faithful secretary."

"She may be more than that."

"*Ah, bon?*" Marine asked, smiling.

"Bruno told me that when he interviewed them yesterday they came in together, holding hands. Mme Devaux was able to fill Bruno in on the missing details."

"So she explained what she was doing in the museum the morning she found the bodies?"

"Yes. She was getting some documents that she'd been working on. A project to bring money into the museum. In her past life she worked for a travel agency, and she'd been working on a business plan to develop a first-class tour agency specializing in the decorative arts. With Achille as tour guide. She'd do all the leg work."

"There's a market for that?"

"Apparently, yes. She had approval from the bank, and a well-known tour operator in Paris had agreed to jump on board once they saw more numbers."

"Which is what she was working on."

"Exactly." They sat down in the sun on the Mazarin's terrace. Marine ordered a sparkling water and Verlaque a beer.

"Congratulations, you two," Fréderic said as he balanced the tray on his forearm. "I hadn't realized . . ."

"The bump keeps getting bigger," Marine said, smiling.

"Keep it well fed," Fréderic said. "I'll be right back with your drinks."

Marine turned to her husband and said, "I thought that the chocolate seller was away for a month. Isn't that what you told me?"

"He was supposed to be. But his meetings in Singapore and Taiwan were canceled, so he came home early."

"Look who it is," Marine whispered.

Faustine Devaux and Achille Formentin walked up the Cours Mirabeau arm in arm. Achille was using an elegant carved wooden walking stick. Verlaque waved and they stopped, then walked over to their table.

"*Salut!*" Verlaque said, getting up and shaking their hands. He introduced Marine and she suggested they join them. Faustine looked at Achille, who smiled and said, "*Pourquoi pas?*"

Fréderic came back and put the drinks on the table while Faustine and Achille each ordered a glass of Martini Rosso. They smiled at each other and Achille put a hand over hers.

"How are you feeling, M Formentin?" Verlaque asked.

"Very well," he replied. "I'm a little wobbly still, but the doctors tell me that it's normal, and I won't need the cane much longer."

"I think he's very elegant with the cane," Faustine swooned. Marine looked down at her drink to hide her smile.

"I was just telling my wife about your tour company plans," Verlaque said.

"We've been celebrating," Faustine said. "Both the bank and the parent travel company in Paris have signed our contract. Achille and I are just fine-tuning the trip—we'll visit all of the stops before the first official tour."

"That sounds like a dream," Marine said. "I'm a ceramics freak."

"Join the club," said Achille, tightening his grip on Faustine's hand.

"It looks like you'll be too busy for the next year or two," Faustine said, glancing at Marine's stomach. "Congratulations."

"Thank you," Marine replied.

"It's a girl," Verlaque said.

Marine laughed. "It's a surprise. We don't actually know . . ."

Verlaque winked at Marine. "Mme Devaux," he said. "One thing's been bothering me. How did Gilbert know that the salesman who lives on the second floor was going to be away for so long?"

"That bothered me as well," she replied. "Until I remembered that Robert gave me his travel schedule one morning at the bottom of the stairs, in the entryway. Gilbert must have overheard, as he always went out to buy bread at that time."

Verlaque nodded, remembering France Dubois's report of Gilbert in the line at the *boulangerie*.

"And now I'd like to ask you something," Faustine said. "You're from the same family as the flour mills, am I correct? I don't want to pry—it's just that my father was a well-known bread maker in Normandy."

"That's us," Verlaque replied. Marine looked at her husband and smiled, as he had replied, for once, with no hesitation or awkwardness as he usually did when the family was brought up. *No more ghosts?* she wondered.

Faustine sighed. "I've already told Achille all about my dull childhood . . ."

"Not at all dull, my dear!" Achille said.

She continued, "One of the highlights of my teenage years was waiting for the Verlaque flour to arrive." She giggled. "I'd get up very early in the morning just to chat with the delivery boy. He was so charming . . . tall, and shy, with so many freckles . . ."

"Freckles?" Verlaque asked, setting his beer glass down.

Faustine went on. "He told me he was keen to learn the

business, all of it. We spoke every morning. The funny thing was, as much as he loved the work, he said he got an upset stomach when he ate bread. I felt sorry for him. We'd call it gluten intolerant now, of course."

Verlaque looked at Marine, who in turn whispered, "*Oh, mon dieu.*"

"What is it?" Faustine asked, looking at both of them.

"I think that was my father," Verlaque said.

"The delivery boy?" Achille asked.

"Yes," Verlaque replied. "Every summer he was sent off to learn the ropes. Where did you live?"

Faustine named a town in Normandy and again Marine and Verlaque exchanged looks. "The flour mills were just down the road, as was my grandparents' house."

Faustine brought her hands up to her face. "Is he . . ."

"Still alive?" Verlaque asked. "Yes, alive and well and living in Paris. He was just here . . ." He didn't bother to tell her about his parents' loveless marriage, his mother's recent death, or his father's new life with a much-younger scholar. But she seemed happy enough with the news that the elder Verlaque was alive and well. She didn't need to ask any more questions.

A ray of sunshine shone down on them, and as France Dubois walked by the café and saw the scene, she was suddenly overcome with emotion. The two couples sat there, laughing, and France quickened her step. She didn't want to be a voyeur. Besides, Isaac was waiting for her at his apartment, as he had promised to make dumplings from a recipe given to him from an elderly Chinese woman when he studied in China. France had even learned the Chinese words for "I'm very happy." She couldn't wait to tell him.